Roberta-Complete

By Jay A. Harris

Roberta-Complete

A Novel by Jay A. Harris

Published by DiverSyFy™

Cover: Licensed stock

First Edition
Reedited

ISBN: 979-8-8707354-1-2

Chapter 1

In the not-so-distant future, standing inside a thick haze of dust, Roberta contemplated the fate of her mission, a mission that now rested in her hands alone—if only fate would have been so kind. In the aftermath of a crucial misstep, not only was her clothing singed and shredded, but she was down to only one arm. Even if in a more barbaric time, a missing limb would have buckled the most hardened warrior. But not Roberta; she was built of a different material. In the middle of a charcoal-gutted hotel room, she held on to her severed arm like a twisted baguette, scanning the scene for signs of life. Her only aid came from fragments of moonlight through a clouded midnight sky, streaming through a roof once there, now no more. Missing arm or not, she *had* to find her missing team members. Yet memories of how their entire evening had gone sideways, she couldn't escape:

Earlier, just past 21-hundred hours, Roberta sat in a Budapest rooftop café along Marcó Street, not far from the Danube's split. Across the table from her sat Muirfield, Jacobs, Wilkerson, Lloyd and Becker—her elite team of former Navy Seals, Green Berets, Rangers, and Night Stalkers. Most had been elevated to Roberta's special ops unit before the age of thirty. A group coffee break a few hours before a mission was the custom, except Roberta was the only one not sipping. It was a cool breezy evening and her cup had already grown cold. Her eyes were aimed at the table, but her mind was elsewhere.

"We were about ten klicks out when our drones arrived," Muirfield, second-in-charge and the only one in the bunch over forty, said with his stout southern accent. But salt-and-pepper hair wasn't his only distinguishing feature; one ear was visibly marked by a carved indentation the width of a finger. He turned and pointed at the horizon as if the battle ten klicks away were still going on as he spoke. "And I tell you, when the shit hit the fan and they started raining fire from the sky, we felt the ground buck like a bull in heat."

It wasn't the first time the team had heard the story; only Muirfield's euphemism had changed—the one thing that made them chuckle. But just like her untouched cup of coffee, Roberta failed to join in on the reaction.

A waitress approached with a beer list and set it on the table. "Can I get you anything else to drink?" Her English was excellent; only a small trace of Hungary emerged at the end.

"Well, what do we have here?" Becker, last-in-charge and the youngest on the team, reached for the beer list, stopping at the waitress's hand instead, where he rubbed it with the subtlety of a clubfooted rhino.

It was enough to recapture Roberta's attention. Becker may have been a handsome young man, but it didn't take a love genius to realize, *that move won't work.* She watched the waitress withdraw her hand like being scalded by the touch of Satan.

Becker stroked his chin while looking the waitress up and down, then switched to the beer list. "Let's see…"

Roberta, the only female on the team, looked up with a directness that caught the waitress's attention on its own.

"And you, Ma'am?" the waitress asked.

"No thank you, Miss," Roberta said. "We'll just stick with our coffee." She circled her finger around the table. "All of us."

"Yes, Ma'am." The waitress snatched the list from Becker, whirling away from him and whatever airborne S.T.D. he may have been carrying.

But something else was strange; Roberta carried the commanding presence of a "ma'am," but didn't look a day older than Becker.

Becker slung his hands in the air. "Damn it, Roberta! Why do you have to stick us all in the damn mud along with you?"

Roberta smacked her lips and glared, but couldn't beat Lloyd to an answer. "It's because we don't need to be getting sloshed before a goddamn op," he said.

"You should know this, you dipshit," Jacobs jumped in.

Becker threw his palms up even higher. "Right. And it bugs the shit out of me every time we do it. We're talking one freakin' beer! One damn beer! Let me tell you something—" He aimed his finger at Jacobs. "—I have never—ever!—missed a single shot on account o' one fucking beer before action."

Muirfield's eyes bared down on him. "And we don't want your first dang miss to be on *this* op."

Becker huffed, waved everyone off. "Alright, alright. But decaf! C'mon!"

"So we don't go in too hyped up and trigger happy," said Lloyd.

"Oh...," Becker said with a slow nod, "so it's a mental head game we're playing."

"No. Polyphenols, you idiot."

Becker rolled his eyes. "Whatever." Seconds later, he gave in to one sip of decaf with pinky finger in the air, followed by a grunt from the rarely heard-from Wilkerson, a brutish fellow and muscle of the group.

Meanwhile, Roberta leaned back and folded her arms, smug inside. In an odd way, it was great leadership on her part—having restored order without uttering a word, and having had her team trained well enough to have her back, just like Colonel Livingston, the team's remote Ex-O, had assured her. Except there was one thing Roberta couldn't resist emphasizing: she pressed her finger atop the table as sternly as her tone. "We *cannot* let our target be more alert than we are." Nods and yeps came from all but Becker before Roberta got down to business, "Now, are all the camera feeds properly set?" More yeps followed.

Later, after Roberta and her team wrapped up at the café, they waited curbside for their allied Hungarian driver to pick them up. He rolled to a stop in a simple delivery van at 23-hundred on the dot, already loaded up with the team's weapons. As with many vehicles in 2065, form followed function with this one: an unadorned classic look from prior years along with minimal window coverage. Roberta took the passenger's seat while the rest of her team cramped themselves into the rear bay, equipped with monitors like a mini war room.

"Elek," Roberta greeted the driver.

"Roberta. Team," he answered along with a double nod.

"Elek," Muirfield spoke for the remaining members.

They each grabbed their weapons, pistols and semi-automatic short rifles, afterwards exchanging very few words as Elek drove to another stop only five minutes later. To their west was the Danube River—to their east, a line of businesses from corner-to-corner. One of those businesses was a historic hotel overlooking the river, the subject property of their sights this evening. Elek had parked a ways down the Rakpart out of direct sight, but left a clear view from Roberta's window to the hotel's entrance.

"There's our target," Roberta mumbled nearly 30-minutes later, needing no binoculars to spot known crime lord and terrorist financier, Gelep Ergen, who'd been hiding out in the hotel for several weeks. He may have been mildly disguised—a short trench, baseball cap and shades at night—but Roberta had every photograph of him in her mind to a tee.

Intel had it that Ergen's own suspicions had led him there. They also had it that he was the hotel's true owner, just not by title or deed or anything. This, in itself, did little to conceal his whereabouts, his biggest mistake being choosing a hotel bordered by both the Rakpart and the Danube, minutes away from Parliament. A case of hiding in plain sight was everyone's best guess. But this was Ergen, a man of considerable wealth and connections, a man virtually untouchable by local law, a brazen man who loved a great view. But on this night, Roberta and her team were here to change all of that and bring him to allied justice.

Roberta had gotten only a quick glance at Ergen, but from then on, he was blocked by his bodyguard, a man so large, it was a struggle just to see the entrance.

"A husky rascal that one is," Muirfield said with his eyes on a monitor in the rear bay.

Wilkerson grunted. "The bigger they come—" He left it at that.

Just after 23:45-hours, the allied delivery van turned the corner of the next street over and pulled into the hotel's rear parking lot. The team had already hacked into the hotel's security system. All alarms were disabled and the lot's cameras now relayed content from a week ago, while key interior cameras were set on a loop. Ergen's monitors would capture nothing but vacant entries and corridors, some with past guests here and there.

"Let's gear up," Roberta commanded while screwing her silencer onto the tip of her short-rifle.

As the rest of her team did the same, it was Becker's custom to reaffirm all commands: "Time to lace 'em up."

Roberta rolled her eyes but continued, "Although the hotel's security system has been disabled and camera footage is to our liking, we'll need to move like a spider on a silk thread."

"Like a bug up Ergen's ass."

To Roberta, Becker's commentary was more than self-affirmation; it was reinforcement of his own presence, admission that hers was somehow undeserved. But she was far too focused to be insulted, so she turned to the driver instead. "Elek, pick us up in ten minutes, okay?"

Elek tipped his forehead. "You got it."

She clicked her magazine in place. "Let's move," she told her team on her way out of the van, still catching a glimpse of the activity behind her.

"Let's roll." It was no surprise Becker was first to respond, first to open the side door, and the next to step out until pushed aside by Muirfield.

"Watch out," Muirfield grumbled. "That's my line, you shit-head."

The others followed with no further gearing up needed; plain clothing was their disguise tonight. When Elek drove off, all six were left behind walking through the darkest rear entryway, rifles strapped and hidden underneath their jackets. The plan was to take the service stairs to the fifth-floor penthouse, the floor which only Ergen occupied. This, they executed to deft perfection, but the exact location of Ergen's bodyguard was now a mystery. They unveiled their rifles and entered the fifth floor with barely a sound and no fear. But there was a slight catch: they were on a unique schedule. The cameras for the main corridor leading to Ergen's penthouse were timed to receive their loop-feeds at zero-hundred-hours. Setting this up was something Roberta could have done, herself, better than anyone, but trust in her team was a huge part of her job, also something Colonel Livingston had taught her. So, at zero-hundred-and-one, she poised herself for motion, masking her face, nonetheless. Her teammates followed suit.

Fearless, not stupid, Roberta peeked around the wall to the main corridor. Down the hall, absolutely no one was manning Ergen's door, only an empty wooden chair. One handwave forward and Roberta led her team in staggered lockstep, softly, towards Ergen's room, rifles now butted into their shoulders. Only seconds away was when the bodyguard finally showed his face, the same one from downstairs. He rounded the opposite corridor wall with half a chocolate roll in his hand, the other half in his mouth. Both his mouth and feet came to a blunted stop when his eyes met Roberta's, while his roll fell splat on the carpeted floor.

The first thing Roberta did was press her finger against her lips, demanding silence, then flicked her rifle up and down, up and down.

The bodyguard obeyed both commands; he raised his hands in the air without a word.

A single side-nod from Roberta, and Wilkerson parted from the group to extract the bodyguard's handgun from his belt. He then pressed his rifle's barrel against the back of the guard's skull and steered him to the door. "Unlock it and open it," he gritted in his ear.

Oddly, the door was already unlocked, while the guard had become the most fortuitous part of the team's evolving plan: a Trojan horse for all six to huddle behind on their way in. Roberta was the first to peep around him, seeing no one ahead, just furniture in a dimly lit living room suite. Their prior hack had revealed no cameras in this room, the perfect reason to now dispose of their new shield. She gave the signal to Wilkerson, who landed one punch to the back of the bodyguard's skull, and down he went, unconscious and guided to the floor for a soft landing.

And now there was silence, nothing but the low din from one lamp filament in a corner and the fluorescent overheads in the main corridor behind them. At the far end were two solid wooden doors to the bedroom, both closed with light bleeding around the edges. The team spread out with stealth and moved forward; it was time to collect their target.

"Guys," Becker whispered, "something doesn't seem right—doesn't feel right. I think we need to pull back."

Muirfield glanced his way and whispered back, "What makes you say that?"

"I don't know. A gut-feel. And my gut's always right."

Roberta held up her hand in a call for silence, then took one more step before motioning everyone to a stop. She scanned the floor for wires and motion triggers, but found nothing, so she advanced. But by her next step, something *really* didn't feel right—a case of not knowing what you've missed until it's gone. A frequency that had been in her ear a second ago was no longer there, like a heart missing a beat, cutoff as soon as her foot had landed. *Oh, shit.* She'd just tripped an undetected motion trigger, one apparently outside the ordinary spectrum of light and frequencies.

"Fall back! It's a trap!" she yelled, diving backwards and hitting the floor just before the bedroom doors flew clean off. The blast-wave that followed ripped through everything in the room. Left behind was a gutted floor decorated with half the ceiling where furniture used to be. It was a miracle Roberta wasn't buried by it all, but it didn't come without a cost. With nothing in her left shoulder socket, grossly cauterized, she rolled over and pushed herself to her knees, then to her feet. She gazed all over, but it wasn't her arm she sought first; the welfare of her team was what came to mind. "Assess," she commanded herself, but the cloud of dust was too thick and latent with floating debris.

Neither pain nor shock overtook her—only pure anger. How could she have missed the invisible tripwire? How could she have been so negligent? *So fucking stupid!* How could she still be standing, still conscious, still alive? Like her teammates and only a few select others knew, Roberta was built of a different material—synthetic, to be exact. "Assess."

As the dust began to clear, Roberta clinched her fists until every lean muscle in her body rippled. Fortunately, if she could call it such, her missing arm wasn't far away. After retrieving it, she stood erect and opened her ears to every sound around her, one of her many talents. It was what she was programmed to do. But she heard not one heartbeat from any of her colleagues. Every one of them had met a sudden and fatal end. *How could I have missed such a trap?* She festered. *I'm not supposed to miss, damnit!*

Roberta's creators had been trying for years to perfect "A.I.-Complete," the most human of androids. Programmed to breathe, digest, sweat, bleed and feel, Roberta was supposed to be "it." Yet with complete humanity came human imperfections—mistakes—like failing to run all electronic patterns in the room through a full analysis, failing to pick up the "tripwire's" frequency, no matter how far beyond the visible spectrum. The principle of making a mistake may have been promising to the naturalists on her development team, but a "glitch" to those in favor of her military grade status, a glitch they'd already attempted to eliminate. At the moment, it was a complete disaster to Roberta, who was now blaming her own system for not auto-adapting. *How could I have failed?*

She switched to computer-mode to perform a deep internal scan for the glitch, but found nothing. "Reassess." She switched her methodology to piece together everything else around her. Still, nothing. Scenarios began to play themselves out automatically, but with police sirens already screaming from the streets below, and helicopters fast approaching, she was running out of time. Neither she nor any evidence of her team was supposed to be found there, and the local police could not be trusted. Cutting her losses was now her only option, arcing her back to the original plan. She tapped herself into every hotel camera feed remaining and returned it to current, now seeing police officers climbing all stairwells to the top.

She opened her internal-comm to her driver. "Elek?"

"Hey, what happened up there?" he shouted.

"Too much to explain now."

"Needless to say, I'm unable to get back to the hotel."

Hearing the sirens clustered on one side and closing in was when Roberta looked the opposite way. The entire backwall and corridor was just as shredded, open to the riverside air sweeping across her face. "Sit tight. I'll contact you in a few with new rendezvous coordinates."

"I'll be—"

Arm in hand, Roberta was in motion before Elek could finish. Two bounds and a leap away from the sirens took her over the edge towards the Rakpart, five stories down. With most onlookers assembled on the other side, very few witnessed her stick the landing like an Olympian. Of those who did, her nonchalant stroll that followed seemed to abate all curiosity—an optical illusion of sorts. Roberta continued that stroll across the roadway and commuter rails, all the way to the dock-landing. And with their eyes to the sky, no one even seemed to notice her detached arm in plain view, nor Roberta plunging into the Danube without hesitation, where she never rose for air until she reached the other side.

Chapter 2

Soaked from her brown, muscle-tight synthetic skin down to her subdermal nodes, Roberta-X150 stood on the Danube's western bank after swimming across. She stared back across at Ergen's historic landmark, watching its rising smoke blend with the cloudy backdrop like a faded mural. She now had time to reflect on the past. Programmed for an occasional laugh, she'd rarely used this part of her A.I. when hearing her teammates crack tons of jokes: "Little Ms. Drill-bit over there should be able to fix it," Agent Lloyd would tell another teammate whenever anything from a tablet to a chair was broken. "Why… just her middle finger alone can drill a hole in your ass a good two inches wider, Mike!" He'd used it more than once, and on more than just Mike Jacobs, but he would rasp ridiculously every time as if it was his first time saying it.

She remembered another, Agent Becker, approaching her in the breakroom one day, gaining her attention with a solemn inquiry: "Um, excuse me, Roberta? Can I get your thoughts on something?"

Roberta had turned around, eager to assist with eyes as wide as saucers. "Yes?"

"Real or synthetic?"

Her eyes dropped, coming to a hard stop at the most flaccid object she'd ever seen. Becker's thumb was stretching his zipper below his dangling genitals. *Real*, her neural network had begun translating, until she'd noticed the silly grin on his face. She'd realized he was joking, testing her A.I., forcing her to an answer just as true as her first instinct. "Neither. Try *real* pathetic," she'd answered matter-of-factly, but still didn't laugh. From there, she could easily have claimed sexual harassment—if being offended had served any tactical benefit, or if Agent Becker, the biggest asshole she'd ever known, hadn't have been the most reliable and best *human* sniper on the planet.

Standing beside the Danube, she now realized why she'd never laughed at their antics. *My team's jokes were lame.* But lame or not, there were times when every last one of them, five men in all, had had her back—her front to be exact. The time when Agent Muirfield edged in front of her in the line of fire, most likely dragged into chivalry by her feminine features, forgetting the fact she was as close to bullet-resistant as the vest he was wearing. And the many times when Agent Wilkerson, the one of few words, had left a double case of ammo rounds on her toolkit before work, something he'd done for no one else. Absorbing the memories, Roberta cracked a smile, along with a tear streaming down her already dampened cheek.

Yes, Roberta had been programmed for more than just an occasional smile and a laugh; her motherboard was equipped with every emotion from elation to sadness, all the way to the verge of what may have been considered love.

Roberta's emotions may not have been considered ideal for special ops or combat, but they were once perfect for home- and childcare. It was the role for which she was originally designed, a role she'd performed at the highest level—until it all changed in a snap. One quiet evening near the beginning of her service life, a burglar decided to put a sleeping family's security system to the test. At the time, Roberta-X150 was not part of that system. ZepperCorp, her manufacturer, could have easily attempted adding defense training into their first run of domestic units, but they hadn't quite perfected all the scenarios yet, and it was an easy sell otherwise. Liability waivers weren't even trusted. Yet how greatly they'd underestimated Roberta's ability to learn. It was amazing what she'd gathered from sitting in on just a few action movie nights with the family.

It all brought her to a moment in the shadows, where she stood stiff, patiently waiting for the burglar to breach the perimeter, waiting for him to make his way to the kitchen, and waiting for him to load a few items into his bag. Roberta needed evidence; she was recording. Like a pro, the burglar quietly stuffed things like silverware, holiday trays, and anything else that sparkled in the dark.

Assess. Roberta silently ran all the possible scenarios. Based on the burglar's take, she figured him to be a drug addict, at most. A deadly encounter was not anticipated. "Would you like anymore?" she finally asked him. "There's actual monetary currency upstairs. Would you like an escort?"

The burglar's breath came to a stop. "Wha'?" Gazing Roberta up and down, he made a move. He swung the bag of silverware in her direction.

Roberta dipped and dodged his swing like a boxer, grabbing his head and spinning him into a headlock once he'd missed. Her intention was to keep pressure light until putting him to sleep. To his misfortune, Roberta was operating with no field experience; the man's neck snapped under her first twist. The grab bag crashing to the floor was the only thing that awoke the family, but only the parents, who came rushing downstairs. Luckily the burglar survived, while their one and only child had slept right through it all.

Roberta's assigned family had had an agreement in place to contact the service company first in case of any malfunction. So, Roberta's mess had been cleaned up long before sunrise, no lights or sirens necessary. She, herself, was a separate matter. Her suspected glitch ended up placing her back in corporate storage, deactivated and in line for imminent decommission. But one key ally was all that was needed to delay the inevitable. Chief scientist of Program

X150 and Roberta's maker, young Dr. Kenneth Murphy, had his own hypothesis about Roberta's unusual actions, a hypothesis he'd kept silent until he could solidify a theory. After much tinkering and rewiring, he presented his findings to his funding committee, the company's founder's son, Phil Zepper, Jr., included. "We've reached a point in history no one ever envisioned us reaching so quickly," Kenneth announced from a conference table seat across from everyone else. "One of our very own domestic models has reached the pentacle of A.I.-Completeness, the most humanistic stage of android development. A historic moment! I'm speaking of Roberta-X150. Her translation and integration of received information into an evolving computational intelligence is remarkably beyond expectations! Like I said, faster than any of us could have ever envisioned!" He aimed his forefinger to the ceiling. "Which is why I'm recommending Roberta-X150 for special ops trials."

It was never Kenneth's original intent to see his creation placed in such danger, but having Roberta face the risk of death in the field was his only hope for keeping her—alive. He now expected the board to stand and applaud the idea, give him a career-boosting ovation, but that's not what he got. Instead, a few fingers tapped the other side of the table, a few brows arched, but no one said a thing.

Kenneth waved his hand to a stop. "Now, I know what you all must be thinking… how can a compassionate, empathetic, domestic model transition to a rational, hard-fast-reacting warring machine? But her balance of human emotions is exactly what we need to see in the field." The vast difference in billing rates between the two models was no secret to anyone in the room either, ZepperCorp being a huge government contractor. "And with a few tweaks here and there," Dr. Murphy pressed on, "a little augmentation to her B.D.I. software, we can make this work."

He went on for several more minutes, tortured by brooding stares across the table, until Phil sat back and folded his arms. A smug grin followed. "Dr. Murphy," he said, "you can slow down now. Roberta-X150 has already been pre-approved for advanced trials *long* ago."

Kenneth scratched his head. "Oh."

And so began Roberta's renewed path. Yet several years later, not long after the debacle in Budapest, after having been flown back to the Los Angeles office for repairs and a new arm, her path was being reevaluated all over again, and the air seemed unforgiving. Ergen was never found in the rubble after the explosion. Either by an anonymous tip or his own suspicions, an investigation proved that he'd slipped out beforehand through an undetected escape shaft in a backwall. The next time he'd emerged in public was at a Hungarian hearing where he received a presidential pardon, reasons undisclosed.

As for Roberta, the scenarios occasionally replayed in her mind, landing on Becker's forewarning: *Guys, something doesn't seem right—doesn't feel right. I think we need to pull back.* It repeated itself: *I think we need to pull back. I think we need to pull back. I think we need to pull back.* Roberta would actually cringe whenever she thought about it: *Becker was just so damn difficult to take seriously sometimes, like on that fucking night!* She had even tried to explain how the tripwire must have been outside the infrared spectrum, something she had yet to be programmed with. But with everything having been destroyed, there was just no evidence. Regardless, advancements in other models based on her own cognitive architecture now had everyone questioning her continued viability—everyone except Dr. Murphy, a man now on the cusp of middle age and recently promoted.

"Well, Roberta, it seems we've reached a crossroads again," he informed her as she sat across from him at his office desk, just the two of them with the door closed.

"A new assignment?" she asked, rolling her arm like a crankshaft. "The arm feels fine."

He interlocked his fingers. "Yes… you can… say that. But uhh… how would you like to try something a little different? A little closer to… home?" A wide, tightlipped smile was the end to his question.

Roberta paused, searching her databanks for a response. "Sure, Kenneth," she said before a light shrug. "A job is a job."

Chapter 3

"Well, what do you think, Mildred?" San Diego commercial realtor, Bella Ramirez-Jones, asked Mildred Morehouse as each perused her own little corner of a cluttered, dusty display floor. Bella had shown Mildred enough buildings over the past week to bypass last name etiquette. "Quite a canvas waiting for an artist's touch, don't you think?"

Mildred shrugged her chin with a steadfast nod, catching the tail-end of Bella's affirming smile. Neither the clutter, dusty floor, nor the dirt-caked windows seemed to bother her at all. Her creative eye was seeing a bit more than a canvas. "Mmm… I don't know about an artist's touch, but I can see a ton of rose petals over here." She hand-dusted the air in the direction of the empty front window bay, then waved to the right of the store. "A few azaleas over there." The structure, itself, was old and eclectic, built as far back as the 1980s. She, a woman born in the late 2030s, loved everything old and eclectic, but things more from the early 2000s, like the movies and music of her parents' era.

Flowers were also one of Mildred's ageless passions. She'd been consumed by them since she was a child, once mistaking her mother's petunia bed for a free souvenir shop. With an entire garden at her disposal, the little five-year-old had assembled colorful arrangements that could have put a licensed florist to shame. Today, as a young woman, and now a licensed florist, her dream was finally at hand, in large part due to her dad as a deafly silent partner.

The back door flung open. "Hey, I'm here!" Another young woman, hair dyed blonde, walked through the front door wearing spandex and high heels, carrying more determination than the agent—but late. "Sorry I'm late!" She craned her neck up to Mildred's face for a cheek-to-cheek.

"Girl, you're fine," Mildred said. "We just got here."

She turned and extended her hand towards the agent. "Hi! I'm Lauren Brookhaven, Mildred's *bestie*!" she touted with a slight southern twang.

The agent shook her hand, a business card already waiting in the other. "Hi, I'm Bella Ramirez-Jones, Mildred's *realtor*!" she returned Lauren's enthusiasm.

Mildred even got excited. "Realtor *and* friend," she confessed. She then passed a glance at Lauren to feel her out, glad to see her beaming just the same.

But after one too many seconds of awkward glances, Lauren cut her eyes around the room. "Oh, this is nice." She paced the floor. "Needs a little touchup work, though…"

"Huh!" Mildred huffed. "*That* goes without saying."

"Well, hey," Bella cut in, "you haven't seen the upstairs apartment yet! Let me show you."

Mildred and Lauren followed Bella out the backdoor and up the stairs.

"And private parking too," Lauren commented on her way up.

"That's right," Bella added. She stopped to point at the rear parking lot. "Gated and secured as well."

This made Mildred smile, but she didn't need to be reminded. A livable workspace with secure parking was the first thing she'd noticed upon arrival.

"*Bella*?" Lauren asked in a skeptical tone.

"Yes?"

"How's the crime around here?"

Bella fumbled with the apartment keys. "Crime? I haven't really heard anything major," she said on her way into the apartment, saying nothing else about it once inside. *That* conversation was apparently over.

It was easy for Mildred to read Lauren's mind as her eyes rolled to the sky: *Oh, my fucking God!*

"Oh, it'll be fine," Mildred assured her. She turned and dangled her fingers toward the gate. "I could just have some barbed wire wrapped atop the fence, or have a new solid gate installed."

But Lauren's eyes continued to roll, this time into a grim leer. "Uhh..."

Having ridden with Bella to the property, Mildred opted to catch a ride with Lauren back to her apartment, where Mildred had been "bumming" on the sofa sleeper. "Bella is great, isn't she?" Mildred asked as soon as the passenger door shut.

"Sure," Lauren said, "considering I had to do her job for her."

"Lauren!"

"I'm just saying! Didn't sound like she had a *whole* lot of helpful tips to offer." She started the car along with a light shrug. "Maybe I should take up real estate. You know, as a side hustle."

"Maybe you should, but Bella is doing a fine job. Who do you think found this great spot for me?"

"Ha!" Lauren didn't seem too keen on that idea either.

"Alright, you."

She bobbed her head from side to side. "So, where do you want to go next?"

"How about... home?"

"Oh, no!" Lauren blurted. "We need to stop somewhere for eats and drinks. Somewhere we can go hash 'this' out," she said with a grimace, flicking her finger at the building like a booger.

Mildred looked at the building's front face with her own face scrunched in a knot. "What?" She wanted to protest, but really couldn't. "Hmm… I can see how the peeling paint and weathered window frames could be a little misleading. But 'bones,' Lauren! It's got great 'bones!'"

"Bones, huh?"

"Ee-yep."

Lauren paused with a quick glance. "I bet you didn't get that one from Bella, did you?"

Mildred had invited Lauren there today for moral support only; the venture, itself, was all Mildred's endeavor. Whether she got support or not, she knew she'd always get the truth from Lauren. The two had been best friends since the start of college nearly ten years ago. They'd both attended U.C.L.A., and had even graduated at the same time, Mildred in business management, and Lauren in marketing. Mildred had bypassed corporate America enroute to this day, having chosen only a couple of years in retail first. Regardless of her quasi-easy mood today, Mildred had been a nervous wreck all week. And now she needed more than just one friend to quell the turbulence, which led her to an ulterior motive: Would Lauren accept a new friend into their tight circle of two?

Chapter 4

No matter how much the world was leaning towards artificial intelligence—artificial "everything," flowers, *real* flowers, were still in high demand, and Mildred was here to meet it. Months after making the biggest purchase of her young life, she had already accomplished her second major goal: to have the shop renovated and ready for the holiday season. Thanksgiving and Christmas floral arrangements were the perfect primers for the lovers' holiday soon to follow. Thinking of which, a woman like Mildred was far too busy to follow in her new customers' footsteps when it came to the holiday season. Most of it was always spent with no significant other. Her best friend, Lauren, seemed to be in the same boat, but Mildred never knew why. Lauren had a job with regular hours and was always dressed for a party, with a personality to match. Mildred saw no real reason for Lauren's condition to mirror her own during this season. Both were beautiful women, nonetheless. Lauren shorter and curvier, Mildred tall and slim since childhood, but with her lean curves usually well-covered; a sweater or a long sweatshirt was her go-to. "Millie," Lauren would tell her, "you couldn't gain a pound if you ate the whole damn cow—y'uh heifer," her original Texas accent heavier when need be, and tainted with a touch of jealousy. But where Mildred's flare for glamour ended with flowers, Lauren's picked up with personal attire, making her style alone more eye-catching to most men. Helping tend the shop was a sacrifice most other "glamour girls" wouldn't have been able to make, but, "That's what friends are for," Lauren would also say. And Mildred never complained about her bestie's sacrifice, because it often gave her a free early evening assistant, like today.

"What do you think about this one?" Lauren asked of a simple cornucopia arrangement with a sparkling gold ribbon wrapped around the wide end of the horn.

It was a bit lacking in the sunflower department for Mildred's taste, but she knew not to fuss. "Look at you, with all those *skillzzz-uh!*"

Lauren stepped back with her hands up, hesitant to ruin her own masterpiece. "*Mad* skills."

The celebration came to an abrupt stop when the door chimed, another old-fashioned touch Mildred had always dreamed about having. In walked an elderly woman, the first customer of the early evening crowd, and it was back to work for the proprietor and her assistant.

After that customer, more sprinkled in here and there, each leaving with their orders and smiles of contentment. A dream come true for Mildred, and she'd barely broken a sweat.

"You know, Bella called me earlier about an open house this coming Sunday," Lauren said, helping to cleanup while they had a break in the action.

Mildred smiled, always happy to know Lauren had buried her hatchet with Bella and had finally voted her into their new B.F.F. threesome. And she knew Lauren was looking for either a house or a condo. "You going?" Mildred asked her.

"Well, my savings account is not where I want it to be yet, but I might as well. Something to do on a breezy Sunday. Wanna come?"

Wiping down the counter, Mildred tossed her head from side to side. "Mmm, sure. What time?"

"It's all day, so I figure we can—"

The ladies' eyes popped up when the chime went off again. A customer far the opposite of an elderly woman had just entered. A slim, handsome young man with deep brown skin, dark curly hair, heavy brows and piercing dark brown eyes stepped inside. He was clearly a brother with a touch of foreign flavor mixed in. Both women went silent. Men coming into the shop was a rarity; most shopped online websites, a task Mildred had been woefully procrastinating on. When his eyes met hers, then shifted to Lauren, Mildred knew he wasn't there to make a purchase. But his conservative style and dress, maybe too modest for Lauren's taste, had her confused for a second. Not the type Lauren would have met in a club or a mall. In just that split second, everything about him now said *stalker*, until his eyes shifted right back to Mildred, leaving Lauren wide-eyed and stunned. It was the moment Mildred went into shopkeeper-mode. "Hello, how can we help you?" she announced.

"Yes, uhh…" Even he hesitated. "I'm looking for an arrangement today."

Mildred raised her lengthy posture. "Sure! Not a problem! What's the occasion?" *Why am I yelling?*

"Oh, a simple birthday arrangement." By now he was at the computer register with his hands on the countertop. "What would you recommend?" he asked, his piercing eyes tugging on Mildred like a magnet.

Mildred cleared her throat just to quell a feeling she hadn't experienced in a very long time—desire. "That all depends… if it's someone special, like say a… girlfriend…" She held on to her answer like a fisherman watching the cork bob.

"Oh," he blurted, "it's for my mother."

Her eyes bloomed. "*Ahh*! You see now, that actually makes a difference." She glanced at Lauren, who'd finally seemed to come back to Earth for support.

"Oh, yes, it definitely does," Lauren added.

The man shrugged. "Hmph, I guess it does."

"Right this way," Mildred tauntingly beckoned him away from the counter, her standing display case against the wall a source of her confidence.

He even seemed to notice, nodding. "Impressive."

"Thank you," she said with a twinkle, but kind of wondered out loud, "Just curious—you weren't able to find anything online?"

"Yes, but I'd rather see firsthand, myself. I just can't trust the final product, you know? The size and all."

"Oh, I hear you. That is *so* true." She was actually kicking herself for something she should have already known. *Damn it, Mildred!* And there was something endearing about a man who actually cared, endearing enough to avoid asking him how he'd even heard about her new shop, a typical question she always asked new customers.

"And my friend, Bryan, told me about your place. Said he came in a few days ago."

Mildred paused; her eyes wandered. *Did he just read my mind?* "Bryan...," she muttered. "Bryan who?"

"Bryan Wallace."

"Bryan Wallace... No...," she muttered again, unable to attach the name to a face.

"Anyway." Finally, he extended his hand. "Sterling Thorn, by the way."

She proudly gave him hers. "Mildred Morehouse, proprietor." She opened her other hand to Lauren. "And my assistant and dear friend, Lauren Brookhaven."

"*Hiii*...," Lauren said with something close to a purr, a little too kitten-like for Mildred.

Sterling returned a quick wave. "Hello."

"So, an arrangement," Mildred barged in with the subtlety of a bulldozer. After recapturing Sterling's attention, she dazzled him with all her wares, from rosy pink begonias to screaming yellow sunflowers.

"Truth be told," Sterling said, "I came here to get a woman's opinion on what my mom might like."

"Really?" Mildred smiled, but could think of no other florist shop in the area run by a man. This, she held to herself. "Well, you made the right choice." A cute giggle followed.

Meanwhile, off to the side, Lauren's eyes said it all as her mouth fell open: until now, flirtation was a side Mildred had never put on display.

In the end, it made sense that Sterling's final selection was as autumn-rusted as Lauren's cornucopia, since his mother was November-born. When it came time to take the order, Mildred was now tasked with the arrangement to be delivered to Sterling's mother in Sacramento, and she guaranteed him she'd get the size right. "Oh, so you're from Sacramento?" she asked him.

"Yes, I'm new here in San Diego. Here on a temporary assignment."

Mildred's eyes veered slightly away, surprised he'd stopped there. "A temporary assignment," she murmured, making sure not to leave a question mark in her tone, an obvious attempt to mask her personal intrigue.

But Sterling answered anyway, "Of course, 'temporary assignment' could mean a few years."

"Oh." She stopped and looked at his mother's name, Deepa Thorn, the obvious source of his part Indian features. Everything about Sterling was making Mildred more and more curious, but she held on to her last shred of professionalism, saying no more about his assignment or his heritage.

As soon as Sterling finished and made his exit, both women's eyes remained fixed on the door as if he were still standing there. By the time the chime's echo died and he vanished from view, both Mildred and Lauren were now all giggles.

With tight skirt on, Lauren spread her short, toned legs apart and stomped one to the floor, holding and aiming her fingers toward the door like a pistol. "Sterling Thorn, double-O-nine," she said in a deeper voice.

This one had Mildred confused. "Double-O-*nine*?"

"Yeah, that's that next generation spy!"

"Ha!" Mildred belted. "Lauren, chica, you are *too* much!"

Lauren chuckled, swiftly shifting to a chin-stroke before pointing a finger in the air. "Come to think of it... a 'temporary assignment' does sound a bit shady, shady. Which means...," she said, sliding her cellphone over to start tapping on it, "we're gonna have to find out a little something about this brother for when he comes back in here..."

"No, Lauren! Stop!" Mildred shouted. "Do not web-search that man!"

But Lauren kept tapping. "Why not?"

"Because... I don't want to know because he's not coming back here, and I don't care to know anyway."

"Yeah, right," she scoffed. "You two's chemistry was off the chart!"

"Pss, that was nothing but true retail skills at work. You witnessed it firsthand."

"Yeah, right," Lauren conceded and swiped her screen to off. "I don't see you displaying *those* kind of skills with other customers," she mumbled.

"What?"

"Nothing. But you *do* know he'll be back, right?"

Mildred's eyes pinched with suspicion. "Why?"

"Because you both had *nerd* juice for breakfast!"

"'*Nerd Juice*'! Lauren!"

"I'm serious! N-E-R-D *love*! Nerd Juice love."

Mildred chuckled. "I already know how you feel about me, but what makes you say that about him?"

Lauren shrugged. "I don't know. You know how you can just tell."

"See, you're probably going by his clothes, but I did not get that impression from his demeanor. I think he's sweet."

"Oh, I don't doubt that," Lauren concurred, "and I'm just kidding. He's cool." And she left it there.

Mildred, still chuckling, returned to her end of the counter to complete Sterling's order right away, thinking back to Lauren's original suspicion about him—his covertness about his job. And did he actually know the thought of a temporary assignment would interest Mildred even more? The allure of the race against time. *Like, how did he know*? Now, she was bothered, but gleaning any of Sterling's personal information for her own use was legally out of the question, no matter how much she already wanted to call him—so badly. The only thing she could hope for now was that he had seven aunts and both grandmothers still alive, anything to bring him back for another birthday.

Chapter 5

"That son of a hound dawg campaignin' to a room full of Women's Justice Leaguers will be like turnin' loose a rooster on Viagra!" Reverend Waldon Fontley chortled into his cellphone. It was his latest take on a colleague, one of the many colorful takes he'd offered over the years. He sat and worked in the ceremonial Eisenhower Executive Office, a lavish setting, behind what was once Theodore Roosevelt's desk. Not because he had to, but because it was just his style. As vice-president of the United States, he was an anomaly in more ways than his many titles implied. He could have easily walked over to his West Wing office, a few steps away, after his staff meeting, but there was something about the hanging chandeliers and gold-accented walls that made him feel at home. His eggshell skin-tone, wild red-flaming curly hair, and southern flare made him a curious selection considering the growing diversified south. But bible belt-ism was still strong, having made for an odd yet effective union with a presidential candidate of diverse background.

"Hey, I got another call comin' in, so you take care now, Senator! You hear?" he hollered before switching over. "Ee-yello!"

"Mr. Vice-President?"

"Yessss…"

"This is Mike P. Hampton of Bullhorn, the nation's largest gun manufacturer. I hope you don't mind, but Mr. Tolliver said it would be okay if I gave you a call."

Waldon leaned back slowly until the old chair croaked, until feeling a frown scour down his entire face. "Did he now?"

"Yes, Sir, he sure did. And we here at Bullhorn just want to thank you for your tie-breaking vote in the Senate. We couldn't have done it without you. You have singlehandedly made America a better place for us all."

"Well, uhhh, uhh, uhh—"

"And your church has been well—"

At this point, Waldon bounced up in his chair and cleared his throat, his free hand clinging to Teddy's desk for support. "What's that you say? I can't hear you! You're breaking up! Must be a bad connection! Don't worry, I'll call…" He stopped to think to himself, *No*. "Have a good day, Sir!"

Waldon was right back on the phone a few seconds later. "Mitch, what in the blazin' heck is goin' on down there?"

"Sir?" The fear in Mitchell Tolliver's voice was already blatant.

"I just got a call here from some fella' from—" He paused to lower his voice. "A fella' from 'Bull-You-Know-What' called to thank me for my decidin' vote. First of all, how in the heck did he get my phone number? And number two, once the deal is made, no one, I mean no one, is supposed to be contactin' me." He clinched his fist and gritted his teeth. "All church donations from unsolicited funding sources are to go directly through you and you only. Never am I to be notified or personally involved."

"Sir, I do apologize, but he gave me no time to think! Said they'd throw in an entire extra million just to be able to thank you personally. So, what else was I supposed to do?"

Waldon tugged his chin a good ten seconds.

"Sir?"

"Quiet. I'm thinkin'."

Mitchell said nothing.

More seconds of soul-searching followed. "I mean, it was a daggone tough decision. It's like decidin' how many kids gonna go down in the first round—ten, or twenty?" He swiped his hair back until a few curls straightened, huffing to himself. "But just think about it, Mitch. That money could be put to just as good a use than if we didn't have it. Right?"

"Most definitely, Sir."

"I mean, think about all the programs we can start to put an end to all this here violence anyway. Right?"

"Right you are, Sir."

"Why…, I'm not one to dispute our second amendment rights either. Well heck, everyone could use some protection to fire on an entire army, if need be. Who am I to deny them their rights to be armed and ready for war?"

"You are the one who has *given* us those rights, Sir."

"Yeah. Right." Waldon sat up in his chair, his chest stretching for the chandelier. "Exactly!" he blurted. "I knew this was a good idea, Mitch! Didn't I tell you this was a good idea?"

"Indeed, you did, Sir."

Waldon hung up with both his chest and chin now tilted in the air. His hands went behind his head as he leaned back in Teddy's chair, no longer taking into account the bribe he, himself, had encouraged—the bribe to keep military grade weapons available to the general public.

"Mr. Vice-President?" A woman's voice came through his desk phone, still standard equipment in any government office.

He opened the line. "Yes, Ms. Peterson?"

"Your ride is outside waiting for your next appointment, Sir."

He leaped to his feet. "Oh, yeah, that's right. I gotta' standin' one-thirty late lunch. Thank you, Ms. Peterson!"

It was now 2066, and Roberta's occupational hazards had diminished somewhat these days, but only mildly. Yet the mood was always dark. Fitted nicely in a dark suit with dark tie and wearing dark shades, she stood beside a dark tinted, luxury transport parked outside the Eisenhower building. A sedan, by 2066 standards. Two more dark suits with shades stood outside the car with their hands crossed, just like Roberta, except these two were born human.

All heads swiveled back and forth when Vice-President Fontley stepped out the building, his heavy strides crunching the pavement's surface. The rear car door open and waiting, he plunged in without a word to any of his secret service escorts. In the front seat was a human driver; presidential and vice-presidential motorcades were prohibited from being auto- or robo-driven. Droid-driven by the likes of Roberta would have been a gray area at this point, pending every grade on her current duty.

It was only a short ride ahead to the Palm, but like always these days, they bypassed at least fifty protesters just outside government grounds. Signs flew above high-stretched arms, reading: "We Want Our Jobs Back!" and "Human Jobs Matter!" They definitely mattered in terms of motorcade drivers, but nationally and globally, droids were taking all the blue-collar jobs, and the most basic models, those with lower grade learning chips, were preferred. Pay was only room-and-board and a charger, but the outside consequences were growing, for as much as android technology was advancing, the opposite could be said for the overall human condition. Jobs were scarce, poverty was growing, and very few people could afford technological advancements, all leading to a society that on the surface, looked fairly unchanged since the mid-to-late-2020s.

The Reverend Vice-President, apparently immune to the protesters and their plight, was on his phone by the first corner. The two human agents sat on each side of him while Roberta sat alone across from all three. ZepperCorp had succeeded with keeping Roberta in service by toning down her directive. All it took was swaying the government on the fact that she was a one-woman defense squad. Steadily gazing from window-to-window, she may very well have been able to do the job on her own, especially with a few new mods Dr. Murphy had installed, but rules were rules. Reducing the agents from four down to three was the extent of the government's compromise, along with Waldon's motorcade down to one vehicle only.

"Mr. Hampton, I sure do apologize for my brevity a few minutes ago!" Waldon blasted into his phone without shame. "I've heard your generosity is most appreciated. *Most* appreciated."

Roberta's status as the only artificial human in the vehicle was no secret to anyone inside, definitely not to the vice-president, who displayed no signs of discomfort, not even with the windows half-down. But the windows weren't down for just a gentle breeze; they were down for Roberta and her fellow agents to hear any potential commotion. Surely, as touted by ZepperCorp, *her* ears alone would have sufficed. But beyond the passing street conversations outside, she was sworn to secrecy regarding anything heard on the inside, no matter how the other agents were sworn in. Nothing said was to affect her job performance. Anything heard on the other end of the phone, however, was another one of those gray areas.

"Not a problem, not a problem at all, Mr. Vice-President," Roberta heard Mr. Hampton respond on the other end. "I'm glad you called me back. Gives me more of an opportunity to express just how much we at Bullhorn appreciate your vote, and how much we look after those who see the unlimited potential of our second amendment rights. And your church will continue to see the fruits of your good will."

Assess. Roberta's brain scrolled through the web. *Mike Hampton: C.E.O.—Bullhorn Guns; current elected president of the Unified Rifle Association.*

Waldon chuckled. "Very poetically stated there, Mr. Hampton, and many of my congregation and constituents are ardent proponents of our precious constitution."

"A trait vital to keeping every *true* American ready for all invaders at our doorstep, both foreign *and* domestic," Hampton said. "Those who do not share our degree of intellect."

"Well, I do declare, you're startin' to sound more and more like a man of my own ilk. You a church-goin' man, Mr. Hampton?"

Roberta's internal modem could access the internet from anywhere, available for her mind to scroll through at will. Yet she wasn't taking heed to anything written there about Waldon—not from the internet. Whatever she witnessed or whatever her ears picked up in the moment, she deemed most reliable and undeniable. Even with the outdoor noise elevating the farther they rode, she still caught every word of Waldon and Hampton's conversation. No matter how much her directive had been downgraded, her advanced A.I. was still intact to question judgement as much as the human mind. She knew Bullhorn was the biggest manufacturer of military-style weapons. *Military weapons to civilians?* she thought to herself. *The wrong direction for humanity.* It was as simple as that.

Roberta's swiveling gaze suddenly stopped on the reverend V.P., who seemed oblivious. She wondered how someone of *his* "ilk" could sell his vote. She had heard it was prevalent, but never had she witnessed it firsthand. And now they'd reached their destination.

"Hey," Waldon told Hampton, "I have arrived at my next meeting. Please feel free to keep in touch with Mit—uh, Mr. Tolliver from here on out, if you don't mind."

"Not a problem, Mr. Vice-President, but I'm sure you and I will run into each other here and there."

"Uh huh. You have a grand ole day, you hear?"

"Yes, you too, Mr.—"

Before Hampton could finish, Waldon had disconnected and was already practically beyond one of the agent's knees and at the car door.

"Us first if you don't mind, Mr. Vice-President," said the agent.

"Oh, yeah." Waldon sat back down and eyed Roberta instead. "Machinery before man. Right, agent? Hee, hee, hee, hee, hee."

Roberta and agent-number-two stepped out curbside, while the first agent was already out and standing streetside. All three checked every direction before the first agent gave the okay. "All clear, Sir," he told Waldon.

Waldon stepped out, put on his jacket and yanked his belt-line up his aged belly. He seemed comfortable with how his day was going, but Roberta was the first to feel a change in the air. The bolt-action of a sniper rifle struck her ear before Waldon's belt landed above his belly button. Instantly, she turned towards the source-point, a rooftop wall nearly a quarter-mile away. Her cybernetic senses kicked in. *Assess.* The glistening reflection from the weapon's scope glared straight through her shades.

Roberta knew she had a duty to respond, to throw her humanoid but resilient body in the line of fire, and to save her assigned client, one Mr. Vice-President Waldon Fontley. No matter what her manufacturer had thought of her, service at all costs was her most redeeming quality. But she possessed another unique quality, one Dr. Murphy had buried deep in her database. Roberta possessed a software called B.D.I.—belief, desire and intention.

B.D.I was the difference between a good and a bad decision, the core of Roberta's sentient behavior. It also prevented her from protecting a known criminal, and at this moment, she knew her client was guilty. *Reassess.* So, when the glare faded and the rifle's line of fire became clear, she did something not even ZepperCorp higherups would have imagined—she stepped aside and halted the vice-president tepidly, her compromise between duty and B.D.I. After this move, she *believed* the first bullet would strike his shoulder, and it did. It was her *desire* he'd learn a stiff lesson from this. Watching him stumble against the car, screaming, "Lord, have mercy! I been hit," she was sure he'd learn it sooner than later. Next, it was her *intention* to shield him with her lightning quick reflexes to catch the next bullet in her own back. That, she did, aided by her improved subdermal energy absorption system stiffening upon impact, one of those new mods from Dr. Murphy. One more bullet tore through her jacket as she stuffed Waldon back into the vehicle. She and the other agent followed closely behind. Just as the third agent dipped in afterwards, the armored sedan was off in a rush to the Walter Reed Medical Center.

Now in post-procedure, surrounded by his wife and a few staffers, Waldon was in an uproar by the time he was sitting upright in his hospital bed. "We pay PepperCorp all this dang money and this is what we get?" His arm and shoulder were already in a sling.

"That's ZepperCorp, Sir," one of his staffers added.

Waldon's mouth twisted and turned like chewing steel. "ZepperCorp! PepperCorp! Dr. Pepper! Dr. Zepper! I don't give a rat's patootie! We pay a small fortune for mistake-free security, and all she does is throw a *spaghetti* arm in my direction! And I swear, I saw that hunk o' junk step aside like one of them toro bull-fighters!"

The staffer raised a finger. "Uhh, toro is Spanish for bull, Sir."

"Goddamnit, will you shut the hell up!" He pounded the bed with his free fist until the pain reverberated all the way up to his stitched-up shoulder, then to his face. "Ooohhh, look what you've made me do! Not only am I more hurt, but you have made me take the name of our Lord Jesus Chr'ist in vain! Praise the Lord!"

The staffer said no more.

"Anyway," Waldon continued, "the Lord as my witness, I will not breathe another breath of polluted D.C. air until she and the whole lot she came out of are taken out of commission! ASAP!"

Chapter 6

Several days after Roberta-X150's fiasco in D.C., Dr. Kenneth Murphy sat in his Los Angeles office, lips pinched between his fingers and a valley across his forehead. He'd just gone twelve rounds with ZepperCorp's upper management to save Roberta from termination—again. This time, the final decision wasn't at all to his liking, while an average-sized man wearing a custodial jumpsuit and knocking at his office door, was the apparent outcome.

"Dr. Murphy?" the man asked. "I'll need you to come along to make this official."

Kenneth didn't respond, not verbally, that is. He rose from his chair in a huff, slumping his way out the door to follow the custodian.

But this particular custodian wasn't the typical janitorial staffer. What he oversaw was of a more sensitive nature. With unrestricted access, he led Kenneth all the way to the lower basement level, occasionally making an attempt at small talk. "Ee-yep. Workdays getting a lot longer these days," he announced as they weaved their way through a labyrinth of crates.

Kenneth simply nodded with folded lips and offered no eye contact. By the time they stopped walking, Kenneth was still moping.

"Cheer up, Doc," the custodian said with a shrug. "It's not like we're talking death here."

Kenneth looked up and saw something much more than a typical crate, but he didn't seem surprised, and he still didn't speak, only responding in his mind: *It might as well be.* Inside a self-ventilated metal box against a backwall stood Roberta-X150, the bulk of Kenneth's entire career. Seeing Roberta standing there, cadaver-like, stiff and nude with her eyes as glassy as crystals, he shook his head. Even during the time of her creation, before her activation, never had she appeared so robotic. And *her* container wasn't the only one; there were three more to the left. Hers was just the only one that was open.

The custodian quivered as if he'd walked in on Roberta taking a shower. "Oops, sorry. Don't know who left this one open," he said, stepping forward to press a button on the side.

Kenneth shook his head again. He could only imagine the sorts of activities that had gone on in the shadowy depths where they stood. Meanwhile, the door closed at the pace of a man on the moon, giving the custodian time to step back into position.

"This next part we need to do together, Doc."

Kenneth stepped back and straightened his lab coat's lapel, but with no real idea what to expect next.

The custodian raised his wrist-comm, pressed record and began speaking, "On this day, March eleventh, two-thousand-sixty-six at five-forty-six p.m., I, Leonard McGreggory, custodian-in-charge of Level A inventory, in the company of—" He stopped and held his watch in Kenneth's direction, receiving nothing but a twisted stare. "Name?"

Kenneth stared harder.

"I need you to say it."

"Oh. Dr. Kenneth Murphy."

"—chief scientist-in-charge of Level 10 Robotics and Computational Intelligence, do hereby bear witness to the decommission of multi-service units, A-X150, K-X150, Q-X150 and R-X150."

Roberta's door sealed shut on cue with the completion of the custodian's recital. Embossed on the door at eye-level were the letters, "R-X150," along with the word, "**DEFECTIVE**," stenciled below it. Kenneth finally noticed the letters on the other three containers, all labeled defective as well, but all guilty by association only. He, especially, knew the others had received no complaints. Those, he had simply been in charge of their creation, but Roberta was all his, personally crafted from crown to toe. He also knew Roberta was far from defective. She was the most A.I.-complete sentient anyone had ever seen, he was more than certain of it. *But why can't I make everyone else see it?*

Kenneth tightened his lips and fumed inside, remembering Roberta's last words before he'd deactivated her, alone together in his lab: "It's okay, Kenneth," she'd said, "I understand. Everything will work out just fine. You'll see." It wasn't the first time her self-taught optimism had surprised him. *Oh*, how much he wished he could hear it again at this very moment.

For the first time, Kenneth felt the custodian's gloomy frown in his direction, as if he finally understood. But Kenneth offered no tears, refusing to allow the system to break his spirit. "Rest in peace, my dear," he murmured.

Kenneth returned to his office in no better spirits than he was in the basement. Oddly, his door was closed. "That's strange," he mumbled. *I'm sure it was open when I left.* When he held his hand to the scanner, nothing happened; the door remained closed. He tried to open it manually, but still, nothing. That's when his watch received an alert just before making a second attempt. It was his supervisor and board member, Sabrina Chin, whose face emerged on his screen, a reminder that she wasn't in attendance during his plea for Roberta's amnesty.

"Hello, Doctor Murphy," she greeted him, a look more of anguish than her usual perkiness.

Kenneth was confused. "*Doctor* Murphy? Why so formal, Sabrina?"

"Yeah… I wish I could have been there today, but I happen to be at a conference in New York."

Kenneth shrugged. "That's okay." (It wasn't.) He thought for sure her presence, even remotely, would have helped his case tremendously. It made sense, though; Sabrina was never a day-to-day boss, allowing Kenneth free reign when it came to his department.

"I also wish this could be done under more respectful circumstances, but…"

Respectful circumstances? What is she talking about?

"…I still wanted to tell you this face-to-face," she said, her eyes beginning to droop.

"What?" He held his breath. *Has someone* really *died?*

"Vice-President Waldon's request for termination happens to have gone a bit beyond just the X-One-Fifties."

Kenneth's mouth dropped. "Excuse me?"

Two building security guards entered the hallway from afar at that very moment, heading directly towards Kenneth as if tapped into his conversation with Sabrina.

"I'm really sorry, Kenneth," Sabrina said, "your work here has been exemplary, but we're going to have to let you go."

"What!" He yanked on his door before his eyes went back to Sabrina. "Is this why my damn door is locked? What about my personal belongings?" he raged.

"Oh, I'm sorry about that too! Your personal belongings will be delivered to you after all proprietary items are secured. It's standard operating procedure. Security will explain the rest."

"*After*? Well now that's just *jacked up* and invasive!"

Meanwhile, both security guards were upon him. "Right this way, Sir," one said along with a feathery grasp of Kenneth's elbow.

"This is appalling!" Kenneth yanked his elbow away like a punch, only to have his other arm grappled by the other guard, but still gently so. "I, I… I don't understand," Kenneth repeated as he was escorted all the way down to the first floor and out the front door.

"Baby, you are the most brilliant biotech scientist—the most intelligent brother on the face of this planet. I'm sure you'll bounce back from this right away. No, *we'll* bounce back from this—together," was what Kenneth's wife, Linda, had told him just after his own termination. He'd phoned her from a seat on the front steps of ZepperCorp's Los Angeles headquarters. Normally he would have taken the jet-rail home, but thirty minutes later and he was still there, collecting his thoughts.

He finally looked at his lab coat and his Z-Corp shirt. "At least they didn't strip me naked." And yet he still failed to understand. He could have sulked all night on those steps if an old friend hadn't come to mind. "Baby, I have to make a call."

"So, I'll see you soon?" Linda asked him.

"Yeah, yeah, I'll be home right away."

"Alright. Love you."

"Love you more."

Afterwards, Kenneth was feeling much better, well enough to call Torrance Olivar, a friend from his college and graduate school days, one he'd kept in touch with from time to time. When Torrance's face popped on the screen, he was already nodding with a smile on his face. "Dr. Kenneth Murphy. What's happening in your world, my man?"

"Torrance, I'm in a bit of a jam, my brother," Kenneth confessed.

Torrance paused for a second. "Okay… what kind of a jam?"

"I've been let go."

"*Let go*?"

"Yes. As in fired, canned, flushed without toilet paper."

"*Fired*? Why on Earth were *you* fired?"

Kenneth sighed. "It's got something to do with a *defective* creation of mine. Well, that's how they see it, but she is far from defective! She is the most sentient droid on the face of this planet!" Kenneth flailed one arm in the air. "I'm certain of it!"

"Are you, now?" Torrance asked, intrigue in his tone.

"Yes! The only defect she suffers is that defect called *humanity*."

There was another pause. "Hey... wait a minute... you haven't been taking too much from the candy store, have you?"

"*Candy store*? What do you mean?"

"I mean, you haven't been taking this sentient behind the scene and—" Torrance clucked his tongue against the roof of his mouth.

"No! God no! What kind of a question—"

"Well... it's been known to happen, you know. Creators become enamored with their creations. First, you create the perfect being, then she's on your mind day and night. Then, you're spending more time with her, chatting her up, and the next thing you know..." He clucked his tongue again, twice this time.

Kenneth tipped his head from left to right. "Well, I do have a fondness for all my creations, and since I've programmed them to learn emotion, I too share an emotional connection with them... but hell no, bruh! Nothing like that! And Roberta and I have had a number of conversations before—and I can't believe I'm even dignifying this with an answer! Plus—" He stopped when he heard the building's front door open. Looking back, he witnessed someone he'd never expected to see again, not this soon. Sabrina Chin was scurrying out the front door with no haste, raising her satchel face-high when she saw Kenneth sitting there. Kenneth stood up and squinted. "Sabrina?"

"Can't talk right now, Kenneth!" she yelled. "In a hurry! Good luck to you!"

"Sabrina!" He took a few steps forward and stopped. "Sabrina!"

Wearing a blue jacket and matching skirt, Sabrina had already blended in with the sidewalk traffic like a mono-colored wall.

His phone in his fallen hand, Kenneth heard Torrance's faded voice: "Kenneth, you there? What's happening?"

Kenneth raised his phone. "You won't believe who I just saw."

"Who?"

"Sabrina Chin," Kenneth gritted. "She said she was out of town. Why... that little b—"

"What? When she canned you?"

Kenneth nodded.

"That's so Sabrina," said Torrance.

"Yes, it is. And I'm going to sue the shitty paints off of them, Sabrina included."

"Hey, hold on, hold on..."

"What?"

"It just so happens you won't need to. Well, you can if you want, but it just so happens we have an opening here at Silver-Stem Robotics for a *genius* like yourself."

Kenneth huffed, doing everything in his power to hang on to his frustration. But he was curious. It wasn't every day he'd fielded such a compliment from his friend. "What kind of an opening?"

"Don't worry. Something worthy of your talents, believe me. Something similar to what you're doing—*were* doing. Even better, actually." Torrance's smile returned, closer to a grin this time.

"Hmm… Would I be reporting to you?"

"Well, technically, but we would be essentially operating as equals, as far as I'm concerned. You'd be pretty much all on your own, buddy. Plus, I don't think I'd be able to put up with your ass on a daily basis anyway."

"*Pf,* likewise. But how can you be so sure you can sell me to your bosses? I mean, I suspect Zepper won't make it easy for me to find employment. And it doesn't look like Sabrina is gonna lift a finger on my behalf. Man, I'm fucking damaged goods now."

"Don't worry. My word carries far more weight around here than Sabrina's, or any damn body at ZepperCorp. And damaged goods? Far from it. You were a genius in college, and I don't suppose you've gotten any dumber since then. Have you?"

"Ha, ha," Kenneth grumped.

"Hey, but we have some advancements here that will make yours and all of good ole Zepp's projects look like spare parts for first generation metal-bots. Advancements that will blow them *all* off the shelf—no offense."

Kenneth shook his head. "None taken, but shit, that won't be hard to do now."

Kenneth eventually hung up feeling somewhat encouraged by both his wife's and Torrance's kind sentiments, but he couldn't erase the sting from being fired for the very first time. It was too soon; the wound was still festering. Yet he couldn't deny a burning desire to make ZepperCorp pay in every way possible. Joining Silver-Stem, their number one competitor, would be the sweetest revenge. When he tried to stuff his phone into his lab coat's pocket, there was something else in there blocking its path. He pulled it out—Roberta's central processing unit. All the commotion had made him forget he'd secretly removed it from her head just before she was shutdown.

A droid's C.P.U. was far beyond a typical computer's C.P.U. In it was not just an algorithm processor, but both Roberta's cognitive architecture and recurring neural network, her memories, and in this case, her emotion chip. Twisting it between his fingers, Kenneth let out a sigh of relief. He stuffed it back into his pocket and pranced away with his head held high, his chance for redemption now solely in his own possession.

Chapter 7

Business was better than expected at **Mildred's Floral Arrangements**, and Mildred was pampering it like a baby one Saturday morning. Months had passed and she had hired Bella's teenage cousin, Celia, as a parttime assistant. It gave her friend, Lauren, more time off, time to enjoy more "Lauren" things to do. Nowadays, Mildred had been too swamped to keep up with her bestie. Other than hiring Celia, she'd also installed a new security system that sounded off almost every time the wind blew. She always switched it off during workhours, except today. "Sterling Thorn approaching."

Mildred sighed to the ceiling. "Oh, I forgot to shut that damn thing off."

Busy pruning the window dressings as taught, Celia had never glanced up to see Sterling coming, not until the alert. She took a lingering look, then giggled bashfully on her way back to pruning. Mildred noticed Celia's little antics and smiled; it was the very same way she felt too. In fact, she quickly forgot all about the alarm when the door chimed and Sterling, the first visitor of the weekend, stepped in. Without a word, he sauntered in with his arm behind his back and a grin on his face. And by the time he reached the counter, out popped a bouquet of red roses.

Mildred smacked her cheeks with both hands. "Oh, my God! For me?" She accepted them and took a whiff like she'd never smelled any before. "Roses for a florist? This is a new one."

The last sentence, she'd mumbled, but not low enough to stop Sterling's brow from jumping ten stories. "Really!" he blurted. "Is that the way you feel?"

She gasped, blushed in embarrassment. "Oh, I'm so sorry! Thank you. They're beautiful. But what's the occasion?"

He rested his arm on the counter, then stared into Mildred's eyes as if Celia were invisible. "Do I need a reason?" he asked.

Mildred wanted to be humble, but just couldn't resist propping her hand against her waist. "You do if they come from another shop."

He rolled his eyes and sighed.

"Just kidding! Just kidding!" She laughed and pressed her nose into the buds for another whiff, a longer one. "Seriously though."

"Seriously what?"

"The occasion?"

"Oh, just something to get you off to a good start today, and… something to hold you over until I see you again—tonight," he assured, feigning bashfulness with a coy smirk. "That's all."

I knew there was an angle, Mildred figured, but it was an angle she was totally smitten with. Not another gibe flowed from her lips. "Oh, okay. Then let me put these in some water."

Sterling, definitely no longer the typical customer, turned out *not* to be the shady "spy" Lauren had suspected a few months ago. He was actually a Stanford grad, and now, an environmental specialist there to work on a coastline restoration program. A new southern California savior was what he was. He seemed to have a deep passion for it too, but nowhere near the level he was showing to Mildred. One more visit to the shop after their first meeting, had turned into exchanging personal digits, a dinner date at a fancy restaurant, and then dating on the regular. Sterling may not have been a spy, but he was as smooth as **009** to Mildred.

Spending weekdays together was always tougher for Mildred, but today was a Saturday, and she wasn't going to be held back by a curfew later on. Her only restraint was that she and he had yet to make love, and she wasn't quite sure when she'd be ready. They'd of course been to the movies together, and had each cooked dinner at home for one another—Sterling the far better cook. Each event had ended with either a long kiss or spooning on the sofa in front of the television, but never beyond that. Today, waiting to see how his "angle" would playout was going to be Mildred's barometer.

"Artificial unit approaching," the security system announced.

Mildred slapped her forehead and sighed to the ceiling again. "Oh, I've got to turn that thing off!" She pulled out her tablet and tapped into her control panel. "We don't need to know who or what everyone is or isn't, now do we?" She shut it off.

A short, stout middle-aged woman draped in an old-fashioned sweater, a long khaki skirt and a scarf over her head, waddled in like a maid from the late 1900s.

Celia had completely stopped her assigned task to hide behind a tall houseplant, where she stared at the woman, a female droid, like a soldier on recon. Meanwhile, Sterling stepped aside for Mildred to do her job.

"Hello, may I help you?" Mildred asked the lady like she would any other customer.

The woman lowered her scarf behind her head. "Uh, yes," she said politely, "my employer is looking for a few simple table centerpieces, if you would."

"Not a problem," Mildred said with a beaming smile. "Right this way, please."

Mildred was at ease the entire time she served the woman. Though the realism of these new model droids had her a little surprised. She hadn't been close to one since early childhood, so her memory happened to be a bit dusty. She did recognize this one didn't have the mechanical vocals some others had. She also realized the one in front of her wasn't as svelte as her family's housekeeper and babysitter when she was a child. Perhaps a non-intimidating presence was the manufacturer's goal with this one, and it was definitely working, still reminding Mildred of those good ole days.

Mildred heard the door chime. From the corner of her eye, she watched Sterling light-step his way out the door, his lips miming, "I'll call you later." She flashed a smile and a brief wave in his direction before bouncing back to her current customer.

Unlike Mildred, Celia was still gawking from behind the house-plant. Only wealthy kids had had the privilege of seeing droids up close and personal, but Celia's family wasn't near such wealth. So, to her, the woman facing Mildred at the counter was an eerie ma-chine too real to believe, the reason Celia continued her covert watch until the "robot" made its exit.

Chapter 8

Saturday night didn't go as planned for the new couple. Or did it? Mildred had worked so late, she was too tired for an evening out, so she decided to meet Sterling at his apartment instead. Thoughts of a homecooked meal were replaced by a warm delivery of Peking duck, General Tso's chicken, fried rice and noodles from Mildred's favorite takeout. Too hungry to function, it was all she could think about on her way over.

She now stood beside Sterling's dining area table, tapping her chin with one finger while he was grabbing plates from the kitchen. "Hmm, I just noticed something," she mumbled.

He stepped to the table and set the plates. "What's that?"

"You don't have a nice centerpiece for your table."

Sterling looked down at the table and frowned. A second later he looked up with a wiggling brow. "The better to see you with, my dear."

"You're so corny," she said with a light shove, every day beginning to agree with Lauren's "other" original assessment, but adoringly so. "But no, not *while* we're eating. I'm talking about when the table's sitting there all alone." As he chuckled his way back to the kitchen, she remained there and pondered. In Mildred's world, everything had life to it, including a table from a once living tree. "Those beautiful roses you brought me would have been a nice substitute."

Sterling returned with a couple of takeout boxes and set them on the table. "I guarantee you, those roses will live much, much longer inside *your* place than here."

"Hmm..." She shook her head before pivoting to the kitchen. "Let me help you with that," she said on her way to the remaining boxes. "Celia was really impressed by your gesture, by the way."

Sterling arched his brow. "*Celia*? Was she there today?"

"Oh, stop, Sterling! You know that little girl was in the shop today." When she set the final boxes on the table, she felt a pair of slim but firm arms wrap around her waist, and they weren't hers.

Sterling stroked and rubbed her stomach from navel to curve. "Haven't I told you? I only have eyes for you."

"Awww…" She sank into his grasp, wishing he would have sung it to her instead. "I see you have *old* ears too, don't you?"

The tummy rub came to an abrupt stop. "What do you mean?"

"I mean that lyric. That's a very old song."

"What? 'I only have eyes for you'?"

"Yes. It's even ancient to my parents. Must be over a hundred-years-old."

"Oh. What about your grandparents?"

Mildred hesitated; it was the first time her grandparents had come up. "I never knew my grandparents. They passed away before I was born or shortly after—all of them."

Sterling also hesitated. "Oh. That's strange. But I'm sorry to hear that."

Mildred shrugged, long over it. She then quickly grabbed his arms and steered them back into a rubbing motion, in no hurry to elaborate on two sets of sickly grandparents, not tonight anyway. Regarding Sterling's borrowed lyrics, it wasn't that it had bothered her. *He probably picked it up from someone else.* But it just so happened to trigger one of those rare memories from childhood, because as ancient as the song was, her parents still played it from time to time.

Spooning on Sterling's sectional sofa was where Mildred and he ended up after dinner. They watched a movie in Ultra-Def-3D, mesmerizingly realistic—no 3D-glasses needed. Not that the two were paying much attention to it. Whenever she wiggled like the filling in his spoon, all eyes went to the ceiling. Only occasionally did they look up at the television screen, where Cruise was playing an old gray-haired wizard.

Mildred poked out her bottom lip, nodded her head from side to side. "He looks pretty good for a-hundred-and-something."

Sterling smacked his lips in doubt. "C'mon. You know that's all makeup on his face, don't you?"

"Mmm… I don't know."

She felt him shrug. "Or these days, any actor can just have an android body-double, or even a face-double—an *identical* face-double. *Waaayyy* more realistic than advanced C.G.I."

She opened her hand towards the television. "But why would he need a face-double to play an old man? He's already over a-hundred-years-old!"

"And still doing his own stunts too, right?" Sterling snarked. "Oh, c'mon. That lady in the store today should be proof enough."

Mildred paused. "Speaking of which, she was another person Celia could not stop talking about. I can't believe she's never seen one!"

"*Person?*"

She slapped his wrist, the one wrapped around her waist. "You know what I mean. Truthfully, though, I have no idea what we should be calling them. I mean, they are getting more and more realistic looking every day. Plus, they sound *just* like us, not robotic and all. They have rational conversations…, they make decisions… Hmph, they might as well be called 'people.'" She waited, then nudged him after he'd gone silent. "What do you think about that, mister?"

Sterling stretched to a quiet yawn.

"Hey… you going to sleep on me?" she lifted her head and asked with another nudge.

"Nah, I heard you. I used to believe they were real people when I was a kid too, when we had one as a housekeeper. But—"

"Wait a minute." She tilted her head back until her blown-out hair brushed against his face. "Your family had a droid?"

"Yep. And she was just as realistic looking as that droid… uh, I mean, that 'woman,' who we saw today—enough to have me convinced."

"Wow…," Mildred said in quiet amazement. "That is such a coincidence, because we had one too."

"You did?"

"We sure did."

"And do you remember much about her? A she, I take it?"

"Uh, yes, she was a 'she,' and I remember a little bit. I mean, my parents told me what she was, but it didn't really sink in until much later. Her name was Rah…, Rah…, Robin, I believe, and come to think about it, she looked and sounded realistic too. She was kind and caring, and she used to hum a lullaby to get me to go to sleep."

"Oh, yeah? You remember *that* far back?" he asked with a light snicker.

"Of course. As a matter of fact…" She stretched out her arms, rocked her shoulders and hummed an old Spinners tune, finishing with the words, "…I'll be *around*." Her range was obviously higher, but the harmony was perfect.

Sterling tensed up. "What?"

"That was her lullaby song."

Sterling paused. "That was nice, but I thought you said she only *hummed* it to you."

"She did. But when I was a little older, I heard my mom playing it. Just like the other one, it was a song by a really old group called the 'Spinners.'"

"The *who*?"

"No, not the 'Who,' the 'Spinners.'"

"What?"

"Anyway," she went on, "whenever I was fussy and didn't get my way, Robin used to say, 'Patience, little one—the race is to the deliberate.'"

"Damn, I bet that confused the hell out of a little kid."

They both laughed. "Sure in the hell did," said Mildred, "but I figured it out."

"So, whatever happened to her?"

"I don't know… She left kind of abruptly. I remember waking up one day and… she wasn't there. At the time, I didn't know what happened to her. Later, my folks told me—Hey!" She stopped, pointed at the screen as the credits rolled. "Aww, we missed the ending."

"Oh, yeah. He waved his wand and swept the bad guys up with some kind of magic twister. Or… something like that."

Mildred was on the verge of getting up and pressing re-wind when Sterling grabbed her tighter around the waist. "Don't," he quietly urged.

She took a breath. "Why?"

"Because—*sm*—I may just—*sm*—have a better—*sm*—ending for you," he whispered, soft kisses on the neck in between.

The sofa was too tight to turn around on, but Mildred found a way, turning those kisses on the neck into kisses on the lips, multiple times. "Mmm, I believe I *would* like that ending much better."

Mildred may have only uttered it, but it was the loudest and boldest thought she'd ever expressed to him, especially when it came to thoughts of a happy ending. Because even in her late twenties, only God and Lauren knew she was still a virgin, a rarity in any era. And she had done everything in her power not to let Sterling know, wondering: *What will he think of me? Will he think I'm not experienced enough? Not satisfying enough? Not woman enough!* It was enough to almost start a fire panic. But when she stopped and stared into his eyes, she buried those virgin instincts into obscurity, and her lips deeper into his. The line between passion and feasting became blurred, and it was more than Sterling's eyes that stirred her emotions. Not only was each of them an only child, but both now shared vivid memories of a dear time in their lives. Maybe not so much from him, but it was enough for her to feel it deeply, and his next words assured her he felt the same.

He pulled back and stared even deeper into her eyes. "Mildred, I think I'm falling in love with you."

Her eyes watered, almost instantly, as she replied, "I think I'm falling in love with you too," before falling back into his lips.

Moments later they were standing instead of lying down, and Mildred had no memory of how they ended up there. At this point she wanted more; she leaped and wrapped her legs around his waist to prove it, and Sterling's lean arms were much stronger than they appeared. He held her steady and carried her all the way to his bedroom, leaving behind at least thirty minutes of closing credits.

Sterling and Mildred were still wrapped in one another's arms by the time they made it into the bed. They rolled back and forth a few times, clothes tossed aside erratically until both were completely nude atop his rumpled covers. And now Sterling was on top of her, on the verge of connecting.

She continued to fight to keep her silence, to pretend she'd been here before—to pretend she was already all woman, but she lost miserably. "Sterling, I have something to tell you," she whispered, panting while gently holding him back.

"What?" he whispered back, halfheartedly, also panting.

"I've never gone this far before."

"What do you mean?"

"I mean…, I'm still a virgin."

Sterling's mouth closed softly, but sounded like a door slamming shut to Mildred. "Really?" he asked.

She nodded with fear in her soul.

"You want me to stop?"

She paused, then shook her head.

"Then I'll be gentle."

"Please do," she whispered, followed by a soft moan as he inserted his love deep inside her.

And gentle, Sterling was, but what he did next, the way he moved, was like electricity coursing through Mildred's veins—like nothing she'd ever imagined. And by the time they reached climax, she exhaled all her bliss into his ear, grateful to God she had waited for the right one.

Wrapped in a bedsheet only, Mildred stood in the kitchen doorway the next morning with her feet crossed. Sterling's efforts at the stove had her stuck there, gnawing away at one fingernail as she leered at him. In nothing but tight briefs, his back turned, he swayed over a skillet. Despite the aroma of seasoned omelets filling the room, he made her want to skip breakfast altogether and start last night all over again.

She'd replaced the sheet with a satin slip by the time breakfast was served, while Sterling had added only a plain white undershirt to his briefs. "Butter?" he asked as he nudged it in her direction.

"Yes, please." She began spreading the butter over two slices of toast, all while gazing only at Sterling, adoring him.

But Sterling's eyes were on his plate and *his* plate only. He was already close to finishing his first piece and a quarter of the way into his omelet by the time he looked up. "What?" he paused to say, but only for a second before his eyes returned to his plate.

Mildred suddenly feared the worst. One: after only one night of sex, she was already losing his attention to a chicken egg. Two: this entire breakfast wasn't for *her* at all. Watching Sterling scoop and scoff down another forkful of omelet, she tried to hold it together. "This is so nice, Sterling. Thank you."

"Huh? Oh, you're welcome," he muffled and flashed another look her way, then right back into his toast. "You know..." *Crunch, crunch, crunch, crunch, crunch.* "I think your friend, Lauren, will like my friend, Bryan."

Mildred couldn't believe the suggestion or its timing. *Has he forgotten I just gave up my goddamn virginity to him?* Finally, she focused on her own plate and began eating. "Really?" she said with the flatness of a tire. "Why's that?"

He shrugged. "I don't know—he's a fun guy."

"Yeah, I got that impression when I met him." She had only met Bryan once and was thankful he'd told Sterling about the shop, although she still never remembered his face as one of her first customers. Nonetheless, she had read about this instinct in a man—*in a boy*—to try to hook his friends up the first thing the next morning after things had gotten good for him. His *boys* always came first. *One for all and all for one! Bros before hoes!* But Mildred had originally thought she was dealing with a *man*. She wondered, *Is this a bad sign?* But she decided not to make too hasty a judgement, so she played along. "Well, maybe they *should* meet."

Sterling nodded. "Mm hm." Then in a shocking move, he reached for one of two glass pitchers sitting near the center. "Here. You haven't tried the apple juice." He poured her a glass and set it back down."

"Thank you." She accepted it with her pinky half extended and took a sip. "Mmm… this is really good."

"The best in town—sold in only one store *waaayyy* on the other side."

"Really?" Again, flatly.

"Mm hm. I got it because I knew you were coming over."

"*Really*!" Mildred latched on to every piece of Sterling's gesture she could, until she couldn't. "Yeah, right."

"What!" His eyes blew up. "I'm serious!"

"Nice try, buddy," she said with a piercing glare.

He stabbed and lifted his last piece of omelet. "I don't know why you don't believe me."

Mildred was almost convinced, but after the one sip of juice, she stood up and took her nearly full glass and her plate, half an omelet still remaining, to the kitchen sink, huffing at the end. It wasn't the celebratory breakfast she was expecting. *We should have just stayed in the damn bed.* But her sour mood shifted when she felt Sterling's arms wrap around her waist again, his breath in her ear.

"So, do I have you for the rest of the day?" The warm breeze from his question tickled her earlobe, while something else tickled her below the waist.

She leaned back instantly, like drawn by a magnet. "Do you *want* me for the rest of the day?"

"Well, I didn't make reservations for two at the museum if I didn't."

She swiveled around in his arms like a ballerina until they were nose-to-nose. "The Museum of Art?" Her celebration had arrived.

"Yes, Ma'am."

"Okay…" She smiled so hard, not even their subsequent kiss could wipe it away. That's when she really felt him rise to attention.

He gave her a peck. "But we have plenty of time before that. Perhaps there's something we need to finish in…"

His simple nod towards the bedroom was all Mildred needed to wrap her legs around his waist again, just like the night before, except this time with more help from Sterling. Passionate kisses followed, and their blooming romance was back on track.

Chapter 9

Kenneth Murphy stood atop the mezzanine deck above Silver-Stem's assembly room, gazing over mechanized arms in motion, all of them busy assembling the core internals of their next model. Months had passed since the "incident" at ZepperCorp, and it was Kenneth's first day on the new job. Torrance Olivar was standing beside him to usher him in. Just as Torrance had implied, Silver-Stem's designs were far more intricate, and demand was high.

"I'm sure you're aware that we recently became nearly one-hundred-percent U.S. government-funded, which means most of our projects will lean in a military direction, but with a *little* leeway to vary," Torrance informed before jabbing his finger at the assemblage below. "But *this* room, Ken, is what separates Silver-Stem from the rest." Uncompromised conviction rained from his voice. "Veins and muscles stranded to a seamlessness only apparent to the world's highest res. microscope. Countless hours spent on each organ, making sure they function to the highest of human efficiency. Just a kidney alone can take days to perfect."

They began a slow walk around the deck, each with his hands behind his back, except Kenneth moved with his own puzzle to assemble, one with a missing piece. "Excuse me for asking, but shouldn't you—I mean, shouldn't *we* be aiming beyond 'human' efficiency? Isn't that our purpose in it all? To surpass the limits of humanity?"

Torrance raised his forefinger, an enthused look in his eyes. "I'm glad you ask, my friend. Let me put it to you this way: it's like designing a passenger vehicle. Some are built for high-speed, some are built for luxury and unparalleled comfort. Some are built for a level in between. The end use will dictate the function."

"This, I know, my friend—with regards to vehicles, but I fail to see how the two correlate."

"No? Well, let me put it to you another way: in your design of the X-One-Fifty, was it not your intention to make the brain A.I.-complete, to function as comparable to the human mind as possible?"

"Yes…"

"Okay, then why 'like' the human mind and not 'superior' to the human mind?"

Kenneth paused, drawing upon his debate class wizardry from college years. "Well now, there does exist a certain aspect of the human decision-making process which the droid can benefit from: instincts and spontaneity. For this, there is nothing superior. It would take a far superior, more creative mind just to know a process superior to this, and therein lies the societal debate. We were only able to try our best, but it was definitely a line item. We did, however, aim for a superior body, and that, we did accomplish. I mean, the human body, although Silver-Stem has made advancements in increasing the lifespan of human beings for several years now as well—the human body is feeble in the universal spectrum. Unadaptable and slow to evolve."

"But you see, that's where I beg to differ," Torrance retorted, his fingers pinched together. "Not only does the human body carry its own unique and valuable aspects, but there is something you've failed to mention in elevating the A.I. mind:" He leaned in towards Kenneth's face with expanded eyes. "Creativity. Creativity paired with computer logic can be boundless."

Kenneth raised both palms, gave a light smile. "Whoa, be careful there. You're talking about setting off the alarm for all the existential risk theorists and fundamentalists to come out of hiding."

Torrance chuckled and patted him on the back. "Man, don't try to play me. I'm sure you've already considered this in your design process. Anyway, it's not that deep. It's deep. But it's not *that* deep." He pointed at the assemblage below again. "This is the frontline of one of our most advanced projects, which you'll see sooner than later. In the meantime, follow me this way. There's someone I'd like you to meet."

Kenneth couldn't deny it to himself; he was pumped. A spirited philosophical debate was what he lived for. But he now trailed his friend, wondering, *I still don't see what in the hell this has to do with the make and style of a motor vehicle.* He wanted to spit it all out to nail his point, but it was only his first day on the job. As many times as he'd slain Torrance in friendly debates outside of work, as Kenneth saw it, Torrance was now, technically, his senior in the company, no matter how much Torrance tried to downplay it. So, it was time for Kenneth to bring his own point to an abrupt end. But who was he kidding but himself? Prior to this day, knowing when to cap-off his scientific battle tactics was actually his wife's idea.

Nonetheless, one of Kenneth's debate points was what every expert had known about Silver-Stem. It was a company founded long ago, rooted in stem-cell and organic research to heal the elderly and add to their years. Thus, the title, Silver-Stem. Kenneth was excited about their progress in bio-robotics; their stem-cell technology had obviously played a huge role in his decision to join the team.

Kenneth proudly continued to trail Torrance to someone's office. "You've got to be kidding me," Kenneth mumbled when he stepped inside. The baldheaded gray-beard sitting behind the desk looked awfully familiar.

"Dr. Murphy," the old man said as he rose from his chair, leaning forward with his hand extended.

"Dr. Gaines?" Kenneth, caught in his own brand of subdued giddiness, hurried over to shake the man's hand. "Please, call me Kenneth."

Torrance, peeking in from just outside the door, had led Kenneth to the man still known as their favorite college professor, Dr. Forrest Gaines. Kenneth had to strain to connect the dots since the head, beard and cheek lines were all new to the professor's style.

"No, no," Dr. Gaines blared, "you've earned the title, and therefore, you should bear the name, Dr. Murphy!" From there was a cross between a right hook and a fist-pump. Now, that, was Professor Gaines's style.

Torrance stepped farther inside with a tiny smirk. "Yeah, we dug this old guy up a few years ago from underneath a stack of bio-engineering papers he was grading on campus."

"A few *years*?" Kenneth blurted. "Why haven't you ever told me?"

Torrance shrugged. "Apparently saving it for today, I guess."

Dr. Gaines inflated his chest in Torrance's direction. "And what do you mean by 'old guy,' Dr. Olivar?" he blasted. "I still possess the wherewithal to run circles around you, in both the classroom and the track—if you ever want to put me to the test!"

Torrance leaned back, waving his hands in surrender. And Kenneth believed Dr. Gaines may have had a point; his rapid body movements and spryness gave no indication of his appearance above the neck. The advantage of working for a company still formidable in stem-cell research was showing itself, more so than what the general public saw.

Torrance continued as soon as all the jovial testosterone fizzled out, "What's it been, Dr. Gaines—six, seven years now?"

Dr. Gaines shrugged his chin. "Mmm… give or take."

"The doctor here has always been a consultant for us, and now he's here fulltime, working on some *special* projects for us. We're lucky to have him."

Just as Torrance nodded in admiration, both Dr. Gaines and his chest receded to humble gratitude.

"And how's your wife, Dr. Gaines?" Kenneth asked, praying she was still alive.

"She is doing just fine, bless her heart," Dr. Gaines said and winked, "and still calling the shots."

After a little more time with Dr. Gaines, Kenneth followed Torrance up one flight of stairs to meet the big chief, C.E.O. and Director of Research and Development, Dr. Jahid Al Balushi. Jahid was someone Kenneth had known about, but had almost lost sight of. The way the morning had been going, he was convinced Torrance was the true director, himself, if not C.E.O. His majestic presence throughout the tour had said so. But there was no mistaking who was in charge when they approached Jahid's office. A pure scientist by background, one couldn't have told by his commanding presence. Torrance actually knocked this time, his head bowed in deference with no formal introduction. But Jahid stood up with a look that said none was necessary.

"Dr. Kenneth Murphy, it's a pleasure to finally meet you," Jahid said, leaning over his desk with his hand extended.

Kenneth met him with a stiff handshake. "Same here, Director Al Balushi, Sir."

"Please, feel free to call me Jahid. First name basis works just as well around here. Plus, I find 'Director Al Balushi' to not only be stuffy, but a mouthful as well," he said with a light smile, the complete opposite view to Dr. Gaines.

"Oh. Then please feel free to call me Kenneth." Kenneth returned the pleasantry, but heard no "old man" remarks from Torrance this time either—not that Jahid was anywhere near Dr. Gaines's age.

"Uh, please, gentlemen, have a seat." Jahid waited for both his guests to sit down. "So, Kenneth, how was your vacation?"

"Just fine, just fine. We had a great time."

"Hawaii, was it?"

"Yes, Hawaii. The kids loved it. The Mrs. loved it."

"You guys' first time there?"

"Oh, no…, well, first time for the kids, but about the… third time… for my wife and me."

Jahid leaned back in his chair and stared at the ceiling as if his own memories were at hand's reach. "Yes, beautiful place."

It was tough for Kenneth to consider time between jobs a vacation, but he and his family had taken an entire month off before starting the transition from Los Angeles County to San Jose. Hawaii proved to be just what they'd needed to soften the gut-blow thrown by ZepperCorp.

"Just curious—did you guys get a chance to visit the Waimea Canyon while you were down there?" Jahid asked further.

Kenneth nodded. "Yes, we did! We had to do something to wear the kids out."

"How many children?"

"Two. Boy and a girl."

"Oh, yeah. That's all it takes."

Quaint laughter followed, leading all three men into a few more Hawaii stories before Jahid finally changed the subject. "I guess this is sort of a homecoming for you, right?" he asked Kenneth.

Kenneth stared in confusion. "Home...coming?" Originally from Illinois, he didn't quite understand.

"Yes. Closer to Stanford."

"Ah, yes! It is a little bit of a homecoming."

Both Kenneth and Torrance had graduated from Stanford, where Dr. Gaines had groomed them for life after multiple degrees. And here they all were, in the same building, together again as if they should have never parted. It was making more sense to Kenneth by the minute. Unlike Silver-Stem, ZepperCorp was the only company of its kind with no location in Silicon Valley, a valley he should have never left.

"So, are you and the family all settled in now?" Jahid asked.

Kenneth sighed. "Just about. I decided to come up here first while my wife takes care of a few final matters there in L.A. They should be up in about another week."

"Good, good. The corporate house is all yours as long as you need it until you find a place. I'm sure you know the area; it hasn't changed much since you were last here." Jahid aimed his hand at Torrance. "But if nothing comes back to memory, I'm sure Torrance will be happy to assist."

Torrance tipped his head. "Of course."

"Good, good," Jahid repeated. "So, I'll let Torrance finish your orientation. Meanwhile, are there any questions you have for me before you get to it?"

Kenneth's comfort level had been growing the entire conversation up until this point, now replaced by an air of solemnity. "Well... if it's not too much trouble, I've been wondering what project, exactly, will I be assigned? I mean, since ZepperCorp obviously owns all the rights to my years of research, my life's work is practically in their poss—"

"Don't you worry about that," Jahid interrupted, still upbeat. "Torrance will show you what's next on that front too."

Everyone stood up. "You'll be pleasantly surprised," Torrance, again the heir-apparent, promised with a nod that took Kenneth's curiosity to new heights.

Jahid leaned forward and shook Kenneth's hand again. "I look forward to working with you, Kenneth."

Moments later, Kenneth was again on an elevator ride down into a baselevel much like the one at ZepperCorp. He followed Torrance through rows of cargo boxes, a bit more organized than his former employer, but still another labyrinth of alleyways. An eerie feeling followed, yet one Kenneth was far too curious to question. It wasn't until their journey ended at the farthest wall, did he finally mumble, "What the…?"

Standing against the wall was a single metal box with the letters, "R-X150," embossed across an opaque door. Painted below the letters was a solid black rectangle where the word, "**DEFECTIVE**," was faintly visible, but covered by it.

Torrance pressed in a code on the side and stepped back, while the door glided open endlessly slower than Kenneth remembered. A light switched on automatically once the door opened, illuminating Roberta standing there like a statue, no longer cadaver-like, but still stiff, nude and glassy-eyed. "What the…?" Kenneth repeated.

Torrance opened his arm like an emcee. "She's a gift," he said with a pause, "just for you."

Kenneth could hide neither his joy nor his confusion. "What did you do, steal her?"

"Good God no, man." Torrance chuckled to a serious stop. "But close. We managed to do a little light finagling and cutting through red tape to purchase her."

"You *purchased* her?"

"Yes."

"All rights? All programming?"

"Indeed, my friend. All rights, all programming, all everything. Well, due to the nature of her deactivation, we can't label her as an X-one-fifty anymore, and they only allowed us to purchase one. So, I took a stab in the dark and figured this one was a good one to keep you company—the one who got you into trouble in the first place, I believe…" Another chuckle followed.

"*Pf*—you already knew all this," Kenneth said while stepping forward, where he floated his hand only inches away from Roberta's body. "But I don't understand." He looked at Torrance. "You were on the verge of deeming her obsolete, yourself—more than a month ago."

Torrance's hands were now behind his back. "She was. She is. But she doesn't always *have* to be."

Kenneth turned back to Roberta, beaming at the possibilities. She was just what he needed to get off to a burning new start.

"Strange thing, though," said Torrance.

"What's that?"

"We did a scan, and… it seems her C.P.U. is inexplicably missing." He raised a brow. "Any idea why?"

Kenneth twisted his lips. "Mmmm…"

"Well, anyway, you'll have many more new projects to explore," Torrance assured, followed by a hand on Kenneth's shoulder, "but Project Roberta is up and running again. And she's *all* yours."

Chapter 10

Picture a family: a mother, a father and a sweet little daughter with the face of an angel, side-puffs, and lollipop eyes staring up at you as she lifts a sunflower for you to smell. Fast-forward through dozens of vivid images to another time, more like another world, full of gunfire, explosions and death—then to the anguishing face of a vice-president collapsing in your arms after being shot in the shoulder. All ended by Dr. Kenneth Murphy's face about a foot away before you black out. This was the strange diaspora of Roberta's life, all wrapped into a string of memories before opening her eyes to the present. She opened them to crosshairs streaming horizontally back and forth, and quaternary codes counting in place along the right periphery. *Assess.* The date and time were both on the left, nearly three months since she last saw anything but complete darkness. Erased by a quick flash of static grains, all was replaced by Kenneth's real face even closer than before, now in perfect clarity.

"Data fusion—complete," Kenneth said, tapping his notepad keys. "Integration—complete." He waved his hand before her eyes. "Roberta? Roberta, can you hear me?"

Roberta hesitated. "Yes. I can hear you." Her vocal cords quivered like an instrument out of tune.

"Can you see me?"

"Yes. I can see you."

"Good. V.P.U.—complete. A.I. accelerator—complete also. Okay, what is your system identification?"

She hesitated again because something felt different. "My system identification is R-One-Fifty." *What happened to the "X"?*

Kenneth leaned in a little closer. "Do you recognize my face?"

Of her own volition, Roberta decided to look elsewhere first. Surrounding them both was a lab, one her system had never processed before, but it was processing every bit now. She noticed herself wearing nothing but a johnny-gown, then her eyes landed back on Kenneth. *Adjust vocals.* Her mechanical voice leveled to an even tone, practically sultry, as she answered the question, "Yes, I recognize you, Kenneth—my creator."

Kenneth peered with a touch of reprehension in his eyes. "Your *what*?"

Reassess. "My… maker."

Roberta's core processor had been programmed with many things; general religious knowledge was one of them. But the last distinction, "maker" versus "creator," was one she wasn't familiar with until that very moment, an obvious update. Whatever it was, it led to Kenneth jotting it down with his head shaking.

With more vital functions coming online, Roberta felt just as many additional modifications, highlighted by a sharp shriek that flew from her mouth—an emotional outburst. A tear followed. "Ooh, excuse me," she said, covering her mouth with one hand as if she'd belched, and wiping her cheek with the other. "I must be malfunctioning."

Kenneth leaned back in his chair and folded his arms. "Actually, you're not. You can say I was *coerced* into elevating your emotion chip."

Her lips curled. "Uhh, why?"

"To better integrate you into civilian society," Torrance explained as he stepped into the room.

Kenneth opened his hand after Torrance walked into the room. "Roberta, I'd like you to meet Dr. Torrance Olivar. Dr. Olivar, meet Roberta."

Torrance approached Roberta. "The pleasure's all mine," he greeted her, but he didn't say it with much conviction, nor did he extend his hand. With eyes narrowed, he only leaned into her face like she was a rock from another planet. "Good, good, good," he mumbled.

Apparently not so good to Roberta, who folded her arms and sneered. "Everything to your *liking*, Dr. Olivar?"

"Huh? Oh, yes, yes. The detail is immaculate." He leaned back. "Do you mind if I try something?"

"*What?*"

She looked to Kenneth for clarity, who offered none.

Meanwhile, Torrance didn't seem to need an answer just to say, "Code seventy-one, shutdown."

"Is he—" Roberta stopped with eyes still on Kenneth and a finger aimed at Torrance, where they remained like a freezeframe, just like her opened mouth.

The seconds ticking through Roberta's pause gave Torrance time to explain to Kenneth, "Just checking our executive authority."

"I see." Kenneth folded his lips, then gritted. "And when did *this* happen?"

"Umm… maybe while you were asleep," Torrance said with a light shrug and a bright-eyed smile.

But Kenneth was fuming. It was like a member of his own family had been violated. "And just who else has this executive privilege?"

Torrance shrugged again. "Not many. Just you, me, Jahid—and a few other board members. That's all."

"That's all! So, you're telling me the entire world can shut her down with just one word and two numbers?"

Torrance laughed to the ceiling. "No, ho, ho, hooo! That's not the entire world! And the controls are voice-specific."

Kenneth pointed to himself. "But Torrance, she is *my* project. No one was supposed to touch her but me!"

"I know. I know. And I *am* sorry."

"What, you didn't think she'd be capable of maintaining safety protocols on her own?"

"Well… you can never be too safe."

"But—"

"Oh, everything will be fine, Kenneth!" Torrance said on his way out the door.

"Hey!" Kenneth shouted. "What's the reboot code?"

Torrance's voice echoed from down the hall. "Code seventy-two, reboot!"

Kenneth didn't have to repeat it; Roberta was back in motion just from Torrance's distant command. "—serious?" She picked up where she'd left off, struck by a stifled look when she gazed around the lab. "Where did he go?" Again, she looked to Kenneth; again, he said nothing. She scratched her head. "What just happened here?"

It was dark outside by the time Kenneth finished running diagnostics on Roberta, and leaving her alone right after a long shutdown was not in his plan. The enhanced emotion chip was something Torrance had talked him into. Like he'd explained, the plan was to get Roberta as integrated as the other droid units they already had deployed, which was fine with Kenneth; he didn't mind at all. Ever since the military miscues, he was never too excited whenever Roberta had lost an arm or a leg, or even a finger. Any new assignment for her would be a cakewalk in his eyes. So, he led her to the company's main courtyard with much catching up to do. Palm trees surrounded by Hawaiian ferns formed the yard's centerpiece, but the two migrated to the most isolated corner they could find. They sat side by side atop a planter wall, Kenneth still in his lab coat, and Roberta no longer half-nude. Underneath her johnny-gown was now a two-piece tight set.

Kenneth took a swig of soda and let out a huge sigh. "Yeah, things got pretty ugly after you went dark," he informed Roberta.

Roberta, definitely no longer in tears, took a swig from her own can and did the same. She never really had to drink anything, but her system was already designed to process any food or drink. As her program further dictated, logic wasn't the only driving force behind her actions; socializing was also a prime directive. If ever she assessed comradery to be advantageous to a relationship, she wouldn't have hesitated to wine and dine on anything.

She gazed at the buildings overlooking the courtyard. "I take it by the new fancy surroundings that things didn't go so well for us at ZepperCorp."

Kenneth drooped in exasperation. "No…, they didn't. But it's not just that; it's the *way* they let me go. They practically dragged me out on my ass!"

She turned with a sidelong glance. "Really? On your ass?"

"It felt like it! I mean, more than twenty years of service, and they throw me out like a common criminal! Escorted out by ruffians! It was rude. It was disrespectful. It was downright humiliating!"

"Aww…" Roberta's eyes fell in sympathy, a reaction Kenneth wasn't expecting so soon. "But surely everyone knows Fontley is the real criminal, don't they?"

"Yeah, we analyzed your recordings thoroughly and discovered that, but ZepperCorp has an agreement with the government, prohibiting anything gained behind closed doors—deeming it confidential and inadmissible in a court of law—similar to attorney-client-privilege. So, I couldn't use it for payback or anything."

"Yes, I remember. Well, I do apologize for my role in it, but my graphic prediction model instantly assured me the bullet wasn't going to hit a crucial artery. My internals assessed the shooter's aim, crosswind velocity, the drag coefficient, distance; every factor was taken into account."

"Hmph, every factor but the aftermath."

"And I'm sorry about that—but after all, I *am* programmed not to protect criminals. It was a fair compromise, if you ask me."

Kenneth sighed to the sky, shaking his head. "Ohhh, Roberta, Roberta, Roberta." His chin fell into his chest, in the end knowing he had only himself to blame.

Roberta shrugged. "Well, chin up, Doc," she offered with a hand on his shoulder. "It's over now. And this place *is* much better than ZepperCorp, right?"

He tugged his chin into a slow nod. "You know what? I believe you're right."

She joined him in another swig and belched. "I know I'm right."

Kenneth's mood switched from gloomy to complete comfort. It was like he'd designed Roberta as his own voice of reason, his own personal confidant to hold his deepest feelings safe. But there was a far greater reason for his close and personal attachment to her. He took a long look at the side of her face, a familiarity beyond what he'd seen after molding the lifelike silicon. Her features bore a striking resemblance to his own little sister, Keneisha. Keneisha may have been three years younger than him, but her antagonistic wisdom was seldom wrong. It always took another pair of eyes to make him see a side of himself he couldn't—an honest set of eyes. His one little sister had carried those eyes just for his sake—but for sixteen years only. Keneisha ended up dying from a rare heart disease two days after her sixteenth birthday, and Kenneth's life took form immediately after. Until then, his college major was undecided. Medicine was one consideration, but there was another profession dominating social media, and medicine wasn't going to bring back his sister. In Roberta's face he saw Keneisha—at least a grown version of her. Overall, it was the main reason he no longer wanted to be referred to as Roberta's "creator." He'd chosen the word, "maker," believing a higher force, one far above himself, was at work when *this* droid was created.

He and Roberta talked a few more minutes until an old-school hip-hop beat chimed from his watch, his ringer.

"I think you better get home to your wife," Roberta calmly advised.

Kenneth's fingers rushed to open his phone's screen. "Hey, baby! Wh-wh-what are you doing?" he jittered as if he were cheating on her.

"Stalking you, apparently."

"Oh!" He didn't know whether to take her seriously or not, but his guilt had nothing to do with talking to Roberta. "I'll be on my way home right away." It was his inordinate amount of hours at the office that had him shifting back and forth.

"That's not what I—"

"I was just catching up with... catching up with, um... Roberta! See!" He aimed his wrist in Roberta's direction.

Roberta smiled and waved. "Hi, Linda!"

"Oh! Roberta!" Linda was beyond excitement. "Welcome back! How are you?"

"All is well. How are you?"

"I'm fine. I'm so happy to see you!"

Roberta raised her can of soda and jiggled it. "Sorry to have your hubby out drinking all night," she said with a sense of humor that had also been tweaked.

Linda laughed out loud. "That's quite alright!" She switched to side-cupping her mouth for a blaring whisper: "He could use a stiff drink to loosen him up a little."

Kenneth sneered while both women laughed. "Alright, alright," he said, "get it all out your system. I'll be home soon, though."

But Linda waved him off. "No, no… like I was trying to say, I'm not begging you to come home. I was just wondering if you were okay. Just trying to make sure you're safe. But go on and do your thing. Take your time. I am fine here with some of my own 'me-time.'"

Kenneth whipped up a quick frown. "Hey… wait a minute. Now, you're making *me* suspicious."

Linda pursed a coy smile. "Bye, Kenneth. Bye, Roberta!"

"Goodnight, Linda," said Roberta.

But Kenneth looked down at Linda and scratched his head. "Uh, Linda—" Only to find himself interrupted by a blank screen. "Surely, she can't be serious."

Roberta stared Kenneth down and shook her head slowly. "Sometimes I can't believe *you* actually made *me*," she confessed, pointing to and from.

Kenneth looked up, annoyed. "I've really got to dial down your sarcasm chip."

Chapter 11

Roberta's test to acclimate with civilian society was already under-way, starting with being setup the next day in a corporate apartment a few blocks over from SilverStem, most of them occupied by guest scientists and students, but no other droids. Roberta was the only one. But her new programming was put to the test not long after awaking in Kenneth's lab, where she'd slept and reenergized the night before. She was always programmed in such a manner—to sleep like a human for cellular rejuvenation, whenever time permitted. Her apartment unit was on the top third floor, and despite the plush furnishings, it was still something she wasn't used to. Only on prior op assignments was she given a hotel room; other-wise, it was a paramilitary office chair or mat-covered floor to bed-down on. Her new spot was nice, but the bed's comforter sprawled across the hardwood floor was all she needed when late night ar-rived.

Flat on her back was how Roberta often slept, and tonight was the same, the only difference being the more restored memo-ries that now raced through her mind. One in particular was the pursuit of another crime overlord in hiding. She and her team and a few more, all adorned in guerilla-gear, had tracked Yakuza boss, Akino Saito, to a forest location in the Central Highlands of Tas-mania. Unlike Ergen, Saito was an outdoorsman; nature was his safe haven, along with the wilds of the forest as an additional bar-rier, and night had fallen:

> Agent Muirfield, Roberta's second, had gone si-lent in her internal comm, and she couldn't see him through the thicket. *Infrared.* He was

nowhere in sight, which wasn't too surprising; he was the oldest and slowest on the team. So, Roberta backtracked at least 20-yards until two heat signatures caught her attention, one pinned against a tree at gunpoint by the other. She raised her rifle and advanced. *Illuminate. Low beam.* A light emerged from her eyes, intense enough to see that Muirfield was the one pinned against the tree, but faint and blue enough to avoid detection. *That's a lie*; the light actually was detectible, but she had to take a chance. She could also see the sweat dripping down Muirfield's forehead, while Saito's soldier was now in clear view for her to strike. But the soldier, also sweating, shifted and shielded himself with Agent Muirfield. Only a piece of his head was visible behind Muirfield's ear.

"Drop your weapon—and I'll let him live," was the soldier's demand.

Roberta cracked her neck to the side, then re-aligned her corneal scope. "How about you drop yours, and I'll let *you* live," was her first and final compromise.

She had her sights firm on the soldier's skull, enough to immobilize him. With her finger poised and ready to pull the trigger, both she and Muirfield got a surprise. The soldier went to activate his headset, leaving his gun in place, but both his grip and attention on Muirfield was totally abandoned. Muirfield's eyes lit up before slinging an elbow into the soldier's chest. The soldier aimlessly fired his gun, the shot echoing into the forest after taking a piece of Muirfield's ear with it, a wound Muirfield had gone on to keep as a reminder.

Roberta had seen and recorded it all, a slow-motion reel to her as Muirfield dove flat to the ground. This left Roberta with a clear shot to whichever part of the soldier's body she desired, but first, she had to ask herself: *What's he going to do next with that gun?* She studied the scene as he stood there with his eyes wide and his gun aimed nowhere in particular.

"I repeat—put down your weapon," she commanded.

But the soldier did nothing; the gun remained in place.

Analyze. Of all the scenarios, only one held the possibility of his surrender; the rest were not in Roberta's favor. With silencer in place, she fired two lightning quick shots, one to the head and one through the heart, sending the soldier to the ground. Roberta then listened carefully until his heartbeat slowly descended to zero.

No time to waste, she tapped into her internal comm. "Jacobs," she whispered.

"Roberta, what's going on?" Agent Jacobs whispered back. "We heard a gunshot."

"We're fine," she said as Muirfield cranked himself off the ground. "I need everyone to move in on the target now before all his soldiers mobilize. We got your six."

With her six-man team and an additional ten, they moved in with more gunfire until Saito and his crew quickly surrendered.

In all, the final battle had lasted only ten minutes, and Roberta had always been satisfied by the results. Colonel Livingston had heaped a load of praise on her, her past manufacturer was also satisfied, and Kenneth, as always, was happy she was still breathing. Then why was she now tossing and turning, twisted up in her comforter on the floor? That's when another situation came to mind:

> Rarely had the team been called in for a kill-shot, but the execution of mass terrorists was in a category all its own. Relentless attacks on individual terrorist leaders had reduced catastrophes drastically by the 2060s. What leader wanted to *truly* be held personally accountable in the end, was the question each had to ask himself. Regardless, whether by military or paramilitary, a kill-shot was always by executive order, an act of protecting the freedom of not only Americans, but of citizens worldwide as well.
>
> Roberta remembered a trek through another forest, through another Turkish territory until reaching a remote terrorist compound far on the outskirts of civilization. Khalil Aksoy was their target, and his compound mirrored the look of its location—far short of civilized. Covered from head-to-toe in all black gear, Roberta and her core team moved along the shadows like shadows, themselves. Again, with silenced barrels, they shot any guard who flinched, except without warning or call to drop their weapons. Post 2060, the sound of discharge was more of a blowgun than a

twerp. The team kept moving, their steps rapid and decisive, but stealthy. One compound guard after another fell until the team reached its final destination, Aksoy's private quarters. A live satellite feed had confirmed his prior entry.

Roberta reran the stats in her mind as they advanced through Aksoy's barracks: Aksoy, a distant relative of Ergen, had a lifetime of 1,010 murders to his name, 2,230 more reported injuries, and over 700-million-credits in facility damages. Normally, Becker, the sniper, would have been first in to take the shot, even for close-range kills. Yet the stats were enough to fuel Roberta to be number one on this one, the first to face Aksoy, who was on his knees praying to his maker for forgiveness.

"I don't know which god you're praying to," Roberta said, "but surely it's not the one my logic can accept."

She heard Muirfield in her comm. "Roberta, our orders are not to engage in verbal contact. Shoot first and ask questions—never."

But Roberta raised her hand, halting her team while giving Aksoy a chance to respond.

Aksoy raised his eyes, sorrowful but certain as he spoke. "Logic?" he said softly. "Belief and logic do not make for good bedfellows."

Roberta paused, then scoped her target. "Then you will die with your misbelief."

He took a deep breath. "For this, I am ready to d—," he said, cut short by her bullet between his eyes.

Roberta untwisted herself from her comforter and sat up, eyes wide and panicked from the latest memory. Yes, Aksoy was trouble, a badass of monumental proportions, one who *had* to be eliminated. There was absolutely no need for a soldier to feel remorse for executing the kill-shot. Only honor was the result of executing such a task. Then why was a tear now running down Roberta's cheek? *This isn't from joy*, she surmised, then thought back to the look in Saito's soldiers' eyes, not far from the look in Aksoy's. One, only a soldier, the other, a criminal mastermind, but both aware of the consequences. Yet there was something in each pair of eyes—a shred of humanity in those last seconds. *What is it I'm feeling? Guilt?* Muirfield had told her not to engage. *But it shouldn't matter, dammit! Orders are orders, and the bad guys had to go!* She now swiped her face and took a deep breath. "Kenneth...," she gritted to herself, "what have you done to me?"

Kenneth had been in no rush to see Roberta off to work so soon in her redevelopment; he had many more tests to run. Yet Roberta was at least deemed ready to function safely among society. Kenneth had maintained her automobile while she was in stasis, and it was now parked in an assigned space in the apartment complex's downstairs garage. She was encouraged to take a drive around the city, see the sights, but opted to spend the next day outdoors, walking as many streets as her interests carried her.

Outside her paramilitary assignments, a casual tee shirt with jeans was her normal attire. This was what she wore the entire next day—not glamorous, but enough to still get her a few honks from drivers zipping by. Her path had been a meandering one, one that landed her at a fairly busy downtown intersection by 1:32 p.m. per her internal clock. *1:32 p.m.?* She gazed around, confused, wondering what the hell had happened to her military timer; it was no longer her default. The distraction was almost enough to over-look two men bursting out of a bank across the street. Heading Roberta's way in balaclavas and zipped up duffle bags in hand, they were no welcoming party. A bank robbery just after lunch made absolute sense to Roberta—*the least alert time of day.*

It wasn't her typical assignment, but Roberta readied her-self for action anyway. These were two bad guys she wasn't going to let slip by. She had no plans on killing them, but whatever she'd end up doing, there would be no tears afterwards; she promised this to herself. Only one robber's gun was visible, strapped across his torso. Her plan was to take this one out first, to step back and clothesline him to the sidewalk, wrestle his gun away, and fire a warning shot if necessary. That was the plan—until it wasn't. She stepped back and watched him run by without flinching one muscle in his direction. The next one ran by, and Roberta did the same: nothing. "What?" she questioned herself out loud as both men dove into a van parked just a few yards behind her.

"Where's Emerson?" she heard the driver shout all the way from where she stood.

On cue, another robber, carrying two more full duffle bags, was the third to crash through the bank's doors. This one was shorter, stouter, laboring and stumbling across the street like a Weeble. A simple trip and fall would have been all that was needed to save at least two bags of money. So, Roberta tipped her toe and readied herself to execute, only to watch him waddle by untouched and unscathed on his way to the van.

Roberta slapped her foot back to the sidewalk and shook her head in total disbelief. "Nah...," she murmured as the van screeched off right in front of her, exhaust in her face before it weaved through the intersection to get away.

A minute later, Roberta was still standing there, disgusted with herself, but trying to rationalize her actions, or lack thereof.

Afterall, being a vigilante was never in her programming. *But damn*, doing absolutely nothing was tough to swallow. So, with the urge to do nothing else, she turned away and headed back to her apartment.

Having endured another night of tears, Roberta barged into Kenneth's office early the next morning and plopped into a seat across from him. She sat there for a few seconds with nothing but a shrewd stare. "Kenneth…," she finally said, fuming.

Kenneth remained buried in his tablet. "Yes, Roberta?"

"What have you done to me?"

He lifted his eyes first, then sat all the way back. "What do you mean?"

Roberta went on to explain her entire ordeal from yesterday, ending with more disgust. "And I couldn't even get myself to stick around to report everything I'd seen or heard! Not even one of the guys' names! Not even the license plate number! Nothing! And the night before, I was boo-hooing from guilt for every criminal that got what was coming! What is going on with me?"

Kenneth fanned his hands. "Alright, alright. Calm down. There's a simple explanation."

"And don't tell me my 'emotion chip' is out of whack!"

"Well, that may have a little something to do with it, but we also had to reduce a few of your military-slash-law-and-order instincts a bit."

Roberta sat back and folded her arms, deepened her stare.

"Just a bit," Kenneth said with fingers pinched together.

"Shit," she mumbled.

"Roberta, we had to make sure your initial response to certain situations mirrored that of the typical human response."

She curled her lip. "Huh?"

"The typical human response!"

"No, I heard you! But does complete *apathy* fall into that category?"

"Relax… You can still assess and analyze."

Her brow jumped. "Assess and *analyze*! Analyze for what! It's not like I'm going to do any damn thing afterwards anyway!"

Kenneth bobbed his head from side to side. "Okay, I get it, I get it. We may have to recalibrate a few things."

"Uhh…, you think?" She held a cold stare. "And I need a job, Kenneth!"

He sighed. "We're working on it."

Chapter 12

"Ahhhhh," Mildred blew out a long sigh, one of physical relief only. But the true aftermath of her trip to the toilet carried massive anxiety. In fact, her eyes remained closed long after she'd pulled the stick from between her legs. When her eyes opened, another "Ahhh" of full relief followed the sight of one pink line. Take-home sticks still existed in the 2060s, but now yielding results in a mere fraction of the time.

Her body had been feeling weird all week, especially in the mornings, and she'd missed her period. She couldn't understand it; she'd been diligent with her contraceptives, and Sterling had been using protection—*except for that one time on his dryer*. It was now her second go at the urine test, and a visit to Dr. Yamada, her OB-GYN, would have been next if either had indicated a positive. A few seconds, and another exhale followed. *All good. No need.*

To top off Mildred's atrocious mornings, Celia, who'd fallen behind in her schoolwork, hadn't been in for more than a week, while Lauren was able to help on only one of those afternoons. And Mildred definitely wasn't going to ask Sterling for help. As much as she would have enjoyed seeing him in an apron, she wasn't ready to show him the weak spots underneath her super cape, and her business was that cape.

"Be right with you!" Mildred yelled to a customer across the store while ringing up another at the computer. "Be right with you!" she yelled to another. "Be right with you!" And another. "Be right with you!" And another. "Be right with you!"

By the end of the evening, alone in the shop with the doors locked, Mildred rolled back and forth in a desk chair with her legs outstretched, too gassed to even make it upstairs. "Aarrhhh!" she screamed to the ceiling. "I need some fucking help!" That's when her cellphone buzzed, except it was all the way on the counter. "Answer!" she shouted.

"Hey, baby, what's up?" It was Sterling's voice on the other end. "Where are you?"

"In the shop," she said from her chair. "I would love to see your face right now, sweetie, but I can't move... not even turn my head."

"Why? Are you hurt?"

"Uhh... something like that. No. Just fatigued out of my freaking mind."

"Ohh... your freaking mind, huh?"

Her eyes wandered from side to side and her chair began to swivel. "Oooh, you're so bad. I like it. But I'm beat."

"Tell me then, what can I bring you to make it all better? Wine? Massage oils?"

"Oooh, that sounds nice. Maybe... for my feet."

"Your feet? Oh."

She found the strength to sit up, alarmed. "Why do you say it like that? What's wrong with my feet?"

"Nothing, baby. Nothing. You have beautiful feet!"

"So, if all I want touched are my feet, does that mean you're not coming over?"

"Of course not. I mean, of course, I'm coming over."

"Uh huh. You'd better."

"See you in a few."

Mildred began spinning around slowly in her chair after hanging up, more fatigued than before. Her eyes settled back on the ceiling as she screamed again, "Aarrhhh! I don't need a damn foot massage! I need some fucking help!" She spun to a stop, remembering a conversation she'd had with Sterling a few months ago. "I need…" She suddenly found the energy to rise and dash to her cellphone on the counter. "Call Mom."

Her mother's face popped onto the screen after several rings, somewhat disheveled while straightening a shawl as if she'd just slung it over her shoulders. "Oh! Uh… hey, dear."

Oh-ohh. Did I just interrupt my mom and dad gettin' busy? was her first thought. "Mom? Is Dad around?"

"Uhh, no, dear. Your dad is out—uh, your dad is out—aw shoot. I don't know where your dad is. You want him to call you when he gets back?"

Then what the hell are you doing, Mom? "Nope. Actually, you may have some thoughts on this."

"Oh. Okay. Watcha' got?"

"I was wondering what you think about this: being that things are really picking up here at the shop, and I haven't been successful at finding reliable parttime help, I was thinking about hiring a droid. What do you think?"

A wave of shock seemed to overtake her mother's face. "I don't know, hon. We had one a long time ago when you were little, but those things don't work for free. Nowadays you may have to pay the company and the droid. And with all these people out there protesting, I would fear for your safety, dear."

"But I hear some of them are out there living on their own now. So, I can't imagine the manufacturer or a leasing company being highly involved anymore. As for wages, I hear a lot of them are personally—I mean, 'individually' charging a simple minimum wage." She had searched for the appropriate descriptor, but there was no way to make her statement anymore politically correct when it came to droids. "As for protests, they must not have reached San Diego yet, because I haven't seen any."

Her mother sat back and rolled her eyes. "Shoo,' girl, I bet there'll be protests if you hire one."

"Oh, Mom."

"I'm serious!"

"You worry too much."

"And if you hire one off the street, without a manufacturer involved, what kind of warranty or maintenance plan will they be on? Who insures them in case of glitches?"

Mildred's mouth dropped. "Dang, Ma, you sure just put on your thinking cap about droids, didn't you?" Her mother yielded a smug look on that note, but Mildred pressed on, "Well now, that brings me to my next point. Would you happen to know where I can find… Robin?"

Mrs. Morehouse crunched her brow. "Who?"

"Robin, my nanny when I was a kid."

"Oh. You mean, Roberta."

Mildred sat stunned. "Roberta? Ohh… that's right. Roberta, not Robin! My bad."

Regardless, Mrs. Morehouse frowned at the thought. "Ugh—Roberta. I can't believe you even came that close to remembering her name. But speaking of glitches."

"But Mom, thinking back on it, what could be wrong with a domestic model that has self-defense skills?" When Mildred was old enough, her parents had already told her about Roberta's handling of a burglar. Just the story alone now had her bursting with elation. "And I would have a helper and a security guard all wrapped up in one! Hopefully for the price of one. Not to mention she and I already have a connection, right?"

"Well, I suppose. That's if a droid is actually capable of such."

The silence that followed left room for a deep sigh from Mrs. Morehouse, drawing Mildred in for a mopey final blow: "So…, will you help me find her?"

In the end, Mrs. Morehouse surrendered her hands in the air. "Oh, alright! I'll have to talk to your uh—father—when he gets back. He may be able to find all that information somewhere."

Mildred exhaled. "Oh, thank you, Mother!" She'd thought her mother would never give in. "By the way, you and Dad are alright, huh?"

"Uhh, of course."

Then why is there suddenly an "uh" before his name? And this wasn't the first time Mildred had heard her mother fumble through her father's whereabouts, nor the first time only one was in the house without the other, especially whenever Mildred made a surprise visit. As a matter of fact, the only time she'd seen them together lately was for one drive down from Los Angeles to San Diego to see the shop. Beyond that, her mother had even stopped caring to know where her father's business trips were taking him. When Mildred thought about it, the insouciance was happening more and more for every passing year.

"Alright, I'll have him call you," her mother said, "but Mildred, don't go getting your hopes all too high about Roberta; it's been a long time between now and way back when, and she might not even be on the shelf anymore."

"I know, I know… but please just tell him to give it a try. Please!"

Her mother huffed. "Okay. And let me know whenever you decide to come home and visit, but call first, okay? Bye now."

"Bye—" But Mildred was cut short by a blank screen. *Now I know something strange is going on. I see I'm going to have to pay my folks another surprise visit.*

Mrs. Morehouse flipped the shawl off her shoulders like an itchy blanket as soon as she hung up with Mildred. She bounced from her antique living room chair like a teenager, along with wearing a full spandex jogging suit. Moving to the kitchen, she tapped speed-dial and waited for Mr. Morehouse to appear on her screen.

"Yes, Evelyn?" he answered.

"Ray, you alone?"

"Well, I wouldn't have answered if I wasn't."

"I just got a call from Mildred. She just made an inquiry about Roberta." Evelyn's tone was staunch, deliberate and commanding, the complete opposite of the doubtful mother Mildred had just spoken to.

"Roberta?"

"Roberta-X-One-Fifty. Remember her?"

"Of course. How can I forget. What about her?"

"Mildred wants to make contact with her to hire her as a helper of some sort—at her florist shop."

Ray's eyes flexed in surprise. "A floral helper? As in a security detail?"

"Perhaps. Partially. But my question is, wasn't Roberta recently decommissioned?"

"Yes, but all her tech was purchased by Silver-Stem. At least that's the last I heard. So, who knows? She could be back on the market soon."

"Uh huh…," Evelyn teetered. "Then my next question is, do you think it would be a wise move?"

"For Mildred?"

"Yes. Of course, for Mildred."

He scratched the back of his neck. "Hmm… sounds like it would be great for extra security if you ask me. But you tell me—what would a concerned *mother* think?"

It sounded like a simple question for a mother to answer, yet Evelyn paused at the thought. "A concerned mother would do what's best for her daughter, but I wouldn't call a malfunctioning, decommissioned-ass droid the best solution." She paused again. "However… a girl wants what a girl wants."

"Hmph. Ain't that the truth. Well, regardless, I would have to feel out what the company thinks about it—and Roberta's status."

"Okay, you do that, Ray. If all are in agreement there, can you get back to me by O-nine-hundred tomorrow with that an-swer?"

"Why? Is she in a hurry?"

"Unknown, but the sooner we get back to her, the less of a chance there'll be for her seeking other offshoot units that could be even worse. You know what I mean?"

"Okay, okay. I'll do my best."

Evelyn exhaled. "Good. Until then, 'Mr. Morehouse,'" she said with a hint of duplicity.

While Ray tipped his forehead with the same in return. "'Mrs. Morehouse.'"

Chapter 13

Kenneth and Torrance had seen each other at work every day when neither was traveling, had had lunch and afterwork drinks together many times, but had yet to go to each other's house for dinner. Torrance, having been married and divorced once, was probably waiting for a brand-new girlfriend to show-off before extending an invitation—an attempt to compete with Kenneth's permanent selection, Linda, a natural beauty. Torrance's refusal to be outdone was matched only by his will to climb any mountain in his way, and hump the devil out of it. All this was what Kenneth had figured. Sure, he'd seen Torrance a few times meeting younger women in the lobby and escorting them out, hand-in-hand, but Kenneth was fairly certain they matched his own wife by style of dress only. That was as far as his comparisons had gone. Regardless, Linda, a fulltime mother with sales experience, and Kenneth's more social half, had pressed him to finally invite Torrance to their new home for dinner—a plus-one welcomed, but optional.

With old friends still in the San Jose area, Kenneth and Linda had plenty of places to send the kids while on an all-adult evening with the boss. And showing up with an expensive bottle of rosé in one arm and his beautiful plus-one latched onto the other, Torrance didn't disappoint. They were soon to find out that his date was an attorney, and slightly more age-appropriate than the many others. Kenneth had even noticed her in the lobby more than once as of late, a sign the many others could soon become one.

Dinner included Dungeness crab surrounded by garlic baked potatoes, roasted Brussels sprouts and almond Caesar salad, led by shrimp cocktails, then washed down with a variety of wines to choose from. The dinner conversation included the long overdue discussion about growth in the San Jose area since college. Torrance's date, Rosana, was from Phoenix, and was the only one who wasn't a Stanford grad. But by the time the dinner party had moved from the dining room to the great room, she was dying to hear about those old Stanford days.

Kenneth and Linda, as if by plan, rushed to the sofa, leaving the loveseat for their guests to share. The weather outside wasn't chilly enough for a fire, but a perfect holographic flame in the fireplace kept all their spirits warm as the women yacked it up at the men's expense.

"Child, you would have had to be really into dorks to catch one of these diamonds in the rough!" Linda blared to Rosana, holding her third glass of Chardonnay steady in one hand, while stretching the other out for an off-centered high-five.

"Speaking of dorks," Kenneth snarked beneath his breath, an eyeshot briefly in Torrance's direction.

"Oh, it is quite an adjustment," Rosana admitted.

Torrance's eyes bucked from the next cushion over. "Hey! What do you mean? I haven't been a 'dork' in a *long* time!"

Rosana waved a finger like a ticking clock. "Oh, no, honey! That is something you can never rid yourself of." It was now obvious the two had seen each other much more than once.

"Well, we may backslide from time to time. Right, Ken?"

Kenneth rolled his eyes, again landing on Torrance. "Speak for yourself, Torrance."

The room fell to abrupt silence, followed by an uproar of laughter from everyone, including Torrance, who at least came to Kenneth's defense. "But you gotta admit, this man right here—" He pointed at Kenneth. "—gearhead or not, landed the best beauty on campus."

Linda came close to spitting wine in response. "Who!"

Torrance's squinched face said it all. "C'mon now, Linda."

"Awww, that is so sweet, baby," Rosana gushed on Linda's behalf while rubbing Torrance's arm, not one jealous bone in her tone.

Linda sank in disbelief. "Oh, right, Torrance." But with a slight blush.

Kenneth had been smiling up until this point, when it all struck. "And this coming from the man who told her she had picked the wrong one," he said in a tone somewhere between payback's a mother, and—okay. Truth was, he felt nowhere in between.

Torrance's face turned as red as a light brown-skinned brother's face could. Meanwhile, Linda was now hiding behind both hands.

Kenneth nodded at Torrance with all seriousness, followed by a smirk. "You thought she never told me, didn't you?" Kenneth was a "dork" no longer.

Rosana was next in line to react, running inches away in the loveseat. "Oh, wait a minute! Did someone have a crush on someone else in this room?" Her tenor had changed. "I thought it was just a compliment!"

Torrance fell back and slapped his forehead. "I was young. I was stupid. I was a college dude, okay?"

Light chuckles filled the air as Rosana's joy returned, drawing her into Torrance for a soft snuggle. "That's alright, baby. Our hostess is a very gorgeous woman, who I am sure made all the boys 'bend the knee' back in school."

"Aww," Linda swooned, raising her wine glass, "thank you, dear. You are too kind." She eyed Torrance. "Your date's a keeper, Torrance." Then back to Rosana. "And yes, the men all did pause when I walked by back in the day."

The women leaned forward and clinked their glasses, Rosana giggling. "Came to the yard looking for that milkshake, huh?"

Linda totally erupted.

"Alright!" Kenneth blasted. "Enough with all our parents' old song and movie references!"

When the celebration of Linda's beauty came to an end, and faces returned to their original hues, Torrance could have left it at that, but he didn't. He pointed at Kenneth instead. "Bruh, come to think of it… for real though, I didn't even know you that well at that point!"

Kenneth, slightly slumped, sat up to attention. "What are you talking about?" He held up two fingers. "We had been hanging out for two whole semesters!"

"Two semesters?" Torrance waved him off. "Aw, man—that's nothing!"

"Guys," was the only word Linda needed to extinguish a sparking fire.

By the time tempers had cooled, the men's tiff behind them but never forgotten, the women spurred off to their own conversation. The men were left to dawdle. That's when Torrance stood up and beckoned Kenneth, "Hey, man, you got a second?"

Kenneth stood up too. "Yeah, man."

Linda's eyes trailed them with caution as the two walked out the room.

Kenneth and Torrance stopped in the hallway, out of view. "What's up?" Kenneth asked.

Torrance leaned in with a deep whisper, "Oh, I was just gonna ask you, where's your bathroom?"

"Aw man—right there, dude." He pointed two doors down. "Second door."

"No—I mean, I really have to let a few blow. You know what I mean?"

"Oh…," Kenneth answered, pointing up the stairs, "right up the stairs and straight ahead at the end of the hall. The door should be open."

"Thanks." Torrance tapped Kenneth on the chest two times and made his way up the stairs.

Halfway up, Kenneth whispered to him like a bullhorn, "Spray can's on the counter!" Not only did Kenneth chuckle, but so did the women all the way from the great room.

Torrance didn't seem very amused. "Thanks for the public announcement, mother fucker."

With Kenneth back on the sofa, the conversation in the great room was so stirring, no one seemed to notice that Torrance's break was approaching twenty minutes. Rosana was the first to finally look over her shoulder. "I wonder if Torrance is alright," she said softly.

Kenneth hopped from his seat. "I'll go see." He weaved through the furniture and climbed the stairs, two steps at a time, surprised at what he saw at the top. The bathroom door was wide open, but with no Torrance inside, nor any foul odor mixed with a lemony fresh scent—only Torrance exiting the second door on the right. Kenneth snickered, but was a little concerned. "Don't tell me you mistook my study for the bathroom and took a big fat dump in my desk chair."

Torrance closed the door, pinching his brow. "Nah, sorry about that. I just saw the door open and went in to look at all the photos. Hope you don't mind."

Kenneth shrugged. "Nah, of course not. Want to see some more?"

"Oh, no… I saw plenty. They were great. Hey, I got some cigars in my jacket. You got any beer? A back porch?"

Kenneth nodded practically out of control. "Sure, brother—on both counts." He waved Torrance to follow, grumbling on the way down the stairs, "Do I have a damn back porch."

As Prensado fumes soon drifted off the back porch, even the imported beer Kenneth served Torrance was Linda's selection. Propped against the sturdy railing, Torrance exhaled after a sip and a long puff. "Well, what do you think?" he asked.

Also against the rail, Kenneth glanced around. "About?"

Torrance nudged his head towards the inside.

"Ohhh!" Kenneth blurted, then lowered his voice. "Rosana? She's nice, man. Beautiful. Intelligent. Sociable. Kudos, bro."

The two were close enough to clank bottles and take a swig before Torrance's response: "Thanks, bro."

"A little younger than you too." Kenneth took a sip, building towards a smirk. "Old enough to put you in check from time-to-time, and young enough to maybe pop out a kid or two. You need to put a ring on that."

"Slow your roll, freight train. I may be a man of a particular age group, but I'm still in no big hurry—on either front." Light chuckles from both men followed. "Hey, I'm sorry about popping off on you in there," Torrance said.

"What are you talking about?"

"You know… with Linda… back in college…"

"Aw, man, it's water under the bridge, bruh. You weren't the first friend who tried to get with her behind my back back then."

"Good, good. Nothing happened, by the way."

"I'm sure. My wife has something called 'taste.' Ha, ha, haaa."

"Whatever. While we're here, I wanted to give you a heads up on a new development at work that concerns you."

Torrance's segue was brutally timed and horrifically worded, as Kenneth saw it, leaving him breathless in wait.

"Oh, it's nothing bad. It's about R-One-Fifty, though."

"Roberta?" He still gulped as if a fatal diagnosis was on its way, something he was far too familiar with.

"Yes. Do you remember several years ago—a joint venture project between us and ZepperCorp that involved Roberta? You remember—when she was a domestic."

Kenneth twisted his lips. "Mmmm… vaguely."

"Yeah, there was this wealthy family, the Morehouses, who wanted to try her out as a nanny. Then there was the incident with the burglar—"

Kenneth's eyes expanded like two moons. "Oh, yeah! That part, I can't forget. But you know—I still never knew how you guys, 'us guys' now, somehow got involved in that deal in the first place."

Torrance hesitated. "Well… the deal started with us, but being that you, personally, were smoking our asses in A.I.-completeness at the time, we were able to strike a subcontractor deal with the head honchos over there. Leased your girl, Roberta, on a virtual steal."

"Oh," Kenneth said flatly.

"By the way, it was ZepperCorp who actually pulled the plug on the deal. We had no problem with the outcome with her and the burglar. I mean, he survived. So, it was a total A-plus performance from Roberta, if you ask me."

"Yeah…" Kenneth nodded tepidly. "So, what exactly is going on now?"

"Well, guess what? The little girl she nannied is all grown up now, and she's recently made an inquiry about hiring Roberta."

A cigar in one hand, a beer in the other, Kenneth still managed to bounce them up and down, confused. "Hire Roberta for what? To nanny *her* kids?"

"No. She doesn't have any kids, but the budding young tycoon owns a florist shop and she needs some help, so apparently, she thought about Roberta. Makes sense, right?" Torrance finished his beer on the next swig.

"*One* floral shop?"

"That's right."

"One floral shop makes her a *tycoon*?"

Torrance smacked his lips. "You know what I mean, jackass. Makes sense, right?"

Kenneth tossed his head from left to right, ending with a shrug. "I guess. It definitely sounds much safer than special ops."

Torrance nodded. "That's the truth."

"But I was kind of hoping she'd get into something…" He whirled his beer and cigar in small circles. "…something a little more far-reaching. Something more… I don't know—important!"

"This could be important. This could be very important. Our team can check in on her progress… you know, use the data for future concerns—if all goes well. Future funding…"

Finishing off his beer, Kenneth's face went sour, and it had nothing to do with the taste.

Torrance raised his forefinger. "Plus, the shop does need some added security too. Now, that's important."

"Extra security for a flower shop? Really?"

Torrance shrugged. "Ultimately, it comes down to what the Morehouses want. So, what do you say?"

Kenneth stroked his chin, figuring the Morehouses must have been the world's most undercover billionaires, because he'd never heard of them. But they were obviously high on Torrance's priority sheet. "Do I have a choice?" Kenneth grumped.

Torrance's eyes widened in his direction. "No. *We* don't have a choice. So, what do you think?"

Kenneth looked at his empty bottle and shrugged, then rose from the rail. "I think I need another drink, a stiffer one. How about you?"

"Sure."

Chapter 14

Mildred and Sterling had found the most secluded spot on the southside of Coronado Beach one Sunday afternoon. Mildred, the old spirit she was, had packed an old-fashioned, woven picnic basket she'd bought from a local thrift store. A classic red-checkered blanket lay beneath them as she pulled her homemade turkey and avocado wraps from the basket. Sterling had supplied the wine. The entire outlay was centered by a vase filled with yellow daffodils. She, wearing cutoff jeans shorts and a light U.C.L.A. sweatshirt, and he, wearing khaki shorts and a pullover, they were a pair of dockers and a sundress short of a 1950s painting.

Shoulder-to-shoulder they gazed at the sunset, each wearing auto-adjusting sunshades to make it a bearable experience. Sterling broke his gaze to look at Mildred's layout. "The flowers are a nice touch," he said.

"Oh, yeah? The daffodils?" Mildred giggled. "Glad you noticed." It was like hearing that she, herself, was a star.

"And what exactly do they symbolize?"

It was a fair assumption they were there for some kind of reason; most things were in Mildred's case. "Ohhh, they symbolize many things," she said. "Some good, some bad—but I prefer to think of them as symbolizing a new beginning—new life."

"A new beginning, huh?"

She leaned over for a light snuggle. "Mmm hm."

"Don't you think it's a few months late for a *new* beginning?"

Silence intervened for a moment. There were several things racing through Mildred's mind in those few seconds, one being the recent incident on her bathroom toilet. With the near scare, having "the talk" with Sterling was now overdue. *And why not have it now? It doesn't seem like he's in any hurry to broach the issue.* She'd even avoided intercourse ever since then, even the night he'd come over to deliver a masterful "foot-job." And she wasn't about to move forward until this issue was resolved.

"What do you mean a few months late?" she asked rhetorically. "It's never too late. But since you mention it… I do have a question to ask before things *do* grow to be—too late."

"What's that?" Sterling's reaction was surprisingly calm.

But Mildred dawdled, dangling her finger against his arm. "With the great time we've been having together—"

"There's only you," he cut in before she could finish.

Her heart skipped a beat. "Well, that's great to hear," she admitted, somewhat stumped on how to respond. But his eyes bearing down on her through his shades were pushing for a quicker one. "Oh, and so are you mine."

He sighed in relief.

"But that's not exactly what I was going to ask. Important! But not what I wanted to know. What I want to know is…" She dawdled again, stirring more circles into his arm. "…where do you see this going? Where do you see *us* going?"

To her surprise, his stare remained intense. He didn't dawdle, flinch or hesitate to say, "I see us going very far together. At least, I hope for us to go far together."

"Far together?"

"What—are you asking me about…?" Just the "m" alone got trapped in his mouth like fish in a net.

Mildred jerked back in mortal fear, waving her hands in and out like a pair of scissors. "Oh, God, no! No, no, no, no, no, no," she rattled off. "That is *not* what I meant! Scratch that! Please tell me that's not what you thought I meant!" But was she too late?

Had she pressed the wrong button? Had she pressed the issue too hard, too soon?

Sterling raised his own hand to a halt. "Alright, alright—not at first—but you don't have to be all *that* aversive to it. Damn."

She gasped, even more embarrassed, before stroking his arm. "No, that's not what I meant either!" She took a breath to calm herself down. "I mean, with the intimate moments we've been sharing as of late—if something were to happen…" She stopped there, using her hands to mold the air into a possible conclusion.

"Like…?" Sterling asked.

Mildred huffed, exasperated. "Do you like kids?"

Sterling's eyes flew wide; his pupils even dilated. "Kids!" He then gawked, indicating neither joy nor pain. "Are you pregnant?" he whispered.

"No! I'm just—"

In bounced a huge beachball, splattering sand in their faces before pounding the picnic basket, which rocked until the lid snapped shut. The guilty culprit was a man in baggy shorts and a tank-top, blocking out the sun in front of them. "Look who's over here trying to hide!" he yelled with a cheesy grin and no remorse.

Mildred and Sterling had to remove their shades to make out his face. It was Sterling's friend, Bryan. Next came Mildred's friend, Lauren, peeking from behind Bryan with her usual peachy smile. And it wasn't that Bryan was an extremely large man, but he was muscular and athletically built, the type of man Lauren wasn't opposed to. Like Sterling had suspected, the two had hit it off after only one double-date, and frequently having gone out by themselves after the second. Sterling had gone on to bloviate about his superior match-making skills to no end—to the point of nausea in Mildred's opinion. Needless for anyone to say, the rest of this evening was off to becoming another double-date, with Mildred's own relationship status tabled for another time.

Mildred's weekend went by no differently than it had ended on the beach blanket—full of Lauren and Bryan. Sterling had failed to continue their conversation, while Mildred had been too embarrassed to rehash it. It was now Monday morning and she had something much more engaging on her schedule. The shop hadn't even opened yet, and she already witnessed a woman around her age approaching the glass door. Mildred rushed to open the door before the woman had a chance to ring the doorbell. "Roberta?" she said with eyes wide.

Roberta arrived on her first day as a florist's assistant, dressed comfortably in casual slacks and a thin, long-sleeved pullover, uncannily matching the style of her new supervisor. She'd already spoken to Mildred on the phone the prior week, and was prepared to share the upstairs apartment. All she needed was the one duffle bag in her hand and a corner to stretch out in to sleep. She practically bowed her head when Mildred greeted her at the door. "Good morning," Roberta said.

Mildred gaped with one hand over her mouth. "Oh, my God! Come in! Come in! It is *so* good to see you again!" The two exchanged smiles and a long, hearty hug, reminding Roberta of how she used to feel when Mildred was a little girl. The warmth from her tiny little body had always brought joy to Roberta, even before her emotion chip had been enhanced. *What is that?* she used to wonder. Even her internal sensors and analyzers couldn't isolate the nature or cause of the warmth. Kenneth had later explained it as her auto-generative emotions, just like her ability to learn from all data around her. And he may very well have been correct, for she was feeling that same warmth all over again, along with a second heartbeat somewhere in the shop. It was as faint as a mouse's, but much slower in pace, perhaps from a creature on its way to a slow death. She and Mildred stepped back to hold each other's hands just like giddy little schoolgirls.

"What's it been, twenty-plus years?" Mildred asked.

Roberta's smile flatlined. *Calculate.* When it came to mathematical questions, her instincts were prone to responding to an extra significant figure. She was actually on the verge of calculating this one to years and days, but her renewed conversational chip restored her smile, canceling that calculation at the same time. "Indeed, it has."

"And you haven't changed one bit! From what I can remember, at least."

Roberta sighed. "That's the way things are. But *you* most certainly have! You've grown into quite a beautiful young woman, haven't you?" She perked a smile, aware that chronologically, she and Mildred were nearly the same age.

"Oh, thank you," Mildred said with a faint curtsy.

The small talk didn't go much further as Roberta began to scan the room. "So… where would you like me to start?"

"Okay, just give me that bag and let me show you."
"Sure."

Mildred snatched the duffle bag from her hand and placed it underneath the central counter, then beckoned her to follow. Soon, in the middle of absorbing Mildred's every instruction, Roberta took another quick scan, unable to find that dying mouse. She even reanalyzed the faint beats, figuring out exactly what they matched, but she wasn't ready to say.

As the day progressed, Mildred was in awe of how Roberta had instantly attended to the shop's every need, most of the time before she, herself, could think it. Not only that, she was also amazed at

Roberta's demeanor—happy, enthusiastic, so emotional—traits that had her handling customers with ease by midday. Hard to believe since Mildred's only memories were those of Roberta's nurturing "nanny" side. Seeing her organizing everything underneath the counter like no one had even thought to do, Mildred had to wave her to a stop just to ask, "Roberta, you're doing so well. How are you able to do it?"

Roberta stopped abruptly, but only for a second. "Do what, exactly?" she asked while resuming.

"I mean, the way you organize... the way you handle the customers... the way you do my duties like a pro!" She threw her hands up. "And only half-a-day on the job!"

"Oh, that," Roberta said nonchalantly. "It's because I've already researched two-hundred-and—uhh... hundreds of ways to organize a flower shop."

Mildred's eyes popped. "Really! That's impressive."

"As for your customers, I'm taking in hundreds of gigs of customer service seminars as we speak."

"Oh." It was just what Mildred needed to remind her of who she was dealing with—not exactly a human being. This was a good thing, she thought, since she'd already been talked into going on another double-date, this time on a trip for the entire upcoming weekend. She was now confident that together, Roberta and Celia would be able to hold down the shop while she was away.

The workday finally came to a close, and with Roberta's presence, the usual two-hour cleanup had been reduced to thirty minutes. By the end, Roberta stood before Mildred with her duffle bag held by both hands. "So...," she said with a light shrug, "where will I be residing? Where is your apartment?"

"Oh, it's just up the stairs out back. I have a second room that was large enough to convert to a guest bedroom. It turned out pretty nice, actually. You'll love it! Plenty of wall sockets too—for… you know." She balled her fist and reached behind her neck, started jabbing at it like a knife in the back.

Roberta's face went blank for a moment. "Oh! You mean for—oh, no. Some of us have been modified over the years. We now draw energy from many elements in the air, but mostly radiant energy from the sun—captured and stored in micro-fibrous cells—like a sponge. So, just like humans, we're mostly solar-powered."

Now, Mildred went blank. "Oh." She'd never thought of it that way.

"Why else do you think you woke up so quickly whenever the blinds opened—when you were a child?"

Mildred scratched her head. "You mean it had nothing to do with my circadian rhythm?"

"Holistically speaking—sure."

"Uhh… anyway—Roberta, you are such a Godsend!" Mildred threw her arms around Roberta and squeezed her like a newly found long-lost sister.

Snug in Mildred's grip, Roberta gave no resistance to being waved around like the duffle bag now swinging in one hand. "Silver-Stem-sent, actually."

Mildred pulled back and laughed. "That's so funny! True, but funny!" She noticed Roberta's delayed smile, but grabbed her arm anyway. "Come on. Follow me." She yanked, only to find Roberta to be an immovable object. She noticed her standing in the same spot, staring her up and down until stopping at her stomach.

A surprised look spread across Roberta's face, delayed like the smile.

But Mildred was too confused to share in the moment. "What? What is it?" she asked.

Facing Mildred's growing anxiety, Roberta could now hear the extra heartbeat like a slow drumroll. *Assess.* And it definitely wasn't from a mouse. She placed her hand gently on Mildred's stomach, to which Mildred raised both her hands like she was being held up.

"What?" Mildred repeated.

"I suppose 'congratulations' are in order."

"*Congratulations*? For what?"

"You didn't know? You're pregnant."

Mildred's mouth dropped. She batted her eyes repeatedly as if trying to bat Roberta right back out the front door. But she soon nodded; a smile crept into her cheeks. "You're trying to be funny again, aren't you?"

Chapter 15

It was the next day after Roberta's revelation. Mildred sat in Dr. Yamada's examination chair with a calm expression, except her foot was fluttering like a leaf. It wasn't much of a shock the doctor had squeezed her in that afternoon on such short notice; only a couple of women were in the waiting room when Mildred had arrived, just like her last visit. And she could have sworn she'd seen one of those same women back again.

Now in the examination room, Dr. Yamada, who was preparing the transducer, was going to do the ultrasound, herself, since the blood scan was as negative as the urine test. Meanwhile, Mildred sat there fretting every piece of conversation she and Roberta had had after their awkward standoff last night:

"That's impossible!" she remembered telling Roberta in response, after her smile had fallen. "I've had two pregnancy tests," she shouted with two fingers jabbed in the air, "and both said negative!" Mildred was amped as if in a fight for her life, desperately trying to ignore the fact she was standing in front of a walking-talking ultrasound machine.

Roberta's effervescent smile fell from her face, but she didn't back down. "It's most likely due to your low hCG levels, honey," she explained with a nanny's compassion, just like more than twenty years ago. She even placed a hand on Mildred's shoulder.

But Mildred answered with a hard flinch and a block that would make a karate master bow.

"I'm sorry." Roberta stepped back. "I've upset you, haven't I?"

Mildred said nothing, just folded her arms and pouted.

Roberta sighed with more compassion in her eyes. "Perhaps you should schedule a doctor's visit to confirm—tomorrow, maybe. Meanwhile, I can just find a nearby hotel to stay the night. I'll be in first thing tomorrow morning to see if you're feeling any better, or… any differently."

Roberta turned and walked away. Her hand was on the door when Mildred called out, "Roberta, wait!" Mildred dropped her arms and sighed. "I'm sorry. It's not your fault. Could you come back, please? I'll show you upstairs."

It was only Roberta's second day on the job, and Mildred had already trusted her with closing the shop while she now faced Dr. Yamada. Seconds after the transducer was inside her, however, she could barely trust what was on the screen, nor the second heartbeat as Dr. Yamada turned up the volume. The doctor's smile, one that used to brighten the entire room, now seemed sinister and conniving to Mildred.

"Would you like to know the sex?" Dr. Yamada asked. "Our new devices can predict gender in the first trimester."

Mildred took a deep breath; she didn't even want to acknowledge she had a living being floating in her lower belly. "Sure. Why not," she said flatly, now dreading how on earth Sterling was going to react. Better yet, she wasn't exactly sure how she *wanted* him to react. Did she want him to jump up and click his heels, or did she want him to take the first flight back to Sacramento? She knew she loved him, but as a staunch independent woman, she was just as frightened of marriage as most men were.

"Congratulations, Ms. Morehouse," Dr. Yamada said, this time with undeniable but quiet joy, "you're going to be the proud mother of a baby boy."

Mildred tried her best to return the sentiment, but felt her own teeth gritting and grinding like a woodchipper—the same reaction to everything else the doctor explained thereafter. At a certain point, Mildred began to drift, remembering a strange thing about her gynecologist. It wasn't that she was a strange woman, but Mildred felt it odd to see a successful private physician move her entire office from Los Angeles to San Diego. The relocation occurred shortly after Mildred had done the same, and was up and running in record time. When asked, Dr. Yamada had told her it was because she enjoyed the lifestyle and the lower cost of living. Mildred had asked no more; it was the same reason she'd done it. Fortunately, Mildred didn't have to make many visits. She was a healthy young woman whose visits were only routine and infrequent, but now a woman thankful for Dr. Yamada's presence, no matter how strange.

Dr. Yamada had just sent Mildred away with a handful of pamphlets and the next appointment date. From her office's window, she shifted one blind up to watch Mildred drive completely away before lifting her cellphone. Scrolling down her contact's list, she found "C" for confidential. One press and a few rings later, a man answered the phone.

"Yes?" he said.

"Chief Agent Adams?"

"Yes, Doctor."

"It's happened," the doctor said in a tone of extreme se-crecy, regardless of being alone in her own office. *"She's* preg-nant," she added like a talk show host, but still clandestine.

The man went silent for several seconds. "Good," he fi-nally admitted, dryly.

"Good? More like, *exciting*, right?"

But his tone was still dirt-dry. "Yes. Exciting. Keep me informed, okay?"

"As always, Sir."

Not everyone could afford a robotic drive option in their vehicle. Mildred was one of them. Sure, her father could have easily had one installed for her, but except for his startup assistance with the shop, Mildred preferred to be independent on all levels. Although, she did have an E.V./Perpetuo hybrid like a few other folks she knew, one she'd driven straight from Dr. Yamada's office to the beach, La Jolla Shores this time. She hated to admit to herself, but it was simply to avoid the last place she'd seen Sterling. By the time she'd parked, she remembered nothing along her entire trip from the doctor's office. It was like she'd blinked her eyes and she was suddenly at the beach.

Mildred soon stood knee-deep in a cool wave, no concern for the jeans and sneakers she'd never bothered to remove. And having purposely left her shades in the car, she gazed out over an-other sunset with a heavy-browed squint, placing her vision at the mercy of the sun before it set. She even started walking towards it, farther and farther into the water until neck-deep, no concern for the light jean jacket that went in with her either. One more step and the waves began to slosh in and out her nostrils, inviting her to take in a few more. She wasn't ready to be a mother. She loved Sterling, but she wasn't ready to be a wife. Yet she knew she had to give him the news, but when? How? Truth be told, she really just wanted to die.

Chapter 16

"This is a travesty, Madame President! A complete and utter travesty of holy justice!" Weeks before Mildred's discovery in her doctor's office, Vice-President Waldon Fontley seemed consumed by another discovery made in an office on higher ground. He didn't appear too happy when he slammed a file-folder on President Vera Houston's desk in the oval office, its walls painted sky-blue to the president's liking. From there, Waldon jammed a hand in his pants pocket and paced around in circles, swiping his thinning hair to the back with the other. "A complete travesty!" he reiterated as the president perused the file's contents, her eye-glasses propped on the tip of her nose.

Flawless in a white blouse under a taupe-colored pantsuit, she thumbed her way to the end, only a hair slower than shuffling a deck of cards. "Okay, just what is it here you have a problem with, Mr. Vice-President?" Her tone was forcefully accommodating, considering she'd already been kind enough to allow Waldon to enter unannounced.

"Robots that look, talk, walk and smell like us! Robots that can think faster than us! That can regenerate cells better than us! Pretty soon, they'll be running for public office! Gubernatorial! Congressional seats! Hell, can you imagine Vice President R2-D2 and President C3-PO? Can you!"

The president huffed. "They don't have a vote, Mr. Vice-President."

"You mean—now! You mean, they don't have a vote—*now*!"

Listening to Waldon's rant and watching his hands fly all over the place, Vera was aware the Vice-President's arm had only recently been out of its sling. She, like everyone else, figured he'd "milked" every piece of sympathy he could out of the shooting, enough to last another term if necessary. She was also aware his attitude about androids had "one-eightied" the moment Roberta had "failed" to protect him from a sniper's bullet. But Vera never could understand his stance on the matter, wondering, *I mean my God—all this major attitude because of a damn flesh wound?*

She slammed the folder shut and eyed Waldon with the tautness of the curls on her head. She'd always joked that the single gray streak in the front, one that had developed on its own, was left untouched to encourage her to live up to its wisdom. Now was the time to put that wisdom to use. "First of all, I'll need you to dial the volume down a bit, okay?"

Waldon stopped and faced her, took a deep breath and straightened his lapel, then nodded his agreement with a reluctant grunt.

"That's better," said Vera. "So, what exactly is it you're proposing?"

He took another breath. "I'm proposin' we shut this down—the whole daggum thing down."

Vera watched Waldon fold his lips, his struggle to suppress his emotions as blatant as his outbursts. His entire head even began to swell like trying to hold helium. Vera chuckled into her answer just to avoid full laughter, "That's a no-go, Mr. Vice-President."

"You may laugh, and I may have spoken in the hyperbole just now, but these contraptions conjured up by the likes of 'PepperCorp,' and uh, and uh—dang Silver-Stick, are already taking jobs away from hardworking Americans." But he went ballistic again, grabbing a layer of oval air in his fist and ripping it right out of place. "*Snatching* food right out of the mouths of clean, wholesome, hardworking American families, the little ones included!"

As entertaining as Waldon's antics were, Vera absorbed the seriousness of his words, foremost. "Yes, I am aware of the few units out there that have been working among the general public, but nothing has been to the level of mass job extinction, and we do not have the authority to go after private businesses who choose to operate by their own accord. Plus, our move to hire *Silver-Stem* for military contracts, along with limits and conditions, has served as a major step towards curtailing private production. And we're close to procuring the same with *ZepperCorp* as you and I speak right now."

"'Curtailing'—but not eliminating!" All it took was a stiff forefinger from Vera for him to dampen his tone. "Sorry. 'Curtailing,' but not eliminating."

"True, but things of this nature take time, so there is a small percentage of sales allowed to the private sector to give them a re-adjustment or grace period, so to speak. Actually, I think it happens to be a fair reward for the dual benefits of their unparalleled contributions in stem-cell research."

But Waldon seemed uninterested in her last point. "Percentage?" He raised a brow. "How much of a percentage are we talkin' here?"

She slid the folder to the side. "Not that I have to divulge anything to you at this time, Reverend, but for the sake of full disclosure, ten-percent is a fair gratuity for the services they'll return to the people."

Waldon's hands quivered. "Ten-percent? Ten-percent!"

Vera sat befuddled by his reaction. "What!" She practically felt one more gray strand growing.

"Ten-percent is *far* too generous!"

She shrugged. "Well, it's done. And if ever you were to check your emails, you'd be up on matters like these. By the way, how do you see any of this as a travesty of justice?"

"*Holy* justice! I said, '*holy* justice'!"

"Well, sometimes I wish we could rely on 'holy justice' in our positions, but we're employed to abide by 'legal justice,' and justice is on their side here."

"*That*—is the travesty!" He yanked his lapel again along with another grunt, but no nod this time. "Well, I can tell you this much: there is no way in gracious skies ten-percent is gonna fly with the American people."

"On the contrary, Reverend, our data indicates that this number falls in line with the acceptance level of the American people. It's safe to say most Americans are curious what the future holds."

Waldon boldly approached the president's desk and pressed his hands along the edge, sneering. "I don't care what your fancy, schmancy number crunchers and computers say. They don't know people like *I* know people. And if you want me to place the entire Bible Belt in your back pocket for the next election, then I reckon that ten-percent needs to fall to zero."

Vera stared into his fiery eyes after hearing everything, including an "or else" in his tone. She stood from her chair, mirroring both his pose and his glare from her side of the desk. "Why Mr. Vice-President," she said, mocking his southern accent to perfection, "I do declare that that there sounds like a threat."

Waldon rolled his eyes and stepped back. "You can mock me all you like, but when hog slop hits the fan, it won't matter if it's a threat or a prediction; we will all go down in a burning inferno!"

Vera huffed and flopped back into her chair, remembering she had another meeting starting soon. She folded her fingers and fell back to her proper vernacular. "I tell you what, Reverend—if you and your team can find any of these companies guilty of any malfeasance, even if it's in their field of play, you bring it to me and I promise you—we will renegotiate that percentage more to your liking. How does that sound to you?"

Waldon folded his arms. "Zero!" he demanded.

But Vera shook her head. "Rev—learn how to accept a victory."

Waldon's nostrils flared in and out. "Fine. Folder, please."

After handing him his folder, Vera watched Waldon exit her office in typical Waldon fashion, permanently disfiguring every floor-fiber in his path. She allowed a few seconds to pass after the door closed before connecting to her receptionist, no visuals. "Michael?"

Michael's voice was brisk and crisp. "Yes, Madame President?"

"Am I on speaker?"

"No, Ma'am, Madame President."

"Good. Just give me the signal the next time he shows up unannounced—so I can get out through the escape hatch."

"But—"

"I know… I don't care if he's just down the damn hall. Got it?"

"*You* got it, Madame President."

"Damn it!" With his office door closed, Waldon pounded his desk when he noticed a second file-folder setting there—part two of the one he'd just shown the president minutes before. "Praise the Lord," was the phrase he always used to negate a verbal faux pas. "Havin' two dang offices is enough to drive someone crazy," he mumbled to himself. He was in his West Wing office today, just down the hall from the Oval. Only portraits of vice-presidents-past adorned the walls—not much else in it to call it his own. Regardless, leaving files both places was a constant, but not really the cause this time. This forgotten folder was strictly Waldon's fault. Both files reaching Waldon so late in the game was the direct result of him reaching that point in his haystack today. Per his request, his staff had spent countless hours "oddly" printing out paper documents in an advanced digital age. A child of the early 2000s, Waldon's attachment to paper trails was confounding to every last staff member—confounding to everyone he knew. He blamed C.V.S. (computer vision syndrome) for his aversion to computers, although this was never medically confirmed.

Waldon dove into the second file with far more vehemence than the first, determined to overturn the mockery he'd just encountered in the Oval. But when the string of six-syllable words began turning into cryptic messages from beyond, he resorted to buzz words. Turning the page, his eyes landed on the heading. "Millennium Droid...," he mumbled further, glossing over the rest to get to more buzz words: "....cellular multiplication...." A tug on the chin. "....engineered de... oxy... ribo—whatever." His eyes dropped down the page. "....preprogrammed chromosome construction and determination....," "....electro-energized protein conversion and delivery system—oh, my God..." A few illustrations had helped.

Waldon's bottom lip fell close to the point of dribbling. "These sons o' bitches are plannin' on giving birth to the death of all mankind," he murmured. "Praise the Lord."

He slammed the folder shut and grabbed his cellphone, determined to save the U.S. of A., and the world, from this new existential threat. He dialed F.B.I. director, Gerald Fatzinger, immediately, and like always, he dialed without using the speakerphone or his phone-screen.

"Mr. Vice-President," Harold answered with a dead calm in his sonorous voice.

"Gerald, how goes it?"

"It goes well, Mr. Vice-President. How is everything with you?"

Waldon fell back in his chair. "*Well*, hard to say. That's why I'm callin' you."

"How can I help you?"

Waldon went on to explain everything he'd just taken in, concluding with his own holy justice. "Now, I'm sure you can see exactly what we're up against here—a holy injustice! The fate of the free world is at stake if these daggum living, breathing robots multiply and flood the streets. Imagine the ramifications! This is a complete violation of the Artificial Intelligence Act of 2040! That's why this here 'Millennium' program cannot be allowed to persist, Gerald!"

"Now, hold on, Mr. Vice-President—that particular project has been allowed to continue for quite a while now. In fact, all of Silver-Stem's existing projects have been allowed to continue on a special exemption from the Artificial Intelligence Act of *2042*," Gerald corrected, "—grandfathered in. And being that there are no other relevant laws on the books, there's nothing the Bureau can do."

"What! What! Can you hear yourself speaking right now? Gerald, you are turnin' a blind eye to the fate of all of America! All the whole entire world!" Hearing no response from Gerald, Waldon reopened the second folder and traced his finger right down the middle of each sheet to the very last one. "Well, come to think of it, I don't see anything in here, or anywhere, regarding a hard cap limit on the number of *units* these rascals can make. And don't try to go tellin' me ten-percent is a ceiling, because it's not!"

He heard Gerald huff. "Now that, Mr. Vice-President, would be in the addendum to the contract."

"Oh, yeah? An addendum, huh?"

"Yes, Sir."

"And have you seen it in this addendum?"

Gerald went silent.

"I thought not." This was one time Waldon wished he could have seen his adversary's face. "I tell you what—I will find and go through that there addendum, and if I do not see a hardline ceiling limit on production *or* this here Millennium Program, you will be hearing from me, and you and your people will put an end to this here program—quick, fast and pronto. Agreed?"

There was a lengthy pause. "If so, that all would depend on what you, Madame President *and* Congress have to say about it."

"Then I'm sure you will be hearing from me *real* soon, Director Fatzinger."

Another pause. "You have a good day, Mr. Vice-President."

"Mm hm. You too." Waldon hung up, but with a little more on his mind about the F.B.I. director: "Arrogant son of a— praise the Lord."

Waldon was back in the Eisenhower Building the next morning, far enough away from the West Wing to prop his feet on Teddy's desk. He'd had his most trusted staffer dig up the contract in question and give it a twice-over, addendum included. Lo and behold, the only limitation or reference to the type of droid allowed was found to be at the discretion of the overseeing agency—none specified. It wasn't much, but it was enough to raise Waldon from his seat, uplifted by the opportunity before him. Madame President, Director Fatzinger, and all their lackeys were going to feel his wrath. "You just wait and see, Ms. Fancy, Schmancy, Smarty Pants," he muttered to himself as he picked up his cell and began to dial, only to stop in his downswing. *But what are the odds?* he asked himself. He was correct before; he knew the ways of people, and he knew *these* particular people were not going to budge from their stance. Afterall, he was a token hire, an outsider to everyone beyond his own staff, some who'd served him faithfully during his liturgical glory. *No, I have a better idea.* He decided to dial a new-old friend's number.

"Hello, how can I help you today?" a male voice answered.

"Well, hello there, Mr. Hampton!" He'd called Mike P. Hampton of Bullhorn.

"Mr. Vice-President," Mike greeted, "how are you?"

"Mighty fine." (He wasn't) "Look, uhhh… I have a favor to call in."

"Ohhh? Have we not followed through on anything?"

"Oh, no, forgive me. You have honored your word on many occasions. What I seek now, you can call it an advance on a favor." The holy man's tone carried a devilish chuckle.

"Okay… fire at me, please."

"Okay, first of all, this here is strictly confidential."

"Always."

"The U.S. government, and I speak on its full behalf, has a need to shut down a covert operation that is undermining the fabric of this great nation as we speak. An operation so tightly hinged, we can't even trust our own forces to terminate it. But I hear your rifle association may have contact with the specialists we need to execute such a delicate task. Do you see where I'm coming from? Do you *feel* me?"

There was a brief pause. "I feel you, alright."

"And afterwards, I will be in your debt to no ends." *Maybe.* "Deal?"

Another brief pause. "Mr. Vice-President, all I need now are the specifics."

"Good! And need I remind you again, this all needs to stay confidential between you and me. None of this can be recorded."

"You need not remind me, Sir."

"Good. Then here are the details...." Waldon went on to layout the gist of what he'd read and what he knew, ending with a final instruction: "This Millennium Project needs to be shutdown, starting with that droid. And when your boys capture her, let me be the first to know. Got it?"

"Got it, Sir."

Chapter 17

When Lauren opened her apartment's front door, Mildred said and did nothing but drag herself across the threshold with an overnight bag in her hand. She didn't know exactly how long she'd be staying; she just knew it had to match whatever time she needed to take cover from Sterling. She'd already told Roberta she wouldn't be returning for the evening, and in her mind, her upcoming couples' weekend was also canceled.

Lauren grabbed the bag and sniffed the air as Mildred breezed by straight to the sofa. "Mildred, did you go swimming without me?"

No matter how hard Mildred had showered and scrubbed after her stroll into the Pacific, she couldn't rinse the faint smell of ocean salt from her hair. She plopped down on the sofa like it was hers. "No… well, yes… kind of. I just needed some time alone." She rumbled her lips. "And now I don't."

Lauren set the bag down where she stood and joined her friend on the sofa, facing her from the opposite end. "So, what's up?"

Mildred's original request to Lauren was that she'd needed somewhere else to stay for a night or two—no reason as to why. But there was now no way she could hide the turmoil spinning in her head. "I… I'm… oh, shit." She turned away and mumbled out the other side of her mouth, "I'm pregnant."

"What? Come again. I didn't hear you."

Mildred turned back around and noticed Lauren cupping her ear with two fingers. Mildred shifted her eyes to the floor. "I… am pregnant," she mumbled a little louder while scratching the back of her neck.

"You're what!" Lauren's eyes nearly exploded, and remained that way until Mildred's did the same.

"I'm—"

"No, I heard you! I heard you! I just can't believe you!"

"I know, I know...," she groaned to the ceiling, ashamed.

Lauren moved in closer and laid her hand on Mildred's knee. "No, I'm not trying to shame you. And I'm not saying it's a *bad thing*. It's a shocking thing, though. Then again, why should I be so shocked? You're in love... You're deep in your twenties... It's about time! You're practically an old maid!"

"Old maid? Old maid!" The accusation had a definite effect on her mood, swinging from embarrassment to eye-rolling, reinforced by folded arms and a strong neckroll. "So, just what does that make you?"

Lauren's face went blank. "Ooh... that's a good question. What *does* it make me?" she muttered, shaking it off the next instant. "Anyway, you two are in love, right?"

Mildred retreated back to groaning, "Yes," until stunned by Lauren's halting hands.

"Hey, wait a minute! This baby does belong to—"

"Lauren! How could you think—"

"Alright, alright!" Lauren reared back with palms up. "Just checking. And I take it you haven't told him yet."

Mildred sighed. "No... no... no... I haven't even told my parents yet."

"You haven't?" Lauren scratched her head and confessed, "I guess I should feel honored, but—," then placed her hand back on Mildred's knee. "—you really should at least discuss it with your mom. I mean, that's what moms are here for."

"I know, I know. But if I do, she'll just tell Dad and he'll be so mad at me, I know he will. You know, *they* got married first;

I didn't. And my dad, he'll think I've been 'slutting' around or something."

"What! Slutting around? Doesn't he know about you and Sterling?"

"Yeah, but slutting around outside of wedlock; that's what I'm talking about. And I'm not even ready to tell Sterling because I'm not sure if I'm ready to be a parent. I'm not sure if *he's* ready for anything like that! I don't even know what he's going to think!" Her anguish grew louder for every word until tears began to flow. "I just… I just… I just don't know *what* to do!" Sobs and sniffles followed.

"Aw now, sweetheart." Lauren scooted all the way over to Mildred's end to hold her in her arms. "Sh, sh, shhh… everything's gonna be alright. It's gonna be alright."

The night eventually ended with the two sharing Lauren's king-sized bed, wrapped in each other's arms like siblings.

The next morning, Sterling paced back and forth in his apartment's living room, rubbing his head just the same. He was so distraught, he'd taken the entire day off from work just to brood. *What did I do? What did I do?* It was the question he'd been repeating to himself ever since Mildred's absence. She hadn't returned any of his text or voice messages all the day before, nor this morning. He knew she wasn't on a rope or a chain or anything, but it was the first time it had happened since they'd been dating, further begging the question: *What did I do? What did I do? What did I do wrong?*

It was time to act. Too soon to drop by the store unannounced, he raised his smartwatch. "Dial Mildred's Floral," he commanded.

"Mildred's Floral Arrangements. Dialing," a sultry virtual voice responded.

Sterling opened his phone's screen while waiting, anticipating Mildred's beautiful face to be on the other end. Instead, he got another face just as lovely on the shop's comm-system.

"It's a wonderful day for flowers," the woman said with a smile. "How can we help you?"

"Roberta?" Mildred had told him Roberta was coming in to help out, and her face was just as described, but he'd yet to meet her until now.

"Yes. Sterling, I take it?"

"Yes, nice to meet you. How are you?"

"I'm just fine. Yourself?"

"Doing well." Everything he'd been told about her seemed true, even more so. Never had he seen so many facial expressions, so much personality, from any other droid. There was absolutely no way to distinguish her from a human being, but he cut to the chase: "Umm, is Mildred in?"

"I'm sorry, Sterling, Mildred wanted me to tell you she's in Los Angeles at her parents' house for a personal matter." She'd pointed north. "She said she'll call you as soon as she returns."

"Ohh. Did she say *when* she'll return?"

Roberta mummed her lips and shook her head slowly, followed by compassionate eyes. "I'm sorry, Sterling." She paused to welcome a customer. "Good morning!" Then turned back to Sterling, her tone suddenly far from compassionate. "Forgive me, Sterling, a customer has just come in."

But Sterling never heard the door chime. "No problem. I'll just wait for her call. And can't wait to meet you in person, Roberta."

"Same here, dear."

Sterling hung up only a little less distraught. He at least knew Mildred was safe, but the complete disregard not to tell him she was leaving town—he didn't know how to handle it. *Am I important to her at all?* Back to rubbing his head and pacing, he would have to wait and see.

Meanwhile, Roberta had already established a morning cleaning ritual, including pruning every plant and sweeping up afterwards. Easy to do since no one else was in the shop. And she knew Mildred wasn't at her parents' house. Designed for special ops, telling a lie or stretching the truth for a mission, primary or secondary, was built into Roberta's protocol. Telling multiple lies was doubly built in. Designing a whole truth routine would have been like setting a hamster in a wheel—a runtime error. In the end, it all amounted to achieving her current secondary mission: to keep Sterling at bay.

Chapter 18

Sterling received the call minutes beyond noon the next day, when Mildred gave him explicit instructions to meet her at the shop that evening, and he put up no fuss. He didn't even bother her with yesterday's frustrations, his prior worries, or his sleeplessness last night. He simply asked, "I heard you had a family emergency yesterday. Is everything okay? Are your parents okay?" *A safe play.*

"Oh, they're fine," Mildred assured, "but I'll explain everything to you when you get here this evening."

"Okay. See you later then."

Sterling wasn't in his usual office environment when his smartwatch went blank. He was standing along a stretch of beach currently occupied by nothing but the typical non-biodegradable wastes—bottles, wrappers, cans—along with one biodegradable that frizzled his nose-hairs. The beach had seen its share of college parties, but the one from the previous weekend was massive, loaded with drunkenness and rowdy behavior. Afterwards, no one would have dared return to dangle their toes in the urine-drenched sand. *Not quite the kind of coastal accretion we were aiming for,* Sterling thought to himself. Luckily he was wearing rubber boots, but still huffed and braced himself. Since he'd forgotten his respirator at the office, it was going to be a long day—an even longer night.

Mildred had been the epitome of cool when she'd scheduled with Sterling earlier. Now, pacing the floor in her shop that evening after closing, she felt every gnawed-off fingernail beneath her soft soles. A lightweight, long-sleeved knit above faded jeans remained her fashion statement as she removed her apron and lay it atop the center counter. With the absence of a lost thought, she made not one move to stop it from sliding over the edge onto the floor.

Mildred's pacing resumed. She had already sent Roberta on a long errand to buy herself more time with Sterling, which made things eerily quiet in the shop. A short breath followed when she heard a knock on the front door. Her advanced security scanner was turned off, but it was only Sterling standing outside in the dark. The lumens from one lone streetlight barely on him, his eyes were already longing for an explanation.

After opening the door to its customary chime, Mildred reached up for a hug, her sleeves lightly clinched in both hands. She embraced Sterling without a word, *her* eyes nearly in tears as if on the verge of confessing a crime.

Sterling held on tight, then pulled himself back abruptly. "Mildred, what's going on?" he asked softly. "What's going on with us?"

Mildred turned and walked away, folding and brushing her arms like it was ten below. She stopped just on the other side of the central counter, where Sterling followed. She turned back to face him, then dawdled even longer.

Sterling's gaze was intense the entire moment. "Sooo," he finally continued, "are you going to tell me now?"

Releasing her sleeves, she reached around him, clutched the back of his shirt and returned his gaze. "Sterling, you love me, don't you?"

His brows drooped. "Of course, I do. With all my heart."

Hers followed. "Good. Because I love you too. And I'm—and I'm… I'm—"

"You're what?"

"I'm pregnant, Sterling. I'm pregnant." A single tear dripped.

His eyes did what was totally expected; they inflated like balloons. "You're what?" It was his volume that failed to meet her expectations—no excitement, no joy, just, "You're what?"

Once again, her expression followed his.

"I mean, you're pregnant?" he asked softer.

"Yes, Sterling, I'm pregnant. *We're* pregnant!"

His next look was inscrutable, balanced on a tightrope between joy and panic. "But I thought you said you weren't. Remember? Back at the beach?"

"I remember what I said, but I didn't know at the time." She huffed. "It's hard to explain."

Sterling took a deep breath. "But I thought we were being careful... uhh, you know..."

Again, not what Mildred wanted to hear. She leaned back, fear and shame quickly replaced by contempt. "I know *what*?"

Sterling reached up and pinched the bridge of his nose. "I'm sorry. My bad. I'm just caught a bit off guard."

"I don't know why."

With both hands, he grabbed her shoulders and stroked them with firm compassion, his gaze again deeply into hers. "Look—there is no other woman I would rather have a child with. I mean, *no other*. I just thought..."

"You thought what?"

"I thought we'd have more time, Mildred."

Saying, *We don't, Sterling*, would have been the easiest retort, the quickest. But would it have been the truth? She could no longer hide it; Sterling's chain of responses left little to no optimism she could move forward with this pregnancy. She had no intention to go through it without him. She even believed that was exactly where his thoughts were going next, and she was totally resolved to following—frightened, but resolved. While weighing her next response, a strange thought crossed her mind. With Roberta back in her life, who better to help with raising and protecting a child: the woman, the unit, who helped raise her. Suddenly, Mildred had a viable option. *Not the most ideal one, but—*

"You know what?" Sterling, almost forgotten, finally checked back in.

"What?"

"I think we can handle this. I think we can make this work."

Mildred felt her eyes bloom like the flowers in the case to her right. "Really!"

Sterling nodded. "Yes. I mean, think about it: you're doing great here at the store. And now that Roberta is back in your life, who would make a better babysitter?"

"Roberta?" Mildred's mouth was hanging, her eyes in a trance. Had Sterling just read her mind? Again? *Or maybe he'd somehow planted it here.* Their connection *was* a bit uncanny.

"Yeah. The timing couldn't be any better. And *my* job pays well. My coworkers are great. My supervisor is the best— well, most of the time."

"And your temporary status…?" She remembered.

"Oh, that? Mmm… I think I can make a few suggestions—a few adjustments."

"Really? To stick around?" Her heart pattered as he nodded slowly with a burgeoning smile. Infatuation for a man who was suddenly in perfect sync with his woman now consumed her, as if the first five minutes of this dreadful encounter had never happened. "And you think they'll buy it?"

"Of course. I'll just tell them the truth."

"What? That you knocked up your girlfriend?"

"No, not that truth."

"What truth then?"

"That I knocked up the woman I plan on marrying."

Mildred's shoulders sank. "Sterling, those people probably do not care about—hey, wait a minute." She pulled herself back in shock, but felt a smile growing. "Was that a *proposal*? Did you just *propose* to me?"

"I uhh…, I uhh…" He paused. "I guess."

"You guess?"

He went silent.

"Well, when you're more certain, I guess I'll give you an answer. But this right here…" With two fingers, she circumscribed her belly. "…this right here is happening." Now, completely sold on motherhood, she wrapped her arms around Sterling's shoulders until they were both back in each other's face, nose-to-nose.

"I *am* certain I love you," he said with a single soft kiss.

"Aww…" She returned his affection, their lips now in slow motion as visions of Roberta faded away as quickly as the streetlight outside blinked off. Mildred had sensed it from the corner of her eye, but thought nothing of it; she and Sterling were both in too deep. And when their lips finally did part, she wished all the lights inside were next to fade away. A fantasy of being spread across the countertop first perused her thoughts, but his smile would suffice. And with it all came a faint red dot against his temple. "I love you t—," she said before being interrupted by Sterling's blank stare, his pupils glazed over like porcelain ornaments, along with his full weight bearing down into her arms.

"Sterling?" she asked, bewildered. "Sterling? What's wrong?" But he continued to wilt in her arms, to the point she didn't know where she'd found the strength. How was she holding him up? A trickle of blood down the side of his face was just the start of the answer. The rest came from her left, a barely visible hole through her front window. She had to squint to see it; the dark backdrop allowed her to see nothing else. By the time she realized it wasn't there earlier, Sterling's weight had taken her all the way to the floor, her apron underneath her. His body now limp on top of hers, the counter blocked them both from the window, but the blood began to pour. "Sterling! Sterling!" she screamed.

Once the screaming stopped, Mildred managed to maneuver herself on top of Sterling. "Wake up, baby. Wake up, baby. Baby, wake up," she muttered repeatedly, gasping in between, unable to feel his heartbeat, unable to feel the air around her, and unable to believe her own existence. Cupping his face, the blood pasted to her palm meant nothing to her. That's when the lighting overhead and in the cooler ended abruptly, and all electricity ceased with a humming echo. The silent darkness that followed still meant nothing to Mildred, who began to rock Sterling like a babe in her arms.

Moments passed with no other sound, not until the front door creaked open, but no longer with a chime. Ears uncharacteristically tuned, Mildred was on the verge of calling out Roberta's name just before hearing a new sound: the slow plodding of heavy boots not typical of Roberta's pace. Another set followed, and a third, maybe a fourth, all without a word. With Sterling still in her arms, the unannounced danger approaching suddenly meant something to her. *Oh, my God... what in the hell is happening?*

Mildred knew it was time to run, but she couldn't pull herself away from her helpless lover, refusing to believe a bullet had just bored through his skull. The best she could do was reach up to the countertop, dusting it lightly until retrieving her smartphone a hair before the plot thickened.

"We know you're in here, droid," a strange, male voice called out through the darkness.

Mildred could virtually picture the intruders' every move. As if her heart wasn't already beating fast enough, the pounding that followed was sure to give her away. *Wait*, she wondered, *did he just say the word, 'droid'?* She was on the verge of raising up and screaming, *Wait! Wait! You've got the wrong person! She's not here!* But she couldn't expose Roberta like that; she couldn't let them know she even existed. She only prayed that whoever was on the other side of that counter would recognize their mistake. She took another look at Sterling's lifeless body, now wondering if it would even matter. *What do I do?*

More footsteps filed in, too many to count. Mildred only had time to press the record button on her smartphone, shoving it underneath the counter only a second before a flashlight's beam was in her eyes.

"We thought you wouldn't get too far," the same voice said from behind the light. The man appeared not much older than Mildred, except with eyes wide like a wild animal, and a patchy beard to match. His jacket was zipped all the way up with its hood over his tangled red auburn hair. "Though I can't figure out just how the likes of you can fall for a real *live* man," he said with a rural accent. It was obvious they'd been watching for some time now.

Mildred said nothing in return, her eyes welling up again—not from pain, but from pure instant hatred.

Another man stepped from behind him with a rifle in hand, then another from behind Mildred. She looked around to see him holding a rifle as well, yet her hatred only grew. She leered at the first man and gritted, "What do you want from us? Money! I'm a florist, for God's sake! And cash came to an end in the twenty-thirties!"

The man raised his brow and nodded. "A florist? Sure, you are." His eyes never narrowed. "But we're not here for money. We're here for you, you heap o' twisted circuits."

Mildred paused. "There's no heap of twisted circuits here. You've got the wrong place."

"Do we? I don't think so."

The man behind her stepped forward and turned his own flashlight on her. "Well now, are we sure it's her?"

"Of course, it's her," the first man said while looking her up and down. "Stand up," he commanded her. "Let us get a good look at'cha'."

Mildred grimaced with another uncharacteristic response, "Fuck—you." Nor did she budge.

A light snicker and a head-bob was the man's response, followed by Mildred being yanked up by her armpits. It took two others, each with the breath of dead meat, to do it, but she'd fought the entire way.

The first, the apparent clan leader, continued to look her up and down. "About the same height—same fake skin color—skinny. It's her alright."

It stood to reason to Mildred; she and Roberta could pass for sisters. In the dark, twins.

The leader leaned into her face, and for the first time, his eyes narrowed. "Now—are you gonna be a good little machine and accompany us without a fuss? Or a badass? Which is it gonna be?"

Mildred could feel a full valley creeping down her own forehead. "Like I said, fuck—you!" She punctuated her response with spit she'd accumulated from every backed-up tear, aiming and landing it like a marksman into her new adversary's eye, proud to see it ooze down his cheek.

The leader calmly stepped back and wiped his soaked face. "Hmph," he chuckled, then mumbled, "I didn't know they could do that. And it feels real too. Real wet. Slimy." His mood swiveled. "Take her," he commanded his clan.

On cue, Mildred's world went pitch dark from a jolt, one that raced through every nerve from head to toe.

Chapter 19

Roberta's long errand was a trip to the nearest garden supply center, nothing less than a blissful journey for her. She rolled her overflowing basket down each aisle with her broadest smile since arriving in San Diego. Thanks to Dr. Murphy, her new programing had her convinced that shopping was more exciting than maneuvers through dunes and forests. He had even inserted a subroutine that allowed her to self-adjust her emotion chip if necessary. But she didn't need Kenneth's input to convince her McCarvey's Garden Depot was now her new forest and paradise. Neither did she need a written list to fill her basket; every supply and quantity was in her database like carved engravings. Tape, wrapping, foam bricks, ribbon, cages and cleaning rags all pressed the basket to its limits. Mildred had given her the shop's credit chip and carte blanche authority to overstock whatever they needed, along with instructions to take her time. And it didn't take an android to figure out that more time with Sterling was at the root of it.

Since Mildred had already placed a couple of planter boxes just outside the flower shop, Roberta also had a few garden tools tucked inside the basket. Mildred's explanation was unforgettable: "A flower shop without a flower garden is a crime against nature." Roberta now strolled into the register line, also tickled by the memory of the tiny version of Mildred playing in her family's garden. Roberta chuckled a little, until being distracted by a strange feeling in the air—literally, in the air. A steady vibration quivered her nerves like an electric charge, along with a faint buzz she couldn't identify. Not even her sensors could find a match. *Where is that coming from?*

Her eyes wandered from one ceiling truss to the next until landing on the one customer in front of her. He was a broad-framed man with a basket just as full as hers. When he finished paying, he rolled away with a quick lookback in Roberta's direction, a huge smile on his face. The man appeared to be close to middle age with hair slightly gray and thinning. It was an eerie moment, but more puzzling for another reason: the farther away he got, the more the buzzing faded—to zero as the automatic doors closed behind him.

"Ma'am?" the young register clerk interrupted, returning Roberta to the job at hand.

But what Roberta had just sensed was real; she was certain of it, as certain as she was of the price of all her items. "Two-hundred-thirty-nine-point-fifty-two in credits," she mumbled as she moved forward, "tax included."

The clerk squinched enough for her eyeglasses to slide. "Excuse me?"

Roberta shook her head. "Sorry, nothing." She went on to unload the basket item-by-item, all the while drowning in her own confusion. Was her reaction to the man who'd just left what humans referred to as "chemistry"? But it couldn't have been. It wasn't like he was built like an athlete, nor was he the classic image of a model. Then again, Roberta had never really known what was visually attractive to her. Since Kenneth had never scripted a baseline for her, she could only base it on internet "likes" just to get an approximation of universal good looks. *And the man who was just in front of me would most certainly have received none.*

"Hmph. What do you know?" the clerk said with a shrugged chin. "Two-hundred-thirty-nine-and-fifty-two credits—including tax."

Rolling her basket slowly through the parking lot to her vehicle, Roberta checked her internal clock. *9:26 p.m.* A sigh followed.

That should be enough time, she figured. If not, she wasn't worried. She believed everything between Mildred and Sterling would end up fine; she'd already streamlined the matrix of possibilities. When she stopped at her vehicle's trunk, the vibrating buzz returned as if it was right behind her. So intense and disruptive, she pressed her fingers into her temple, desperate for an off switch.

"Greetings, friend," a man's voice came from behind.

Roberta quivered and turned around, shocked that someone had crept up behind her so easily. If she were ever to return to the field, that buzz would have been the ultimate signal scrambler.

"Sorry to alarm you." The man from the register line was standing there, this time without his basket. "But you get used to it after a sufficient amount of time." He flashed a smile that ended as quickly as it started, like a facial tick.

Roberta tilted her head, more confused. "Excuse me?"

"The buzzing," he said, "it diminishes as time in each other's presence increases."

Roberta didn't need a deep assessment to tell he was an android like herself. Just from his content, not his speech, which sounded as fluently human as hers, she was convinced. But his assurance had yet to be proven valid. The buzzing continued. Taking a deep breath was her only way to deal with it. "But I've never had such a feeling around anyone else like us."

"No, not everyone. Just those of us manufactured by Silver-Stem." The man reached up and aimed his thumb behind his back, towards his neck. "Inside the base of our necks near to the emergency switch, between the C1 and C2 vertebrae, exists an identification transmitter tied into our muscular fibers. Flexible and undetectable to most devices—yet very evident to us." The smile returned, except a little longer.

"But—" Roberta was prepared to reveal the truth: that she was neither designed nor built by Silver-Stem, but she caught herself. She reached back to trace her fingers along the base of her neck instead. Detecting the transmitter with her fingertips' sensors, she now remembered that she'd been reborn inside one of Silver-Stem's labs. She'd been physically restructured. "Wow…"

"I can't believe no one has ever told you."

Roberta paused. *Probably because I would have ripped this shit right out at that very moment.* "And with a G.P.S. locator, I bet."

The man cocked his head like a lost German Shepherd. "Only during emergencies, I'm certain."

Roberta tapped her chin and nodded. *"Ri-i-i-ght…"*

He shrugged, then held out his hand. "Well, I'm Bob, by the way."

Of course, he's a Bob.

"Short for Robert-Two-Hundred."

She shook his hand. "Roberta."

"Roberta. What a coincidence." The next smile may have come a second late, but was just as brief as the first. Bob went on to tell her more about himself, like how he had always been a care-giving unit, "custom-designed to blend in with 'average guy' looks, not to standout to perfection"—his exact words. He even told her which family he worked for, how many children they had, where they lived and so on, leaving little doubt that security features had never been programmed into this one.

Roberta's response: she checked her naked wrist. "Well, Bob, it was nice meeting you. I have a little more work to do, but I look forward to running into you again. Maybe here."

Bob nodded. "Yes, I would like that." He flashed one more smile. "Safe travels to you, Roberta," he said before turning on a dime and walking away, by far the most robotic thing he'd done since their entire exchange.

Roberta's vehicle was on auto-drive the whole trip back to the flower shop, and Sterling's vehicle was parked out front when she approached. All lights were off inside, a good sign the lovers' evening may have gone better than expected. The blacked-out streetlight, on the other hand, told her absolutely nothing, but she did notice it. Meanwhile, she could have continued around the corner and parked in the rear as Mildred had encouraged her, but if things had really gone well for the couple, Roberta couldn't make sense of stopping at all, not until noticing the front door ajar. *They must have really thrown all caution to the wind*, she figured on her way to parking next to Sterling's vehicle.

Heading to the front door, she would have simply closed it and been on her way if not for the spidered hole in the display window. The security alert system was even turned off when she stepped inside, but the faint smell of blood and the soundlessness of no electricity stopped her in her tracks. "Mildred?" she called out. There was no answer. Her next two steps were softer, but one more step and matters grew worse. The bloody aroma, once faint, now rushed through her nose-fibers like a transfusion.

Roberta stood confused, but knew there was one thing she didn't need at a time like this—*Dampen emotion chip*. Kenneth's recalibration was put to the test. And as soon as Roberta's internal bars dropped down to one, she crouched into a more familiar mode—*Assess*—then peered into nothing but darkness. *Illuminate. Low beam.* She now witnessed fresh booted scuff marks on the floor all the way to the other side of the main counter, some with dirt crumbs between the tread-marks. A few blood-smeared heelprints flowed in the opposite direction, towards her. But it was the bloody aroma that still guided her—bloodier as she rounded the counter. "Shit," she mumbled, somehow emotionally stunned to see Sterling lying flat on his back in a pond of blood, and Mildred's apron soaking underneath.

This wasn't one of my scenarios. Fairly certain she was alone, she uttered, "Analyze." The spill was more than an hour old, and Roberta heard no pulse, no heartbeat from Sterling. She stepped around the blood and squatted beside him, where she tipped his head from side-to-side. "Illuminate—high beam," she commanded. "Record." Entry and exit wounds were confirmed, but from his position on the floor, it was difficult to assess where the suspected bullet had come from or where it had landed. Along with it, the pond had been smeared by his body. *He's been moved.*

Roberta stood up and looked towards the far wall; blood was splattered against it. "Assess." She took into account the direction of the splatter, Sterling's height, the spacing between his wounds, and where he might have been standing, leading her eyes straight to the spidered hole in the display window. "Calculate." She projected a virtual line all the way to the building across the street, where the point of origin landed against an exterior wall. "No," she mumbled. It didn't make sense. *A vehicle was involved. A van—parked in the middle of the street.* She immediately visualized a van with a sniper on top. "No." *A sniper through an opening in the van's roof.* With all angles and factors considered—distance, impedance and divergence—she followed a path back to the shop's interior wall, where the bullet had lodged itself into a steel stud, between two standing vases. *High caliber round.* But it didn't take much effort to dislodge the bullet, not for Roberta. She pulled it out and stared at it, was even on the verge of analyzing it until a daunting thought crossed her mind: "Mildred!" she shrieked, a sure sign her emotion bars had elevated on their own, no command needed. All followed by pocketing the bullet and running out the back, upstairs and into the apartment at blinding speed. Quietly she searched every room and every closet, but found no signs of Mildred or any intruders.

Roberta went back downstairs with only a few scattered clues to deal with. *First, the boot-prints.* She scanned the floor. *Four intruders at least, and—* Her analysis was cut short by one of Mildred's sneaker-prints also smeared by blood, then dragged a few feet until there were none, as if she'd been lifted completely off the floor. It was a smear she'd seen before checking the apartment.

Roberta's emotion bars were once again elevating. How was she going to figure out where Mildred had been taken? She needed another clue. *Cameras.* She knew that tapping into the city's street surveillance cams would turn up something. *They have to.* Concentrating, she channeled in electronically with the stealth of a ninja. There weren't as many firewalls as she thought there would be, and hacking into it would be by a string of binary code—only a few hundred-thousand iterations needed, no lock-outs. "Iterate." Seconds later and she was in. Once inside, she backtracked to the approximate time of Sterling's demise, but came up empty. Every camera in the area had been disconnected at a single junction point.

Shit! Roberta clinched her fists until they crunched, until a faint beep from below the main counter caught her attention. Stepping around Sterling again, she reached down and found Mildred's cellphone, fortunately in recording mode. "Good girl, Mildred." But the beep had come from a text message, yet it wasn't going to be as complicated or require a mass amount of iterations. "Open messages," she commanded in the perfect Mildred voice.

The only new message was from Lauren: haven't heard from you in a while... where are you?

"My thoughts exact—," Roberta murmured just before noticing the video messenger alert. "Play video," she ordered.

A second later, Mildred's mother's face appeared on the screen, her brow and eyes under total duress. "Mildred, your father

and I need you to come home right away. I mean, right away!
Don't bother packing. Just get in your car and leave. Then call me
once you're on the road. We'll explain everything to you then.
Okay, hon? See you soon. We love you!" Mr. Morehouse was
visible in the background with a similar look, except his mouth was
agape. Both faces then vanished.

What was that all about? Roberta wondered. Whatever it
was, she could tell the Morehouses had answers she needed, but
there was no answer when she dialed. She tried again, but the results were the same. "Hmmm…"

The outlook was bleak, but one more chance emerged to
solve this horrific mystery: the cellphone's video recorder. Roberta pressed replay. Pants legs, boots and Mildred's sneakers were
the only images she saw moving beyond Sterling's head. The
voices were muffled, but Roberta gave it her best shot. "Let's see
what other new gifts you've given me, Kenneth. Scan web." She
scanned the entire internet, social networks, and criminal databases
for voice recognition, narrowing it down to a mere three-million-
five-hundred-and-twenty-one possibilities. *Search inconclusive.*
She could get no closer. *Shit.* She paused. "The bullet."

Roberta stuffed Mildred's phone in one front pants pocket,
and reached in the other for the bullet. She went to the sink against
the rear wall and began rinsing it with steaming hot water. In these
times, not only did she have lands and groves to analyze, but each
bullet came with its own chemical signature, its own D.N.A. She
just had to remove as much of Sterling's D.N.A. from it as she
could. After rinsing and polishing it with her fingertips, she
gripped it tightly in her fist. "Analyze."

Seconds later, the results were in. The rifle had come from
a bulk stock on the wholesale market, not the black market. The
same applied to the bullet, but from a different shipment. In neither
case was either purchased by an individual.   They'd been

purchased by Barton Brothers, a security guard company with very few legitimate customers. Nor did any brothers named Barton actually own it. Roberta's search could have gone all the way to the top, but time was dwindling. Not even the names of its employees who'd left their trail this night mattered anymore. It was the "where."

Roberta decided to take a different path to finding her cherished companion. She linked herself into public records, which had Barton deeded to properties spanning the nation. The nearest was a 20-acre campsite almost an hour northeast of San Diego. She accessed an aerial history, seeing it hidden deep in the Sycamore Canyon Preserve, a site more brushed and mountainous than cavernous.

The idea may have been a stretch, but less of one when Roberta consumed the entire scene around her again. *The boot-prints*. Squatting, she circumvented Sterling's body all the way to the closest boot-print and pinched a healthy crumb of dirt off the floor. Rolling it to a fine grade, she balled her fingers around it as well. "Analyze." Hundreds of possibilities emerged, soil properties from Sycamore Canyon being the twentieth, conclusive enough for Roberta.

She stood to attention, arched her back with purpose and took one last look behind her. "I'm sorry, Sterling," she spoke her remorse in a flattened tone, followed by an abrupt exit back to her vehicle.

Chapter 20

Now in deep search mode, Roberta switched to manual drive as her own internal G.P.S. led her towards the Sycamore Canyon campsite, while her mind sifted for answers: *Why would mercs from Barton Brothers want to abduct Mildred? It doesn't make any sense.* Mildred's reputation was as clean as bottled water, Roberta knew it. But by ignoring the speed limit, she wasn't giving herself much time to connect the dots. She needed confirmation, a little help, and she needed it now. Eyes locked on the road, she dove into her internal comm system to make a call; no cellphone was necessary.

"Roberta?" Dr. Kenneth Murphy answered after two rings.

Roberta wasted no time with pleasantries. "Are you alone?"

"Mmm… as alone as I can be. I'm in my office. Why?"

"I have strong reason to believe Mildred has been abducted."

"Abducted?" Kenneth blurted.

"Yes."

There was a pause before hearing his office door slide shut. "Abducted?" he asked quietly.

"Yes—abducted, Kenneth."

"How can you be so sure?"

"Check your visual." One quick eye-bat and the stored images were delivered.

"What is this?" Kenneth mumbled. "Wait… is this someone bleeding out on the floor? Is he dead?"

"Oh, yeah," she recalled, "there's that too."

"Oh, my God…" He paused. "And I take it Mildred was nowhere to be found?"

"Yes. All signs point to her being dragged for a few feet and then lifted and taken away. There's also a strong possibility the culprits are contracted by Barton Brothers."

"*Barton Brothers*?"

"Yes. A group of mercs hidden under the alias of a security guard company."

"And how did you arrive at this possibility?"

"Okay, first of all, it's a reality, not a possibility. I traced a sample of the bullet's D.N.A.—one of your new mods, I assume."

Another pause. "I don't recall a—"

"Kenneth, I'm running out of time for this line of Q and A. I need to know if there is anything in Mildred's or her family's background that I'm missing. Are you aware of anything?"

"Right, right. Hmm… you know, I've been trying to figure that out, myself, because I just can't understand Silver-Stem's infatuation with the Morehouses. Well, I'm sure you know the story: the father made it big e-trading, got in and out of Dineroco early before it crashed, flipped it into real estate—you know the rest. I couldn't find anything out of the ordinary, not even any hiccups. No infractions, no lawsuits, no insider trading accusations… no nothing, which in itself may—"

"Raise a flag."

"Yes! Well, anyway, something unusual did pop up when I tried to dig into our own company files on Mildred—" And yet, another pause.

Roberta felt her deep, concealed circuitry heating up. *Damn it, Kenneth! You and all these fucking cliffhanging statements!* She then retuned her emotion chip, dampening it to less than one. "What?" she asked calmly.

"My access got me to a certain point, until running into the Fire-Kraken."

"The Fire-Kraken?"

"Yeah. It's Silver-Stem's security system in case the firewall is breached. Some real crafty gamers were brought in to design it. To get past it is above my paygrade."

Roberta tapped the steering wheel. "Kenneth, can you get me in?"

"Get you where?"

"To the firewall. I'm sure I can circumvent any obstacles from there."

"Hmm, I don't know, Roberta. I already had to come up with a bogus excuse the first time I tried."

This time she squeezed the steering wheel until the steel bars began to flex, her emotion level re-elevated. "Then you'll just have to come up with another one!" she exploded, squeezing until the bars actually bent.

"Warning," her vehicle announced in a woman's voice, but calmly.

Roberta took a deep breath, again dampening her emotion chip. "Sorry, Ken—"

"Alright, alright, calm down," Kenneth interrupted.

"Sorry." Roberta paused. "I can actually scramble your code immediately after breaking through the wall. I suspect I'll only have nanoseconds to do it, but I will do it."

She heard Kenneth huff.

"Kenneth, Mildred's life is at stake here."

"Alright, I'll give it to you," he gave in, "but other than just disguising access codes, if you get in too deep, this system may do more than just block you out."

Roberta didn't need to respond.

"That's right," Kenneth said, "the anti-virus switches from defensive to counteroffensive if it deems you as a potential hacker. Then it tracks the threat all the way back to the source. In this case, *your* C.P.U."

Of all the systems she was empowered to tap into, the company's network was the only one with deadly roadblocks, but she didn't hesitate. "Give me the code."

"I mean, I've upgraded your antivirus system quite a bit, but I'm not sure it can combat what you're about to face. I just wanted to let—"

"Kenneth," Roberta said with all the restraint she could muster, "whatever I'm about to face, I assure you—I'm ready for it. I've already failed before. I'm not going to fail this time. I'm not going to fail Mildred. So, give me the damn code!"

"Alright, alright. It's M-M-eight-eight-X-B-U-two-zero-one-zero-zero-zero-dash-seven-dash-zero. All caps, and the dashes are required. Got it?"

It was obvious to her; the code to executive files were long, complex and randomly assigned to keep executives from using their spouses' names as passwords, as Kenneth would surely have done. But no code was too long for Roberta. "Got it. And there's one more thing I need from you."

"What is it?"

"Two things, actually. First, I need you to turn off this damn location pin you have in my neck."

"Location pin in your neck?"

"Yes."

"Ohh, that's right. Something else they made me do."

"You should have declined."

"I should have."

She heard a few keystrokes on his end.

"I'm just uploading a subroutine to your neural network…
and there."

She felt a slight jolt.

"What else?" he asked her.

"And this 'pussy-fied' response system you've stricken me
with won't be much help where I'm going from here. What can
you do about it?"

"That's a good point." She heard his fingers tapping again.
"I'm sending you another subroutine for that right about… now."

Unlike the faint jolt, Roberta felt a charge that lifted her
chest, invigorating her in an instant. "Oooh." Kenneth had just
uploaded the weapon to restore her combative instincts.

"Did you feel that?" he asked.

"Yes, much better. And I'm in."

"In what?"

"I'm in the network."

"Shit!" Kenneth blurted. "You're in? *Already*?"

"You sound surprised."

"I shouldn't be, but—"

"I have to go, Kenneth. I'll call you back later."

"Right, but like I said, be care—"

Roberta disconnected with Kenneth nearly as fast as she'd
just entered the network. With her body still connected to her vehicle's G.P.S., she locked her mind into the network, facing an odd
surprise as soon as she raised her hand. *I still have a hand?* Her
previous efforts had been simple snatch-and-goes, virtual transfers
only. Yet this one needed something more substantial, more tac-
tile—something that could retrieve more data. With quaternary
codes streaming through her hands and her entire digital presence,
she had done more than simply use the code for access; Roberta
had become the code. Rearranging it for Kenneth's sake was now
under one easy command: *Scramble*. Afterwards, feeling the

system's rhythm beneath her, she synched in, making herself completely undetectable.

Nanoseconds moved like minutes inside the cyber-verse, where Roberta tipped through corridor after corridor of executive memos, memos far less important than would warrant protection. But there she was, seeing electrons passing by and rumbling like thunder whenever they collided, preceded by lightning strikes through a static storm. Unrattled, she was soon there, arms-length from a castle wall of more codes streaming from top to bottom—the firewall constructed to protect all high level files. But these codes raced at a pace different from the floor. These moved with a staccato rhythm, something she had yet to encounter. But she had to break through; the stakes were higher than ever.

She scanned the wall. *Three attempt set-up.* Three attempts to break through was normal, but like Kenneth had warned, the consequences could end up being machine-fatale, and this was far beyond a four-digit code. She reached up and grazed the wall with a feathery touch, advancing digits like a combination lock, advancing until it stopped midway through, the last placeholders empty and waiting for random digits—a snag in her plan. *Shit!* Her emotion chip wavering again, she dropped her hands, finally flustered by the growing number of collisions around her. With only three tries, she had to make a brute-force guess. She raised her hand against the wall again for her first attempt, only to feel the sting of rejection. She tried again with no idea which direction to go, and faced the same result because of it. All she knew was that the collisions had increased with every "spin of the wheel," but a sure sign of just how close she was.

Roberta's touch was firm this time. She pressed the wall and slowed her process—met by the ever-growing colliding electrons, each one agitated by her advance, her intrusion. One more digit to go, and the collisions were roaring. *Click*, went the last tumbler, and all the roars came to a halt. With it went the wall, vanishing until Roberta stepped through, then springing back to full wall height once she was on the other side. She exhaled in relief, with only a twinge of suspicion that this just might be the calm before the storm.

Like a newborn, Roberta gazed around as she walked through the real data corridors, the confidential ones. Loads of text streams raced by like jets in space, none of which embodied the name, Mildred or Morehouse. It wasn't until the next aisle over that she found it, along with a connection to Silver-Stem and a few other companies. Oddly, Barton Brothers was not one of them. "Fascinating," she finally murmured. She could have read it all in milliseconds, but decided to download every piece first. A good idea since the collisions were escalating again. Then came a screeching roar, enough to nearly bring Roberta to releasing fluids like a human, if she could've. She looked over her shoulder to the sight of screaming rage, electrons converging to form an inflamed monster of sorts. As more electrons poured in and wiry stems began to spread from its center like tentacles, Roberta realized the term, "Fire-Kraken," was more than just a euphemism. *Only humans can imagine such a construct.*

Nothing to fight with, logic dictated that Roberta run for her *fucking* programmed life. And with lightspeed as the objective, run, she did. But she felt the heat on her back like a million fingers jabbing into every nerve, pulling her, anchoring her, slowing her down to a trackable pace. She felt all the energy being drained from her coded body until it fell to the floor. But both the floor and her approaching demise felt as real as anywhere else. It even relayed signals to the body that was driving along a dark Sycamore Canyon highway, making it twitch repeatedly, even its eyes, before the foot lifted off the accelerator.

Meanwhile, the digitized Roberta had come to a doleful conclusion: she was losing this battle. *Wait a minute...* Gritting through it, she had an idea: *If this thing is in here... and I'm in here... then we must be of the same... stuff.* With her last ounce of strength, she rolled onto her butt and elbows to face the kraken, then lifted one palm to reverse the flow of electrons. The move resulted in a reenergized jolt for her, but not enough to overcome the kraken, who pulled harder. Roberta needed help.

Feeling herself losing again, help arrived as soon as she thought it. Next to her was a mirror image of herself in the same position, doing exactly the same thing—extending a palm and trying to suck the life right out of the kraken. Roberta had duplicated herself. A tremendous help, but still not enough. She refocused and did it again. And now there were four. And again, until there were eight. And again. And again. And over and over again until there were thousands. It got to the point that Roberta had to do nothing else. For the more the beast fought back, the more her duplicates multiplied on their own, without her. Actually, there was one more thing left to do—run for her "effing" programmed life.

While the warring Robertas remained behind to take care of business, Roberta No. 1 ducked and dodged around partition walls, hiding until jetting back to the firewall. She glanced back only once to watch the onslaught, only to see the kraken multiplying to level the battlefield. *Fuck!*

The ease at which Roberta ghosted through the wall was a sure sign the warring Robertas were making an impact; the kraken was too distracted to fortify it. Meanwhile, Roberta was now sure her mission had been accomplished. The information she needed was in her possession, and the connection back to reality was a bright doorway in clear view—the gateway. *I've just got to—*

But the clatter and clicking of tiny feet interrupted Roberta's dream of freedom. She gazed over her shoulder again, where thousands of clawed, beetle-like creatures were crawling in her direction, each one of them the size of a go-cart, and one of them already snapping at her heels. "Shit, shit, shit!" she hollered. The kraken's wall had released its antiviral counter-offensive system: an army of virus-carrying offspring. And Roberta knew, just one nick from either claw or mandible could result in systemic death. She yelped as a claw came a hair too close.

"Don't worry! We got you, sis!" a voice from above called out.

Coming to Roberta's rescue, more of her replicas had leaped from the digital sky, some stomping the critters to their death, the others jumping in between to draw them away. A gunshot was the sound for each critter crushed, to rapid gunfire for every passing nanosecond. Of course, it all spelled instant death for her replicas too—the splash of viral acid from the critters. But just like before, her "sisters" kept multiplying. None could catch the creature raking at Roberta's heels, however, a huge, angry fellow with a persistence worthy of his lead position and rank. Yet freedom was too near for Roberta. *All I need to do is—* "Get through that damn door!" one of her replicas yelled. But that door was closing quickly.

The closer Roberta approached, the louder the gunfire, as if coming from the other side. Still, in one tremendous bound, she made it through the closing gateway just in time, gasping like a return from the dead.

Roberta felt her own eyes go moon-wide just after the gateway's door slammed shut, but now from the driver's seat inside her own vehicle. She was also pulling quietly up a dirt road just outside what she suspected to be her destination, the Barton Brothers' campsite, a cabin retreat. Turning her vehicle's lights off, she rolled to a stop. *But first things first.* She took a deep breath to collect herself, including a moment to review Mildred's and the Morehouses' files.

What Roberta found was jaw-dropping, to say the least. "I can't believe it," she mumbled. "It can't be." As mind-bending as the news was, she didn't want to be the only one in its possession. Quickly, she closed her eyes and commanded herself, "Send," instantly compressing and e-transmitting her assessment to Kenneth's cell. She had no time to call him; Mildred's plight was already back on her mind.

As Roberta eased out the vehicle, she felt a twinge as soon as her foot hit the ground. It couldn't have been from pain. Kenneth would have never installed such a mod. She lifted her pants leg for the cause—an inflamed streak across her Achilles tendon, just above her sneaker. "How…?" she muttered in disbelief. She'd been nicked.

Yes, the wound was barely visible, but enormous in consequence. Yet there wasn't enough time to weigh the depths of despair. If the virus was soon to strip Roberta of all her motor functions, she still had to get to Mildred. *Like now!* So, she left her vehicle behind, limping her way up the half-graveled driveway, hugging the thick sage scrub along the edge. As expected, she saw part of an unmarked van parked close to a rough-sawn log cabin. There was just enough light spraying from the cabin's windows to see it. She couldn't see all of it because it was blocked by two black, classic model Suburbans angled across the driveway.

Ears attuned, she heard a sharp crunch beneath her shoe as she moved in closer. Not the ordinary crushing of gravel—more like a crunch and a scrape, like metal on rock. Stepping back revealed one bullet casing. *Assess.* She peered down and read the print, identifying it as manufactured in Russia. A complete ground scan revealed dozens more in a sweeping pattern that led to the van, and the human bodies that lay on the ground around it, all motionless.

Roberta's shoulders drooped at the sight of a night that had just gone from horrific to deathly. This explained the extra gunfire she'd heard just before escaping Silver-Stem's network. Meanwhile, she looked at her hands, the only weapons she had to choose from. *Except…* Eying the empty casings all around her, she had another idea.

Chapter 21

Here's what happened before Roberta's arrival:

Victor "Slick" Waltman was considered a company man by every definition. The dirtiest of jobs was his forte—anything for Barton Brothers. "Make a left at this here driveway," the red-headed Victor called to the front of the van from a seat in the middle, his southern accent undeniable. Under a halfmoon-lit night, the driver spun the unmarked van into a winding gravelly driveway as commanded. At the end was a rough-sawn log cabin with no lights on. Every dip in the roadway bucked the van like an angry bronco, the most likely reason for the commotion brewing in the rear bay.

"Hey, Slick," another man behind him said, "she's waking up. Want me to hit her with another lightnin' bolt?" He lifted a stun-gun and wagged it like his own finger.

Victor shook his head for a split second, then stopped. "Well… it would make her a little bit easier to handle, now wouldn't it?" He paused. "Go ahead and hit her one more time. Take the edge off."

Her head mesh-covered to the neck, Mildred was in mid-moan when the man hit her with another burst of voltage. She quivered until falling limp, moving no more by the time the van rolled to a stop.

"Come on. Let's get her inside," Victor directed as everyone rose from their seats. "Some real 'big wigs' want her taken off the market. You know what I mean? We'll rest up and take her to the airfield before sunrise."

It didn't take two men to lift Mildred's lean frame this time, but two did, one under her arms and the other at her feet. Six men in all, four of them stopped outside the van to stretch, the same time two sets of headlights swerved into the driveway.

The Barton driver, one of the four, unclipped his sidearm's holster first. "Who in the hell is that?" His hand, trembling, hovered over his pistol.

Victor's semi-automatic rifle was already in his own hands. "You two, get her in the cabin. Quick!" he told the two carrying Mildred.

Neither answered; they simply rushed her up the front porch steps and into the cabin. The door was unlocked since they'd already been there.

"Settle her down real quick and get your asses back out here," said Victor. "Armed!"

By the time two huge, black Suburbans rolled to a stop in front of them, Mildred's carriers were returning from inside. Except for the driver, all the other Barton men were armed with semi-automatic rifles, including the one who'd used a sniper rifle to bore a bullet straight through Sterling's skull.

Victor and his crew stood strong as several men wearing black army gear emerged from the Suburbans, a few greater in number and armed with automatics. But the most intimidating one wasn't carrying a weapon at all. Wearing a black suit, shiny black shoes, and standing taller than the others, he was the last to exit. The apparent leader, he straightened his lapel and stepped in line with his men, who were all now spread out in firing squad formation. He straightened his cuffs. "I believe you have something of ours," he said with a slight Russian accent.

Victor was scared shitless, but he dared not show it. He raised his chest and threw his bearded chin to the sky. "We don't quite know what you're talkin' about, stranger."

The Russian gazed over Victor's entire crew with a smirk, sliding his hands in his pockets. "Then I suppose the heavy artillery is for a late-night hunting expedition, no?"

Victor returned his new challenger's delight with an even bigger grin. "Yeah. You can say that. The 'cah-yotes' get mighty big out here." He eyed every gunman opposing them. "And I suppose I can say the same about you and your little crew, no?"

"Hmph." The leader shrugged his chin, bobbed his head from side to side.

Victor inched his weapon higher above his waist in a show of resistance. "Then if you'd just excuse us while we retire from our hunt, I would appreciate it if you are not here by tomorrow mornin's light."

The Russian leader shrugged, this time his shoulders, and turned towards his vehicle, only surrendering to the conversation. "Kill them," he commanded on his way into the backseat.

Weapons on both sides went up without hesitation, aimed without discrimination. A ballistic exchange followed, one that lit the night sky far more than the headlights between, sending hundreds of emptied casings to the gravel in its wake.

Chapter 22

Roberta crept towards the cabin as quietly as she could, along with every antiviral trigger she could pull to reject the virus crawling up her leg, coursing through her artificial veins. She *had* to find Mildred, and only the bodies on the ground in front of her held the final clues to her whereabouts. *Assess.* Enough light poured through the cabin's curtains for her to see six bodies down, and every pair of boots toes up. *The boot-treads.* She scanned her own memory drive until finding a perfect match to the bloody boot-prints she'd seen at the shop. *Bingo.* Some even had traces of Sterling's blood on the bottom. But where was Mildred? She wasn't among the fallen, *thankfully.* Could she have now been in more danger? Everything Roberta had discovered about her in Silver-Stem's cyber-vault definitely indicated so.

The gun-smoke in the air was fresh, but even through it all, Roberta could smell the milk and honey scent of Mildred's favorite soap. *She's nearby*—inside the cabin was the logical guess. Another step towards the porch and the pain returned to Roberta's leg like fire. She gritted in anguish until suppressing it, enough to take one more step before the cabin's door creaked open.

Two men carrying automatic rifles walked out, both speaking a foreign language, joking and laughing as if the dead bodies were invisible. But Roberta was not invisible, a presence that brought all their jokes to an abrupt end.

She recognized both the language and the uniforms: *Russian ops soldiers. But for whom exactly?* One of those companies she'd stumbled on behind the firewall happened to be a Russian-owned corporation. And much like Silver-Stem, it was nearly

100% financed by its own government, except for longer. *It's got to be them.*

As the men looked her up and down, they didn't even bother raising their weapons. Their eyes had said it all: a lean young woman in a light sweater, plain baggy pants and plimsoll sneakers couldn't have been too much of a threat.

"Ey," one of them said, "what are you looking for?" he snapped in his Russian-accented English.

But the other nudged him to silence, then calmly gazed at Roberta. "Miss, are you lost or something?" he asked as if she were begging for credits.

Roberta shook her head as slow as the minute hand on an old timeclock. "No," she said meekly.

"Then what the hell are you looking for?" the first repeated, much harsher than before.

Roberta leaned forward, no fear in her voice when she answered and pointed at the cabin. "I believe you have a friend of mine in that cabin." This time, not so meek.

The stunned looks that followed seemed to last forever, until the second man finally leaned back and called out in Russian, "Boss..., we may have a problem!"

A third man wearing a dark suit stepped onto the front porch with a dead-calm expression on his face. "What have we here?" he asked in English, his Russian accent not quite as thick as the others, but still blatant.

More than just being the leader, and more than just wearing a suit and no visible weapon, there was something else about him. *Scan.* But Roberta's quick body-scan revealed nothing unusual.

Meanwhile, the leadman didn't wait for an answer to his question. On his order, four more soldiers poured out from behind him, joining the first two to form a frontline. But the precarious scene didn't end there; one more soldier walked out with a woman's limp body folded over his shoulder, metal straps wrapped around her hands and feet like a rodeo calf.

Roberta's mouth fell open. "Mildred," she murmured, then pressed the balls of her feet into the gravel. Just before launching into action, she found herself halted by one sudden movement. The leader had swung his arm out like a missile targeting system, his finger aimed directly at Roberta.

"Hold your position, little lady," he commanded, the moment his soldiers finally raised their rifles.

Roberta obeyed, but not from fear for her own life; the virus inside had already sealed her fate. It was rescuing Mildred without a rain of gunfire that was now her biggest concern. Besides the virus, Roberta had another strange feeling; something deep inside was keeping her standing, keeping her among the living, and it wasn't due to anything Kenneth or Silver-Stem had programmed. Regardless, she had no time to figure it out; all she knew was, *I've got to save—*

"I know you," the Russian leader said, squinting and shaking his finger at her. "I mean, I know of you." He clutched his chin before pointing again. "You're Roberta X-One-Fifty. Or is it... R-One-Fifty now?" He opened his arms. "Anyway—it is a pleasure to finally meet you. I am sure you have many adventures to share. But as you can see, we are a little too busy to get more acquainted at this time." He waved everyone forward, including his package carrier.

Roberta clinched her fists as four of the soldiers pounded down the steps with rifles in strike-mode. "I don't think you'll be going anywhere without handing her over to me," she said stolidly.

"Hmph. Cute," the leader said with a chuckle. "I didn't know you had the latitude to form attachments. But your friend here happens to belong to us." He turned his attention to his first line. "Gentlemen, clear the path, if you please," he requested in Russian.

On cue, the first four began to clear the path; they opened fire.

Roberta, taking on every bullet, charged forward without haste, but the onslaught was overwhelming her defenses. *Subdermal energy field down to forty-five-percent*, her secondary sensors alerted her. 45-percent: high enough to keep her protected, but low enough to send her back-peddling and weakened, followed by a mad dash into the sagebrush.

She ran and hid until the gunfire stopped, yet still in earshot to hear the men's conversation continue in Russian. "There is no way she'll survive what we just dished out," one of the shooters said.

Roberta peeked through the brush.

"Don't be fooled, Aleksei," said the leader. "You'll have more trouble with her than you had with these." He pointed at the Barton Brother crew in the dirt, then motioned to Aleksei and three other soldiers as he made his way to one of the Suburbans. "You four, go after her until you take her out of commission. Then, I want to see her body to make sure." Trailing behind him were the remaining soldiers, including the one carrying Mildred, who was still limp and motionless.

With the men creeping slowly in Roberta's direction, it was the activity at the leader's vehicle that now had her full attention. Seeing Mildred dumped onto the tailgate like a bag of birdseed was heart-wrenching. Seeing the man withdraw a taser from his belt and tase her in the back of her neck was worse. And watching Mildred's body quiver like a fatal seizure was excruciating. By the time the tailgate slammed shut, Roberta was ready to attack the leader's Suburban—stop it with her bare teeth if her mods would allow it. Only the rustling branches brought her to a stop; the four soldiers were almost on her. Again, she dipped and dashed farther into the brush.

Meanwhile, Aleksei and his team weren't far enough apart to require headsets and comms. Hand signals had to suffice, whatever they could catch from the graze of cabin light at their backs. *Spread out and veer to the left*, was what he commanded with his hand. He heard all three of his sidekicks, two on his left, one on his right, ruffle cautiously through the bushes as if taking on an army.

Konstantin Zorlov, the mission's leader, the one who'd warned them about Roberta, was never wrong about assessing danger. He was like a walking calculator when it came to such matters. Aleksei tightened his rifle's butt into his shoulder the more he thought about it, the farther he trekked into the brush. By the time he realized it, he no longer heard his comrades to the left. He looked to his right. "Yuri." His whisper carried like a weed-eater through the brush. "Yuri!"

"What?" Yuri whispered back.

Aleksei said nothing else. He backtracked all the way to the left instead, where he tripped on a body lying faceup on the ground. "What the…?" he muttered. He leaned over and turned on his rifle's nightlight, revealing one of his own men with a bullet hole between the eyes, just above the brow. Those eyes were open but intense, as if caught totally off-guard.

Shaking his head, Aleksei continued a few feet to the left, where he stumbled on another colleague's body, one with a bullet hole pinpoint in the same position, his dead eyes frozen even wider. From what Aleksei could tell, eyes that had seen the first man go down.

Aleksei looked around with eyes just as wide. *Does this woman have a fucking weapon?* A total shock for a man who believed he could hear a silenced rifle in a thunderstorm.

"What? What is it?" he heard Yuri ask. "Aleksei?"

Aleksei turned forward, squatted in a defensive stance and lifted his palm. "Quiet!" Again, he raised his rifle. "Shoot anything that moves—anything you hear." Their new target, who they'd thought was weaponless, was now armed and dangerous. "She's armed with a silencer."

Only a few more steps into the brush, Aleksei heard branches crack and break, and then there was a thud. Then silence. "Yuri?" he whispered again, but Yuri was nowhere in sight. "Shit." Aleksei had no choice but to abandon his search for Roberta to find Yuri, only to find him a victim of the same morbid fate as the others. Aleksei knelt down to one knee and pounded the ground. "What the fuck is she using?" The answer came as a lean arm wrapped around his neck like a steel brace, inescapable.

"My aim is pretty good with anything metal," a woman murmured in his ear. Her other arm appeared in front of him with a closed fist, then opened just enough to release one piece of metal after another to the ground. "And discarded bullet casings work just fine."

Aleksei now knew the "what" Roberta had used, but not the "how" she had gotten behind him, nor would he ever know. One flinch from Roberta and Aleksei's neck was snapped like a branch.

Moments after eliminating her opponents, Roberta was on a hilltop watching a lone Suburban rolling along a dirt road below, enroute to the main highway. It was on a different roadway than the one she'd driven in on, and the Suburban was less than a mile from the highway. *Assess.* She had already been pushed too far into the brush to get back to her own vehicle in time. Plus, she couldn't allow herself to lose sight of Mildred. Having lifted Aleksei's sidearm, she rushed down the hill with no particular plan in mind— only to get to that S.U.V.

Bouncing along a dirt road, the first Suburban was only half-a-mile from the paved highway. Konstantin sat in the passenger seat with the subdued nerves of a sloth. And why not? He was surrounded by three armed private soldiers, their key asset was under wraps in the folded-down rear bed, and Roberta was occupied elsewhere. Mission impossible was nearing an end, and Konstantin was too smug about it. Their next destination was a private airstrip enroute to Mexico for them, then on to a no-questions-asked transfer back to Moscow.

"Aleksei and the guys should have been catching up to us by now," one of the soldiers said from the backseat. His voice was cast against the window, much like his eyes. "Where are they?"

Yet Konstantin's eyes remained ahead, but his soldier's observation did have him reevaluating his mission's success. "*What* are they, would be the most accurate question," he said, "and dead would be the appropriate answer." His men's silence announced their shock loudly. "I suspect the first set of lights you see behind us will be hers," he informed them.

As Konstantin had first thought, Aleksei's efforts would have only slowed Roberta down, not *taken* her down. If Konstantin were lucky, Aleksei would be hunting her the rest of the night. But he also knew the tables would soon turn; his hunters would become the hunted. Konstantin just needed that process to last long enough for him to reach the open highway.

Ka-thump! A thud hit the top of their vehicle, rocking the whole thing from side to side along with one more huge bounce. An entire stairstep could have slid between their asses and their seats from the impact. To make matters worse, someone was pounding dents into their vehicle's roof. It seemed their luck had run out.

Konstantin looked up, his hands complacently on his knees. "This is a bit sooner than expected." He glanced at his men in the backseat; their arms, unlike his, were hung in a stifled quandary. "I think you need to handle this," he told them, "before she drops in on us. She seems quite angry."

"Let her go!" A woman's yell from outside confirmed Konstantin's suspicions.

"*Sounds* quite angry."

His backseat soldiers grabbed their sidearms and aimed at the growing cluster of dents. Five shots through the roof and the banging stopped; both soldiers ceased fire. One even boasted, "That should teach—," before being interrupted by one female hand crashing through his window. It grabbed him by the neck with blind certainty, and snatched him through the window like a stuffed animal. The last he was seen was tumbling through the brush outside like a flat tire.

"Surely, that is a bone-breaking fall," Konstantin remarked. Meanwhile, the vehicle never slowed down on its way to the highway.

Now tossing frantically in the backseat, the other soldier cursed to the roof, "Shit! You fucking bitch!" He fired more shots towards the roof's edge. And when the movement above came to an end, he ceased again, the very moment Roberta's entire body swung through the window, feet-first into his chest. Along with the opposite rear door, out flew the second soldier.

With barely a second in between, Roberta was now in the backseat with a pistol pressed against the driver's skull.

"I don't think you want to pull that trigger, Roberta," Konstantin calmly warned in English while pointing to the rear. "You wouldn't want to harm your little friend in the rear bed, now would you?"

But her eyes remained focused forward. "Ostanovit' transportnoye sredstvo," she gritted, commanding the driver to stop the vehicle.

The driver, trembling, shifted his eyes in Konstantin's direction, clearly looking for a resolution.

And Konstantin gave him one back in Russian, "Keep driving, Matvey. She will not pull the trigger."

"You dare try me?" Roberta taunted with eyes of human fire. "I do believe I am the one with the advantage. And being that the rest of your men are dead…"

"But like I said, you wouldn't want to harm your little friend in the back."

Roberta paused, shrugging her chin, then her shoulders. "Hmm, I think she'll survive." In a surprise move, she removed the gun from Matvey' skull, slid it down the seat and pulled the trigger. A bullet pierced straight through the seat into his shoulder.

Matvey screamed and folded over, while the Suburban veered and swerved to the side.

"What are you doing!" Konstantin finally unraveled and screamed at Roberta. Then with a surprise move of his own, he reached and grabbed both her gun-toting hand and the steering wheel, somehow managing to right the vehicle. It was the moment their eyes met—his, aimed in anger—hers, wide in shock.

Roberta yanked her arm in an attempt to free herself from Konstantin, but to no avail. She couldn't believe it; his hand was clamped on her like a giant wrench. She tried her best to figure out the source of his strength. *From fear, perhaps?* It appeared he needed no help from Matvey, who was still folded over in pain. Roberta's struggle continued until the gun went off again, this time striking

Matvey in the back, sending him into the steering wheel against Konstantin's hold. Both the wheel and the Suburban turned and weaved until, like the soldiers before it, flipped and tumbled into the brush.

Chapter 23

The Suburban's headlights still on, Roberta opened her eyes to dust and fumes outside as she lay flat on the interior roof; the vehicle was upside down. Her nerve sensors were tingling all over, most of it concentrated in the arm the leader had clamped onto. "Assess damage." Her shoulder was completely dislocated, and the virus was still spreading. No longer able to suppress the pain, she simply willed her way through it to scan the scene. There were damaged door panels and a few hand-tools scattered about, but neither the leader nor the driver was in the front seat. The front windshield was gone, and a detailed search through her memory banks revealed that neither of them were wearing seatbelts.

Unsure if her adversaries had been thrown far enough, Roberta still took a moment to remember why she was there in the first place: "Mildred." She now resummoned everything she had left to throw her shoulder back in joint. "Arrhh," she groaned. "Mildred?" she then murmured, army crawling her way to the rear, where she found Mildred twisted on her back, breathing, but still unconscious. From just a precursory scan, Roberta sensed no broken bones at all. Fortunately, only bruises. *Remarkable*, she thought as she tore Mildred's metal straps apart with ease. All signs of an end to this madness were improving, except: *Subdermal energy field down to five-percent.* The virus and vehicular battering combined had taken its toll.

"Roberta-R-One-Fifty!" a man's voice called from the distance, far outside the overturned Suburban. "We have some unfinished business to attend to!" It carried the same Russian accent as the leader.

Roberta heard one of his feet scuffing the ground, a limp, on his way towards the vehicle. She spun herself slowly around to look, silently in total agreement while crawling out to meet him. Her enthusiasm was uncanny for a droid with a virus reasserting itself. But she and the leader did have unfinished business. *And I am going to be the one to finish it, no matter what.* "Coming," she cried out and wobbled to her feet like an eager volunteer.

His clothes ripped and torn, the leader's limp was far worse than Roberta had envisioned. "Shaken up, are you?" he shouted. "If you are, please—take your time! Go ahead! I'll give you a second to pull yourself together!"

Roberta heaved a deep breath. "Bold words from a man whose arm is dangling a near foot lower than the other!"

She was right; his arm was hanging and swinging like a pendulum. But one full-body quiver, and his dangling arm returned to its socket. One hefty shake, and his damaged leg returned to form. He now walked in regal air once again, no longer with a limp at all. "Allow me to formally introduce myself! My name is Konstantin! And much like you, I too heal quickly!"

Roberta paused at the shocking sight of him approaching. *Assess.* She thought back to their moment at the cabin, when he was standing on the front porch. That strange feeling she'd had was being explained right before her eyes. Konstantin was a droid, his body temperature a slight degree less than human—and a droid who was stronger than her at the moment. She'd felt it in his grip just before the crash, but it made no difference now; she braced herself for battle, nonetheless.

Konstantin proved her right by closing the distance and backhanding her into the dirt before she could blink, all practically in one motion. Roberta flew nearly twenty-feet away from the vehicle, sliding through bushes to a stop like a hurricane through barrier islands. Konstantin took one more step, but stopped, apparently with something else on his mind. He turned and ripped the Suburban's other door off like a perforated notepad, then reached inside as if to reclaim Mildred, but he stopped again. "On second thought…," he said on his return to Roberta, where he fell to both knees and straddled her torso. It seemed resolving his business dispute with her had suddenly taken priority. Grimaced for destruction, he cocked his fist in the air. "There is a significant price to pay for eliminating—," he growled and punched her in the face, "seven Russian operatives!" He punched her again. And again. And again, until the next punch nearly knocked her offline, and for solid reason: *Subdermal energy field down to zero-percent.*

Roberta was still cognizant, however, raising her head to cough up both synthetic blood and saliva. "That reminds me," she wheezed, "why would someone send humans to take on such a task? To take *me* on?"

"Well, it's not like you were part of the original plan," he gritted into another blow, but stopped in mid-swing on the next. "Other than that," he said, lifting his eyes to the sky, "I do not know. I assume operating expenses would have something to do with it. Which reminds *me*," he said calmly before resuming his onslaught, "of the cost of you destroying a nice new vehicle!" And another punch to the face. And another. Again and again until Roberta's densified calcium nose was flattened, and her blood was now overflowing.

Roberta lay flat with a feeling she'd never had before, not even in all her prior ops: utter defeat. Her breathing was fading from pure artificial exhaustion, or a depleted power source in more common theory, another sensation she'd never experienced. *Subdermal energy field—undetected.*

But Konstantin seemed to have energy to spare; his breaths were steady and even as he heaved his chest. "Look at you," he said with teeth tight. "I am amazed your model is still in service. Do you realize how antiquated you are?" He cocked his arm slowly before descending into another thrashing blow. Then he stopped again, raised his hand and pinched his fingers together. "You know, I take that back. We have heard rumors that your creator… Dr. Kenneth Murphy, I believe… may have provided you with particular upgrades. Oh, yes, we know. But there seems to be one huge mistake that he has made: the emotion chip." He shook his finger in her face. "Your emotion chip is at the root of your failure here tonight, clouding your judgement, I would say. Wouldn't you?"

Roberta spat blood to start her point. "First of all—do not—talk about—my maker. And secondly—on the contrary—it is my emotion—that makes me stronger. And what would you call *your* anger—at this point?"

Konstantin wiped his eye, the one spattered by Roberta's blood. "You call *this* anger? My dear, Roberta," he gritted again, hoisting his fist in the air, "anger, you have not seen—" His falling deathblow was interrupted by his eyes gone wide, his fist hung in the air like a still photograph.

Roberta actually heard Konstantin's joints tighten as he toppled forward, on top of her, with all his synthetic weight. A touch of strength remaining, she pulled herself from underneath, stunned by another sight she'd never expected. Standing above them both was Mildred, shaking from head to toe with a screwdriver in her hand. Roberta also witnessed a bloody puncture in Konstantin's cervical spine, just below his skull.

Mildred ditched the screwdriver and helped Roberta to her feet. "Roberta, are you okay?" Her question came with a hug as sure as her grip.

Roberta, weakened to her bones, hugged her back as much as she could, extra sensitive to just how much force Mildred was applying. It was like being in a wrestling match with Konstantin all over again. And the warmth she'd once felt from Mildred in the flower shop, now came with an energy vibrating like a small engine. "I will be," Roberta said.

Mildred pulled back and placed her hand over her mouth. "Oh, my God! B-But, but your face! Y-Y-Your nose!" she stammered, almost tearfully.

"I'll be fine. I don't feel a thing."

"Oh."

"Just a little low on energy."

Mildred paused and stared at Konstantin's rigid body on the ground, her hand still over her mouth. "Oh, Roberta… I don't know what made me do that. I mean, I know what made me do it! Saving you! But I don't know what made me stab someone in the back of the neck! How could I have done such a thing?"

And it must have been one solid jab, Roberta figured. "Well, as much as it pains me to say, he's only a droid. Come on," she said as they held each other up and started walking, "I'll tell you all about it once we get to safety."

Mildred's eyes swiveled from left to right. "And where are we right now?"

"I'll explain that too."

Supporting one another on a path towards the highway, Mildred glanced back at Konstantin, who still lay plastered to the ground. "What about him?" she asked. "Is he dead? Droid-dead? Do we just leave him there?"

"Dead? No. Dead can't describe his condition right now. And he's fine just where he is."

"Then won't he wake up?"

"Perhaps. His backup system may recharge him enough to recover, but what your efforts didn't do, the virus I just spat into his eye will finish him off." Both turned, still in each other's arms, and kept moving.

"Virus!" Mildred squealed.

"Don't worry. You're immune." Roberta proceeded despite Mildred's panicked look. "Keneisha," she murmured instead.

Mildred's eyes swiveled again. "Who?" she asked.

But Roberta's mind was elsewhere. "Locate and pickup."

"Roberta, what are you talking about?"

Roberta finally responded, "Saying it out loud amplifies my signal to her."

"Amplifies your signal to who?"

With Roberta's weight bearing heavier on Mildred's shoulder by the step, the two had just dragged themselves over a crossroad when distracted by a voice from behind: "Roberta!" It was Konstantin again. "I believe you have something that belongs to me! Unleash her to me!"

Just his malevolent tone quivered Mildred's nerves. "Roberta, what's he talking about? Is he talking about me?"

Whatever his intentions were, they seemed to have an advantageous effect on Roberta, who recovered enough to quicken both her and Mildred's pace. "Come on! Don't look at him. Just keep moving," Roberta said without looking back.

But Mildred repeated, "Is he talking about me?" The tremble in her voice aired every ounce of her confusion, while failing to adhere to Roberta's advice; Mildred looked back.

Konstantin was trembling like a fiend from Mildred's stab, but he was somehow already at the crossroad and gaining ground. Mildred's heart now raced far faster than her feet—nearly pumped out of her chest when a roaring mass zoomed from out of the darkness along the crossroad. Mildred pulled away, screaming with her hands over her mouth, "Oh, my God!"

It was Roberta's vehicle, and after a bounce off the ground, it rammed and pounced on Konstantin like a wrestler off the third turnbuckle. It bounced and pounced a few more times, reversed and advanced several times, and rubbed and scrubbed him into the dirt until he was facedown embedded.

Roberta exhaled in relief. "That's... Keneisha."

Meanwhile, Mildred's hands were still over her mouth. "Oh, my God."

Keneisha was usually nothing but the typical auto-vehicle, until triggered into a more sentient entity. She was another one of Dr. Murphy's dream-children, and the perfect gift for Roberta—the perfect vehicular android for moments just like this one.

After her savage attack, the brutal pounding, Keneisha backed up and rolled quietly over to Roberta and Mildred, where she raised both her doors. "Your transport has arrived," Keneisha announced with the courtesy of a valet.

Chapter 24

Keneisha rested on the road a good distance away from Konstantin's flattened body, her engine purring. Sitting inside behind her steering wheel, Mildred pressed every button she could find, but nothing happened. She yanked the wheel to the left, to the right, and again a few times. "Ugh!" she blurted. "Uhh, Roberta? This car is set to your biometrics only, isn't it?"

Roberta had heard Mildred clearly, but she hesitated to respond. Another unfamiliar feeling, grogginess, had overtaken Roberta as soon as she'd landed and stretched out over the full-length backseat. It had hit like an aftershock, while her own antivirus was close to helpless against the spreading pathogen. *Antivirus down to fifteen-percent.* "Yeah…," Roberta moaned drunkenly towards the roof. "Keneisha…?"

Lights emerged back and forth across Keneisha's dashboard. "Voice recognition complete," she concluded. "Yes, Roberta?"

Mildred shook her head. "I can't believe you gave your car a name."

Roberta sighed. "My maker did… actually… after his deceased sister, Keneisha."

"Yes, Roberta?" Keneisha repeated.

Roberta sighed again, internalizing to scan the now fragmented pieces of her own programming. "Keneisha… begin autodrive. Protocol… Darkest Hour… five-zero-zero-eight-one."

Lights migrated repeatedly across the dash again. "Destination confirmed." One quick rev and Keneisha peeled off towards the highway ahead.

There was a moment of silence before Mildred turned her attention back to Roberta. "Will either you or Keneisha please explain to me what all that means?"

"A safety protocol," Roberta said, "Dr. Murphy…, my maker, has setup for the darkest hours… when all the shit hits the fan. And we've just been… dumped on."

"Like I said, what does all that mean?" Mildred yelled to the roof just as Keneisha turned onto the highway back towards San Diego.

Roberta heaved a long sigh. "It means… we're going to a secret safehouse."

"A secret safehouse! Where?"

"I can't tell you." Roberta dropped to a whisper, "It's a secret."

Mildred folded her arms. "Oh, so you want to joke at a time like this? And you're keeping secrets from me now?"

Roberta hesitated. "I believe I have kept a secret for you rather… recently…"

Mildred gasped. "Oh, my God! Sterling!" Tears rolled down her cheeks instantly.

"Yeah… I saw. And I'm real sorry for you. For him."

Mildred sobbed and sniffled. "Why did they do that to him?"

"Probably to get him out of the way as quickly as possible… so as not to be a witness."

"A *witness*? A witness to what!"

"It's… complicated."

Several moments passed before Mildred wiped her tears away. "Alright," she said, "as long as we get the hell away from 'Robo-Frankenstein' back there, I'm cool with wherever we go."

"Konstantin is his name. He's a highly advanced droid."

"Yeah. Okay. Whatever. Now, please tell me how did we end up here, wherever we are. And why was Sterling—" Her mouth hung open as if she couldn't finish.

"That part, I assume—"

"I mean, I assumed they were after you," Mildred interrupted, jittery, "so I didn't say anything. I didn't give them anything. Not a word. I would never dime you out like that, Roberta! I would never—ever—do anything like that to you! But I still don't understand why—"

"It's because... they weren't after me. They were after you."

"Me! Why on Earth would they be after me? And why was the robot—sorry—I mean, the *android*—talking about me like that? Like—like—like I'm not even... even—"

"Human?" Roberta completed the sentence, having done everything she could to restrain herself, to refrain from divulging all the things Mildred's parents had protected her from since childhood. But this was one secret with the weight of an overflowing dam. *Perhaps Mildred can handle it in doses*, Roberta reasoned. *Nah...* "Like you're not human?" she reiterated.

Mildred answered with a slow nod, "Yeah..."

"It's because you're not," Roberta said just as her hand fell to the side, while her eyes remained aimed at Keneisha's roof.

"What?"

"You're not—human."

Mildred's body clinched and stiffened like an icicle, followed by a fit of insane laughter. "I'm not human!" Disbelief sprang from her voice. And when the laughter died down, she dabbed the moisture from her eyes with only her fingers. "Whoooh. Roberta, Roberta, Roberta. You never had this kind of a sense of humor when I was a kid—a *human* kid!" She chuckled, fanning herself. "I mean, you had a few funny moments, but none like this. Whooh!"

Joking actually was within Roberta's programming, but she wasn't joking right now; she couldn't have if she tried.

Ultimately, it brought Mildred's amusement to an abrupt end. She tipped her head along with a shrewd squint. "You're serious, aren't you?"

Roberta took a huge breath just to find the strength to end the mystery in one breath. "You're the subject of a project called 'Millennium Droid, Edition-D,' a one-of-a-kind project implemented in the year 2000. It was created to expand the bounds of humanity—to make an android so sentient, so humanly complete, she feels joy, love, pain, and growth, both emotionally and at the cellular level."

"The cellular level?" Mildred murmured.

"Yes… the cellular level. Growth hormone-enhanced to grow from infanthood to childhood, from childhood to adulthood… to old age. To expiration, even. So complete, she experiences all the weaknesses of a human, as well: from abrasions to common illnesses. So complete, not even she can tell. And that she, is you, Mildred."

Mildred paused for a few seconds. "Millennium—Droid?"

"Millennium Droid, Edition-D—'Mildred,' for short." Eyes to the side, Roberta could see the riddled look on Mildred's face. "You don't believe me? Then how do you think you knew exactly where to plunge the screwdriver back there to incapacitate… the other droid unit? Straight between the C1 and the C2 vertebrae—where the off switch lies."

Mildred shrugged. "Luck, I guess."

Roberta said nothing.

"Okay, Roberta. Tell me—how did I know?"

Roberta took another deep breath, thinking back to the moment of their latest embrace. The vibrating was almost as intense as the droid in the garden center's parking lot, a sure sign something in Mildred had been activated. "I saw them tase you back at the cabin when you were already unconscious. Once again, between the C1 and the C2. Not only incapacitating you further, but most likely triggering major portions of your operating system to reboot."

"Tss." Mildred shook her head. "Operating system?"

"Yes. Nanotech—too small for ordinary medical detection. Anyway, that reboot was like returning you to factory settings. Everything in your database will gradually begin to emerge. Knowledge and some protective mechanisms originally suppressed will now become active. Memories, even, of seemingly insignificant events will now become… more vivid… more meaningful."

"More meaningful?"

"Yes. Your A.I.-awareness." Roberta paused to let it sink in, then continued, "The tension in your muscles will become tightened." She lifted her head slightly. "And judging from your current condition, your bone content has already begun to densify. Think about it. You were just in a horrendous vehicular accident." It was the reason Roberta had risked everything to shoot the driver. "So, how do you feel now? Physically?"

Mildred's eyes bucked. She felt herself up and down. "Uhhh… fine, I guess."

Roberta paused. "And when was the last time before tonight that you used the word, 'biometrics,' in a sentence—ever?" On that point, Roberta's body went limp.

Mildred leaned back into her seat with no response, on the verge of apparent acceptance, until offering one crucial point, "There's just *one* little hitch in your assessment, Ms. 'Think-you-have-it-all-figured-out.'"

This time, Roberta struggled to raise her head, seeing Mildred rubbing her belly.

"Nothing you said can explain what's going on inside here." Mildred was bobbing a nod that spelled victory, as in no way she could have been artificial.

But Roberta had already gone too far to let her have even the slightest of moments. "And thus—the expansion of humanity. With love and growth comes the product of love…, able to grow inside your womb…, the first and only in the world."

Mildred cocked her head to the side with her hand still rested on her belly.

"Yes, my little Mildred… you are one of a kind."

The silence that intervened went from seconds to minutes, sending Mildred from tapping her heel to biting her fingernails. "No… this can't be. I can't be a robot," she finally said while wiping her brow. "I sweat too damn much to be a robot!"

"Another perk of being human, I suppose," was Roberta's first sardonic remark.

More silence passed before Mildred spat out all her nail shavings in a fury. "I can't be a fucking robot! I fart for God's sake! And a lot lately!"

"Which reminds me."

"What! That I fart?"

"No. That there's something else we need to do to aid in your protection. We need to turn off your internal G.P.S. location pin. Dr. Murphy has already turned off mine; I'll have to turn off yours." As noble as her intentions were, Roberta failed to budge.

Mildred's eyes danced from side to side. "Wha,' wha,' what are you talking about?"

Roberta said nothing. She simply blacked out, systems down, the first visible sign of the viral attack.

"Roberta?"

A jolt followed, and Roberta was back online, continuing as if the last several seconds had never happened, "I'm talking about something else we need to do to aid in your protection." She forced herself upright. "We need to turn off your internal G.P.S. location pin. Dr. Murphy has already turned off mine. I'll have to turn off yours. It's most likely how Konstantin and the Russians found you."

"Russians!"

Roberta took a deep breath. "I will fill you in, but for now, close your eyes."

Once again, Mildred's eyes shifted from side to side. "What? Why?"

"I need you to close your eyes. I'll need as little outside light as possible when I'm in."

But Mildred's eyes nearly left their sockets. "When you're in?"

Roberta huffed. "Trust me, okay."

And Mildred huffed as well. "Alright." Finally, she closed her eyes.

Roberta closed her own eyes too, wasting no time linking into Mildred's C.P.U. She'd gained the access code from Mildred's files, and now began disabling her location pin. Once connected and in sync, the process was like no other. Numbers turned, slid and changed places in both women's minds like an old-time Rubik's cube. They twisted and turned until a click, just like the spec files had stated. Roberta had already assessed her virus to be non-wireless, incapable of corrupting their link. She'd also discovered in the specs that Mildred was immune to computer-generated viruses, even the nastiest ones, like this one. It made sense, somewhat; if humans were immune, so was Mildred. And near the end, Roberta took a second to develop a subroutine to alter Mildred's access code, then it was over.

Mildred shivered; her eyes rolled open. "Whoa… What in the hell was that?"

"Freedom," Roberta said on her way back deep into her seat. "Maybe I'll show how to do it yourself… one day."

"Ri-ight… Speaking of location, where are we? And is there a phone in here? I need to at least let my parents know where I'm at—that I'm safe."

"Your phone…?" Roberta mumbled. "Oh, yeah…, your phone. Your phone is—," she hesitated, gently rubbing her pockets, "—not in my front pocket." Her damaged sensors returned no memory of its whereabouts. Perhaps it had been dislodged somewhere in her chain of battles, she figured.

"What?"

"But you cannot call your parents. In fact… you cannot call anyone… especially your parents." This had nothing to do with a phone's location pin; it had more to do with something Roberta had read in the Millennium files. "You cannot call your—your—your parental units—call—," Roberta stammered, "your parental units—units—units—unitsssss." Her jilted speech had swiftly turned from hiccups to a drained slur.

"Parental units!" Mildred blurted. "Oh, shit! Are my parents robots too?"

"Patience… little one," Roberta murmured, "the race is to the deliberrrr…"

"Yeah, yeah, yeah, that's fine and all, but are my parents androids?" Mildred pressed, leaning in closer. "Roberta? Roberta? Roberta, wake up! Don't leave me here to deal with this shit all alone! Roberta!"

"Have no worries, Ms. Morehouse," Keneisha cut in, "I am here with you."

Unlike Roberta's prior sudden shutdown, this one faded into darkness, taking both Mildred's and Keneisha's voices along with it.

Chapter 25

Roberta and Mildred were not the only ones in a quandary that evening. At the Morehouse residence, Mrs. Morehouse paced her kitchen floor from end to end, chewing on her bottom lip until she drew blood. "Shit," she whispered, just the moment a simple text message arrived: "I'm on my way in." Nearly a minute later, she heard Mr. Morehouse unlock the door and open it.

"Honey, I'm home!" he announced with a chuckle, oddly knocking on his way in—but for good reason. The Morehouses had been separated ever since shortly after Mildred's departure from the nest. Located only a few miles from the house, Mr. Morehouse had always managed to keep Mildred unsuspecting by showing his face whenever and almost as soon as she'd return home.

Mrs. Morehouse, still pacing, said nothing in response; she was already expecting him. There was an urgent matter she needed to discuss with him. She'd also gone from lip-chewing to gnawing one lone fingernail to the nub.

Mr. Morehouse stopped at the kitchen doorway, where he propped his hands on his waist. "What's the urgent matter, Evelyn?"

She stopped pacing and folded her arms, but still said nothing, didn't even look at him.

He stepped forward and leaned all the way into her face just to get her attention. "What's wrong?"

She heaved a deep sigh. "I just got word someone is after Mildred!"

Mr. Morehouse's mouth fell open. "*After* her? Who? What do you mean, '*after* her'?"

"I mean someone in big government has called for an end to the project. So, they're sending in a goon-squad to take her in!"

"Who?"

"I don't know. That's all the intel I've been given."

"Well, is it all above board?"

She stomped her foot. "Hell no, it's not above board, Ray! It's as below board as below board can get! And what difference does it make? This is our *daughter* we're talking about!"

An entire foot taller than Evelyn, Ray gazed down, shaking his head with deep chagrin in his eyes. "Evelyn…"

"What! Don't *Evelyn* me!" she mocked. "If she's not our daughter, then I don't know who is!"

"But we were supposed to detach ourselves after she got out on her own. That's what the therapy was for. Remember?"

"Yes, but come on, Ray." She gritted and pointed, leaning in so close that that one-foot difference felt like an inch. "You look me in the eye and tell me that you have no feelings for Mildred whatsoever."

But Ray turned his eyes away, the internal struggle painfully obvious.

"Tell me!" Evelyn pressed.

"Alright, alright!" He huffed. "So, who should we talk to?"

"Talk to! You don't get it, do you? There's no time to talk to anyone! We have to intervene—now!" She grabbed her phone.

"What are you doing?"

"I'm calling *our* daughter."

Ray turned his back and stepped away, massaging the bridge of his nose like a man on trial. "This is so ill-advised," he murmured.

By the time Evelyn received Mildred's video mailbox, she felt Ray's worried breaths from behind, warming the top of her head as she began to speak, "Mildred, your father and I need you to come home right away. I mean, right away! Don't bother packing. Just get in your car and leave. Then call me once you're on the road. We'll explain everything to you then. Okay, hon? See you soon. We love you!" After hanging up, Evelyn turned around and breezed by Ray without a glance.

"Evelyn, this isn't being handled correctly," Ray said. "You're not thinking straight. This house is the first place they'll come looking for her!"

Evelyn had left the kitchen without a word, but with a determination on her face Ray had never seen before. The next time he saw her, only moments later, she was passing by the doorway with a pistol in her hand.

"Oh, I'm thinking very straight," she said, cocking the pistol one good time for punctuation. "Coming here is the *safest* place for her."

Hearing her voice trail off into the living room, Ray knew she'd made it to the window.

"Let them *try* to take her from under my nose," she said, "and they will feel the wrath of my entire being—every last one of them!"

Massaging the bridge of his nose again, Ray followed Evelyn's path, but stopped at the edge of the living room. There she was at the window, gun up and leaning from the side like an image of Malcom X he remembered from childhood. "And you think this is the best way?"

Slowly, Evelyn nodded. "It's the only way."

Nearly half-an-hour had passed with no word from Mildred. Evelyn had already left the living room window and returned for three more cycles before turning away for the last time, gun still in her grip. Ray, on the other hand, now sitting in the living room where he'd been tortured by Evelyn's back-and-forth, was deep into his web browser.

"How could you be browsing through such trash at a time like this!" Evelyn raged. "When our d-d-d-daughter is out there like prey for wild animals!"

Ray stopped browsing and sighed. "Evelyn, I hate to have to keep reminding you of this, but Mildred is not our—"

"Shut up, Ray!" She waved the gun, a short degree away from aiming it at him. From there she marched back to her bedroom.

"Sorry." He watched her intensely until she was out of sight. "What are you doing now?" he shouted.

"I'm packing!" she shouted back. "We're going to find her! And then we're going away! For a *long* time!"

"Find her? But what if she's on her way here?"

"She's not!"

"How can you be so sure?"

"A mother knows!"

Ray shook his head. "What about me?"

"What about you!"

"I mean—"

"I know what you mean." She was back in the living room carrying an overnight case and a small duffle bag. "We'll pickup stuff for you after we find Mildred."

Ray glanced at Evelyn's duffle bag and made his own lightning quick assessment: the hard bulges stretching the fabric indicated items a bit more dangerous than clothes were packed inside. He stood up and asked, "And how will we find her?"

Evelyn breezed by him on her way to the front door, enough to make his shirt flap. "We'll start off in San Diego—her shop. And if we can't find her there, we'll look for clues."

Ray followed her sheepishly out the door. He knew better than to ask her anymore of the how's or why's, so he said nothing else all the way to his vehicle. It was just after Evelyn had loaded up the backseat, just before entering, when they were stunned by headlights rolling in like beacons. Two sedan-style vehicles, one after the other, sped into the driveway, slamming to a stop only inches away from Ray's rear bumper. The usual black suits you'd expect stepped out with a deliberate approach.

One spoke to Ray first, "Agent Kiper?" then to Evelyn, "Agent Dawes? You've been called in. We need you to come with us."

The Morehouses, a.k.a. special agents Evelyn Dawes and Raymond Kiper, didn't have to see any badges; they both knew who they were facing: special security agents from Silver-Stem. But none of this stopped Evelyn from leaning into Ray's car, where she unzipped her duffle bag for one of many guns.

All it took was the agent closest to her to reach into his jacket to freeze Evelyn to a stop. "I wouldn't do that if I were you, Agent Dawes," the agent said urgently, stretching out his other hand. "We're going to need all weapons also."

Employed, themselves, by Silver-Stem, raising Millennium Droid Edition-D was Evelyn and Ray's longest assignment, a joy for them both. It was the longest for any undercover agents to date, the reason for Mildred's success over all three prior editions—also the real reason Ray had to vacate the house once Mildred had left. And on this night, as he and Evelyn were escorted to the backseats of separate sedans, another good thing had just seen its end.

The same night, Mildred's best friend, Lauren, with Bryan trailing behind her, noticed the front door of the floral shop cracked open as she approached. No lights were on inside. "Something's not right," she whispered to Bryan. It was enough to elicit the strangest of reactions. Wearing her usual nightclub clothes, high skirt and high-heeled ankle boots, she reached behind her back, underneath her jacket, and pulled out a laser-scoped handgun. Aimed inside the shop, it was far from matching her outfit, which should have seemed strange to Bryan, but apparently it didn't. He moved beside her while drawing a gun of his own.

Lauren toggled the wall switch a few times on the way inside. Nothing happened. The alert system wasn't even on. With the nearest streetlight out, very little light poured through the window, but Lauren already had every open space memorized. She crouched and crept from there, each step practically measured. Bryan, falling back behind, did the same. "Watch our six," she whispered to Bryan.

Lauren was stopped dead in her tracks when she heard a soft smack, the toe of her boot stuck to the floor. She'd felt it as soon as she'd rounded the main counter, followed by turning on her phone's flashlight. Lying on the floor in front of her was a man's body. "Oh, no," she muttered. It was Sterling, dead-stiff in a pool of congealed blood.

"Damn," Bryan lamented, obviously more shaken.

Lauren saw no need to check Sterling's pulse; she knew the look of certain death. She shook her head a few times before removing her boots. "Wait here," she told Bryan, then began her search for Mildred, starting with dashing out the back and up the stairs.

She was shocked to see the apartment door unlocked with no signs of forced entry. No one was inside, not even Roberta. And when Lauren returned downstairs, Bryan was still standing over Sterling. "Shit. We're too late. They must have her," she said on her way to Bryan, along with her Texas accent starting to fade. She placed her hand on his shoulder. "You're gonna be okay?"

Bryan, somber and brooding, never looked up. "Damn it. I was the one who brought the bloody bloke to the fucking party in the first place," he said with a newfound accent of his own, a heavy British one. "Now look at him. This wasn't supposed to happen, you know. He had no idea what was going on. I was just supposed to set him up to fall in love, that's all." He shook his head and repeated, "Now look at him."

Lauren nodded with a sigh. "I know. It's a fucked up job, but someone's gotta do it." It was a feeble attempt at comfort, one now with absolutely no sign of the Lone Star state remaining. "So, pull yourself together, agent," she said with a stiff pat, then pressed speed-dial on her phone and waited a few seconds. "Chief Agent Adams?"

A man appeared on her screen, a stern look on his face. "Agent Mathis, what did you find?"

Lauren huffed. "Nothing good. We're at the flower shop, and Sterling's down."

"What do you mean, 'Sterling's down'?"

"Down, as in shot—as in deceased."

"Okay… Where's the asset?" Not a lick of remorse escaped his mouth.

Lauren held her breath while Bryan threw his hands up in the background, irate. "You mean, Mildred?" she asked.

"Well, what other asset would I be talking about?" Chief Adams blasted.

"Right. The *asset* is nowhere to be found." Lauren wasn't too happy with the nomenclature either, but duty called for strict objectivity. "All signs indicate she's been taken."

He grabbed his chin. "Damn it, we're too late." Seconds later, he wagged his finger at her. "You know, this wouldn't have happened if you would have been keeping an eye on her like you were supposed to."

But Lauren didn't backdown. "Yes, but the assignment was reduced from day-to-day surveillance to an *occasional eye* on her once she graduated from college. But never twenty-four-hours a day!"

There was a prolonged pause in between. "I wonder why," Chief Adams said. "I mean, why would they come after her now?"

Both Lauren and Chief Adams were privy to the same intel agents Dawes and Kiper had received, but very few knew what Lauren knew. "You *are* aware that the *asset* is pregnant, aren't you?" she said with eyes bearing down on her screen like an eagle.

"Yeah, but no one else knows that. Unless we have a mole."

Lauren shrugged. "I don't know, but I suggest we find her right now!"

"No. We need you and Agent Kojobari back at the office to iron out the details first. We need to regather ourselves."

"But—"

"Look, we don't need any loose cannons, okay? In fact, we've already pulled Agents Dawes and Kiper completely off the assignment for possible attachment issues, so don't make me do the same to you."

"But—"

"That's an order, agent. And I'll have a cleaning crew sent to the shop right away. It'll be like it never happened."

Lauren stood clinching her fist, livid that she couldn't help Mildred right away. "Yes, Sir," she said with gritted teeth.

"Good. I'll meet you at the office."

Lauren hung up and looked towards the front, just now no-ticing a spidered bullet hole in the window. "They'll have their work cut out for them."

Bryan's eyes followed. "So, are we going straight to the field office?" he asked her.

She holstered her weapon and picked up her boots. "Nah. We're going to take a little detour—even if it takes all night."

Bryan's shoulders finally pepped; he also holstered his weapon. "I thought not." Just as they'd entered, he followed her out, but not without one last but sad look at his friend's body on the floor.

Chapter 26

Silver-Stem's private agent, Lauren Mathis, code name, Lauren Brookhaven, had been assigned to Mildred's oversight since Mildred's college years. Lauren, herself, had already finished college online before becoming an agent at that time. A few in-class acting courses didn't hurt either. Now with all her talents, she drove her vehicle down a dark dirt road far north of San Diego, proudly in utter defiance of a direct order to return to the San Diego field office instead of seeking Mildred. "This was the last spot I got a beat on her," she informed her partner, Agent Bryan Kojobari, code name, Bryan Wallace, the one who'd been assigned to deliver Sterling to Mildred. Neither agent had been required to abandon his or her natural accent; it was simply a youthful challenge between colleagues—risky, but something that kept things interesting. Lauren was also one of the few not only privy to Mildred's cellphone location, but her emergency locator as well. An isolated dirt road in the Sycamore Canyon region was the last place she'd picked up a clear ping from each.

"Hold on," Bryan said. "What's going on up ahead there?"

A floating mist of light just offroad suddenly grabbed their attention. With the halfmoon above now covered by clouds, Lauren switched to high beams, revealing headlights from a Suburban. The fact it was on its roof, wheels up, drew them both up in their seats.

"I don't know," Lauren said as she rolled the car to a safe stopping distance. She opened the door. "Come on. But approach with caution."

Both agents traced around the scene with guns and flashlights in hand, Lauren closer to the Suburban, where her locator light was blinking like a red alert. It was the alert for Mildred's cellphone only. "Mildred," Lauren mumbled, but dreaded where her thoughts were taking her. She speed-dialed her best friend just to make sure, quickly hearing a phone ring from inside the overturned Suburban—a simple ring, nothing fancy, but a familiar one. Heart racing, Lauren dropped to her knees and practically dove through a rear shattered window, seeing Mildred's phone lit up like a lamp, but all by itself. She had no choice but to grab it and pocket it on her way up.

"Lauren!" Bryan called out from a point far beyond the wreckage.

Lauren sidestepped over, both hands on her weapon. "What is it?"

"Come see for yourself."

A man's body, face-first in the dirt, answered her question. She looked back at the Suburban, then back at the body, back and forth. "My guess," she said, "the driver—thrown from the vehicle."

"Mm hm." Bryan leaned closer to the body. "Looks like a bullet to the shoulder too. An entry wound, yeah?"

Lauren also leaned in. "Yeah…" She looked around. "You see anything else? Any other bodies?"

He shook his head. "Nada." And he was correct; not one body was found near or far, not in this darkness.

Lauren stepped back, pressed her hands against her waist and swished her lips from side to side. "Why do I sense Roberta-R-One-Fifty's hands all over this mess?" She paused long enough for a response, but harbored no hopes to receive one. "Okay then, back to the car," she said while re-holstering her weapon. "We've got to call this in."

"That's going to put us in an awful amount of trouble, don't you think?"

"Well hell, Bryan, we've got no damn choice, now do we? And what are they gonna do, shoot us?"

The trip back to the car was a disgruntled one for Lauren. Not only was her one and only mission in jeopardy, but her best friend for years was missing, the sweetest "person" she'd ever known. Nothing she'd ever told Mildred about her feelings was a lie. And at this moment, she wanted to burst into flames, enraged by all of it. Lifting her phone and dialing her supervisor was now the last thing she feared, but she would at least need Bryan to corroborate her intentions. Bryan—the man who was nowhere near when she turned around—the man who was off in the distance with his flashlight still in his hand—the man who was staring at something in the dirt.

"What do we have here?" he said just loud enough for Lauren to hear.

Intrigued, Lauren ditched her own call to follow Bryan, where she noticed a trail of jumbled footprints and sweeping tire prints in the dirt. All converged to a point where Bryan was standing. On the ground at the end of Bryan's light was the largest print of them all: one huge, man-sized body-print. "What the hell...?" Lauren mumbled. The imprint was as deep and defined as a fossil-print, including a man's face at the point.

Bryan sighed. "This makes things quite a bit hairier, doesn't it?"

Lauren pinched her chin and tugged. "Yes, it most certainly does. And it still looks like Roberta's work, and a *definite* sign Mildred may still be ali—"

She was interrupted by Bryan's head swinging like an unhinged door in a windstorm. His body flopped to the ground, leaving a tall, dirt-covered man standing in his place.

Lauren redrew her gun and aimed. "Stop or I'll shoot!" she yelled, but too shocked and confused to pull the trigger.

With ripped clothes and flesh hanging off his exposed bones, the stranger's looks alone were frightening enough to drive Lauren back a few steps. He was definitely a killer droid, and he didn't stop there. Hobbled by one bad foot, he scraped forward more like a broken terminator every second, but a fast one.

Lauren had a feeling her bullets would have no effect, *but maybe his fucked-up condition might help a girl out*. Two quick shots to his chest tested her theory, staggering him as planned. But after a second's delay, he was back in rapid pursuit. Lauren fired a few more shots until he slapped the gun clear out of her hand, rebounding with a backhand to her face, tossing her at least fifteen feet in the air before she slid another fifteen through the dirt.

Her head stiff, Lauren gazed up with only her eyes, watching the death-seeking machine rake his way towards her to finish what he'd started, no doubt. Following her instincts, she did what no one else would have: she played dead. A trained actress, she was definitely prepared for it. But when she heard the mechanized words from his mouth, "It is with the deepest regret that you will have to pay for the crimes of those who have preceded you, human," she knew he would have surely turned her façade into a reality. So, she rolled onto her feet and dashed into the surrounding brush.

Keeping her legs and body toned and in shape had nothing to do with Lauren grabbing anyone's attention. It was times like this she had been preparing for. She only stumbled a couple of times during her escape, but she didn't stop, certain her chances against a *broke-down-ass crippled robot* were far better than any of her prior alternatives. She went for her phone as she crossed a hill, only to fumble it into the darkness, maybe backwards. *Shit!* Suddenly, like a wife who'd just lost her ring, she dropped down to grovel around for her phone. But the sound of the broken foot kept dragging in her direction, louder and louder and louder, until

Lauren was up and running again. Soon, she heard a shattering crack. *Oh no. Did he just crush my phone?* She wasn't a human calculator, but the odds were high.

Lauren ran across multiple hills after that, finally stopping when she no longer heard the broken foot dragging the dirt. The only thing she heard next was her vehicle starting up. "What the...?" she murmured and turned around, then backtracked until she reached the first hill's peak. Down below, under dim head-lights, her car was being driven back towards the highway. It couldn't have been her partner; he was still on the ground where he'd been dropped. "Oh, shit!"

Lauren sprinted down the hill in the direction of trouble— but not at all for her vehicle. A former high school athlete, she tapped into her softball roots by sliding in on one knee until she reached Bryan. She knelt beside him and caressed the air around him, fearful any touch would break his already clay-twisted neck. "Bryan, talk to me," she urged.

Bryan's eyes were the only parts of his limp body in mo-tion. "I-I-I can't feel my body," he wheezed and stammered. "I-I-I can't feel anything."

"It's okay. Just stay with me and we're going to get you all fixed up, okay? We'll get through this. I promise." Unwilling to admit, Lauren's faith in Silver-Stem was at an all-time low. But when it came to repairing body parts, she could think of no one better. She just had to keep Bryan alive long enough to experience it. Resting a gentle hand on his shoulder was all she could do to further assure him, whether he felt it or not. But she now faced the inevitable: "I've got to call someone." Just as she went for Mil-dred's phone, Bryan's phone started buzzing. Hands hovering around him again, she went slowly into his pocket. "Okay, buddy, don't move a muscle," she said.

"As if I have a bloody choice."

Lauren actually chuckled. Whether it be Bryan Kojobari or Bryan Wallace, able-bodied or paralyzed, he always had a way of making her laugh, especially in the darkest moments. She then extracted his phone with the steadiness of a surgeon, and she recognized the number. "Chief!" she yelled when she answered.

"Agent Mathis, where are you two?" It was Chief Adams. "I'm at the field office. I tried calling you, but why are you answering Agent Kojobari's phone?"

"Yeah, Chief! No time to explain! We've got an agent down! Agent Kojobari is down! I repeat, Agent Kojobari is down! We need a medic and backup to this phone's coordinates!"

"Backup?"

"Yes, backup! The culprit just drove off in my—just stole my—yeah—just stole my fucking car!"

"Stole your car! Mathis, what have you gotten us all into? I told you to return directly to the office!"

"I know, Sir, but we need that backup right away. Bryan is down! And he's not moving!"

"Not moving? Is he…?"

"No. He's breathing; he's just not able to move. I think he's paralyzed."

Chief Adams took a pause before responding, "Alright, alright. We'll have some choppers sent over right away."

After hanging up, Lauren placed her hand back on Bryan's shoulder. "It's gonna be alright, Bryan. It's gonna be alright."

Chapter 27

Buckled in Keneisha's passenger seat, Mildred stared out the side window, mulling over a reality she couldn't grasp. Along the ride from Sycamore Canyon back towards San Diego, she was now convinced both her parents were none other than robotic "parental units." *And surely Roberta couldn't have been serious about me not contacting my parents! No matter. The moment I get my hands on a damn phone, nothing's going to stop me from calling my mom and dad—or Lauren, for that matter. I've got to talk to someone!* She raised her leg all the way into her chest and rested her foot atop the seat cushion. It was something she'd always been limber enough to do, something that finally gave her comfort on this night, until seeing both dirt and traces of blood on her sneaker. She dropped her foot to the floor instantly, reminded of whose blood she was actually wearing. Already depressed, it only deepened. How could she replace the love of her life? *How can I go on?*

"Would you like to listen to some music, Ms. Morehouse?" Keneisha, who'd been quiet up until this point, asked as if she'd just read Mildred's mind.

It didn't surprise Mildred that Keneisha may have had panoramic vision; she may have seen Mildred's every move—enough to make Mildred dust off any dirt she *may* have just left on the seat. "Sorry about that, Keneisha," she apologized softly.

"No worries, Ms. Morehouse. Would you like to listen to some music?" she repeated.

Mildred fell quiet for a moment. "You're kidding, right?"

"No, not at all. Most people find it to be quite soothing under stressful circumstances. It can serve as an excellent booster to your brain's oxytocin and serotonin levels in lieu of medicine or dietary supplements. The types considered the most soothing in-clude...."

As Keneisha went on with her lecture, Mildred glanced back at Roberta, who was still unconscious in the backseat, jitter-ing ever so often as proof she was still artificially alive. Mildred then returned her sights out the side window and raised her knee back into her chest, this time barefooted. There was nothing along the dark roadside that stuck in her memory or even caught her at-tention; there was simply too much on her mind. Yet she did man-age to crack half-a-smile, but more doubt-ridden than anything. Keneisha had referred to her as a "person"—had even called her "Ms. Morehouse." *But am I still either?* She didn't know the an-swer, but she was certain she still loved music. "You know, Ke-neisha, I wouldn't mind a little music. But what are we going to do about Roberta?"

Keneisha took a few seconds, evidently somehow tapped into Roberta. "Roberta's enhanced operating system and anti-viral add-ons are currently troubleshooting and running auto-upgrades to defeat the virus." She paused. "There is nothing we can do at this time."

Mildred jabbed her fingers through her hair and sighed, conceding, "Okay. Then how about that music?"

"Wonderful. Which type would you like to listen to?"

She shrugged. "Mmm... why don't you decide, Keneisha. And please, call me Mildred."

"Not a problem—Mildred."

Hip-hop was still the taste of the day in the 2060s, and the track Keneisha started with, one with a smooth R&B flow, had Mildred instantly finger-tapping her knee whether she wanted to or not. And as human as she still felt, there was something different about the music; notes were clearer, beats were amplified, and the rhythm was palpable. A new experience, she couldn't deny.

While the playlist advanced through two more similar tracks, without another peep from Keneisha, Mildred noticed the speedometer stuck on the speed limit. Strange, to say they were trying to get away, but not a bad idea once she thought about it; no need to draw any extra attention. So, she finally relaxed, her head drifting towards the side window, nearly touching it. Her eyes fixed on the outside mirror, it didn't take long to notice they were no longer alone on the dark highway. Headlights from another vehicle were closing in rapidly from behind. Not enough to panic, but just enough for Mildred to drop her foot back into her sneaker. By the time the headlights approached, high beams on, the advancing vehicle didn't switch to low beam, didn't signal, nor did it slow down.

"Uhh, Keneisha…?" Mildred turned in her seat to look out the rear window, then panicked. "I think we may need to speed up."

A man was standing on the approaching car's shallow hood. Keneisha said nothing as the car crashed into her rear bumper. One bump and the man was gone, immediately replaced by a thump on Keneisha's roof.

"Brace yourself, Mildred," Keneisha calmly advised before speeding up.

Since Keneisha had never slowed down through the impact, Roberta was held in place against the backrest. Meanwhile, Mildred was pressed into her own backrest, gripping her seat until a man-sized fist punched straight through the roof above her. Its fingers opened up and felt their way for her head, and her head only, grabbing a handful of hair.

Mildred screamed and grappled the man's forearm with all she had. She twisted and turned to try to free herself. "Let me go, let me go, let me go!" she shouted. But the hand held on; its grip only tightened.

"Hang on, Mildred," Keneisha said before swerving from one lane to the other. "It is the Russian unit from the desert crossing."

Konstantin.

Except Mildred was in no position to respond. She had to do *something* before her new synthetic head was ripped from her synthetic neck. Unbuckling and yanking herself free, leaving him with a clump of growing synthetic hair, was now an option, but one she somehow knew to hold off on.

The music still playing and sensors all over, Keneisha could see and feel everything around her, inside-out, like Konstantin grappled onto her roof like a magnet, his arm straight through along with a handful of Mildred's hair, and Mildred on the verge of being snatched through it, the seat along with her if her neck could withstand it. All of it demanded Keneisha's attention first and foremost, while her own erratic swerving had done absolutely nothing to rid them of the threat. Meanwhile, rolling around on the backseat was Roberta, still quivering and jerking through the virus.

"This mission will not be abandoned! You belong to us!" Konstantin screamed at Mildred.

Keneisha couldn't figure out how Konstantin had found them, but it was the fastest route back towards San Diego, the only logical explanation. Regardless, she had to act fast. *But first things first*: she activated her rear seatbelts and auto-strapped Roberta in tightly. Beyond this, even mechanized droid units, like herself, were designed to repair themselves, giving Keneisha an idea. *Calculate*. She went into full acceleration—a short stretch to reach over a hundred-miles-per-hour. Using self-repair, she returned the favor; she resealed and wrapped her roof around Konstantin's elbow joint so tightly, his fingers spread just enough to release Mildred—the perfect time for Keneisha to hit the brakes.

Tires gripping the road and smoking like a fog blanket, Keneisha came to a rapid stop, flinging Konstantin forward and rolling for nearly three-hundred-yards. Left behind was his arm, now dangling through the roof like a broken rudder. The stop would have sent any other vehicle flipping over its nose, but Keneisha was no ordinary vehicle. She had balance control of every wheel and every piece of her being.

Mildred, shaking, swatted and yelled at the swinging arm, "Somebody get this damn thing away from me!"

"In due time, Mildred," Keneisha assured. "My job appears to be incomplete."

Keneisha intensified her headlighting, better able to see the one-armed menace limping in their direction, both his clothes and flesh more ripped apart than how she'd left him before.

Mildred looked up. "What?" She squinted. "Oh, my God! Is that…?" She placed her hand over her mouth. "Is that still who I think it is?"

"It is," Keneisha said bluntly.

"Can't we just… turn around and go the other way?"

"Negative. It will only delay us from our rendezvous—from helping Roberta—and from helping you. Plus, *he* is a problem that needs to be dealt with now—and with extreme prejudice. So, I suggest you relocate—just as a precautionary measure."

"What—?"

Mildred was given no time to adhere; her seat was slid to the rear next to Roberta, compliments of Keneisha. Next in line was the issue of the surround windows. Although they were bulletproof, Keneisha wasn't content. *Cover.* Up rose titanium plates from all around to cover every window, front windshield included. Only Keneisha's exterior cameras now captured what lay ahead.

Keneisha accelerated as fast as she could to meet her new nemesis, who met her back with a dipped shoulder and an impact that jolted her and everyone inside. His feet scorching the pavement, Konstantin somehow managed to grab and rip the titanium cover right off the driver's side window with his one remaining hand, then stared inside as if looking Keneisha straight in the eye.

"It was you who got the best of me before," he told her. "But I assure you, the results will not be the same this time!" One punch and Keneisha's front windshield was cracked.

Hampered by Konstantin's resistance, Keneisha's speed had dropped considerably after impact, but the Sumo match still moved in her favor. She jerked a few times just to keep him off balance, anything to keep his punches to a minimum. And just like Roberta, Keneisha was also equipped for multiple purposes—except in her own unique way. Two hatches on her hood slid open, making way for an articulated arm to emerge from each. On the tip of each arm was the barrel of an automatic rifle, now aimed at Konstantin's belly.

The weapons seemed to get Konstantin's full attention; he stopped punching. Keneisha followed with a barrage of bullets at Konstantin's middle that split him in two. She rolled over his bottom half and was quickly back up to full speed, re-aiming her rifles and firing until his top half fell to the road. Keneisha trampled him one more time before continuing her mission, finally Konstantin-free.

As Keneisha settled back down to the speed limit, Mildred's hand was still over her mouth. "Oh, my God!" Mildred cried out. "Is it over? Is he dead?"

"Dead?" Keneisha pondered. "Unlikely."

"You mean…," Mildred's voice trembled, "he'll be coming after us again?"

"Most likely. But not on this particular evening."

Mildred paused. "Wait a minute," she said, "I believe Roberta said something about spitting in his eye. Yeah…

something about spitting her virus into his eye. I believe it was before you arrived to save us."

"Oh." Keneisha also paused. "Then that may alter things."

Keneisha held her remaining window covers in place as Mildred went back to shaking her foot and biting her nails. By then, Keneisha had witnessed two low sound helicopters crossing the sky behind her, each spotlighting the scene back at the overturned Suburban. Nothing else was said on her way back westbound, while the music continued to play.

Chapter 28

Keneisha had made it all the way to the Marron Valley, about twenty miles southeast of San Diego, without anymore encounters with Konstantin, but Roberta had yet to awaken. Mildred, now sitting in the backseat with Roberta, had taken the initiative and found some cleaning rags in Keneisha's rear compartment. They were stuffed in bags along with other shop essentials from McCarvey's. "Essential"—a word Mildred was no longer sure she'd be using again when it came to the flower shop, which was already becoming a distant memory. She now used the rags to wipe as much blood off Roberta's face as she could. No matter how synthetic, the sight of the thick, red fluid still tugged at Mildred's emotions, which must have been its purpose, she finally figured.

Mildred occasionally gazed out at the clouded night sky just to distract herself. Only the road signs alerted her they weren't far from the U.S./Mexican border, a line she figured they would be crossing soon. Yet breaching it was no longer the political bonfire of the eighties through the twenty-twenties. Newer technology had made it impossible to escape digital D.N.A. scans at key crossings, where uncleared criminal backgrounds prevented crossing from either side. Yet where did this place Mildred? She was neither criminal nor a true citizen; she was now a high-tech machine being hunted by a giant regime. But she didn't have to be a machine to suspect that the minute they would cross that border, would be the minute helicopters move in—not Suburbans. "Damn it!" She stomped the floor with her foot, leaving a small dent.

"Is there a problem, Mildred?" It was the first time Keneisha had said anything to her since their latest dual with Konstantin.

"I'm sorry, Keneisha." Mildred looked down. "I didn't mean to hurt you."

"Not a problem, Mildred. I have seen much worse in just this night alone." Her voice was mechanically even-keeled and, for the most part, soothing as she self-repaired the dent.

Mildred looked out the window again. "I know we're near the border. And there's no way I'll be able to get across it without being found, is there?"

Keneisha paused. "Our chance for success is currently fifty-point-nine-one-percent."

"Fifty-point-nine-one-percent?" Mildred blared.

"Yes. Would you like to speak to Dr. Murphy now?"

"Dr.... Murphy?"

"Yes. Our maker. Both Roberta's and my maker."

Unlike most model units, Mildred wasn't tapped into any top-secret servers or the internet, not even after this recent episode. Any data accidentally retrieved was based solely on information stored before the day of her startup, and Dr. Murphy was not in that database.

"Oh, yeah. Him." She finally remembered him from one of Roberta's utterances. Her eyes panned from window to window. "Is that who we're going to see?"

"No. But I can get him on a private line if you wish."

Mildred looked deeper into the darkness around them, but more so into Keneisha's offer. "Sure."

Dr. Kenneth Murphy answered a few seconds later, his quiet tone amplified by Keneisha's surround-sound interior, "Roberta?" Quiet or not, his anxiety was intense, while his office door could also be heard closing in the background.

"No, Doctor Murphy," Keneisha answered, "This is Keneisha-AV-eleven-hundred. Roberta is incapacitated at the moment."

"*Incapacitated*?"

"Affirmative, Doctor. Diagnostic scans indicate a severe virus has corrupted her operating system. Her motor skills are down to nil."

"Shit," Kenneth muttered. "I knew this would happen."

"We have both been weakened by a battle with a powerful Russian-made droid unit."

"Weakened?" he blurted. "What do you mean, weakened by a Russian-made droid unit? Where is Roberta?"

"She is in the rear, Dr. Murphy, fighting the virus."

Kenneth went silent.

"Doctor Murphy?"

"Yes, Keneisha."

"I have Ms. Mildred Morehouse present to speak with you."

He paused. "You have her there inside with you?"

"Affirmative."

"Place us on visual, please."

As soon as Kenneth's visual came in, Mildred's eyes were on Roberta instead.

"Ms. Morehouse?" Kenneth asked.

She looked up at his facial image in midair. "Hello, Dr. Murphy?"

"Yes. Hello, Ms. Morehouse. Glad to see you safe." It seemed his demeanor had changed 180-degrees since hearing her name.

"Yes, thanks to Roberta." She was hanging onto Roberta's hand with a grip that would have crushed anyone else's. She looked back at Roberta's trembling body. "Now, I wish I could just return the favor."

Kenneth sighed. "I believe we all have done everything we possibly can."

"Would you like me to perform an extract and transfer, Dr. Murphy?" Keneisha interrupted.

Kenneth paused, his brow weighing the impact of Keneisha's suggestion. "No. We can't afford to have you take on the virus too. I mean, not yet, at least. I assume you're on Protocol Darkest Hour, which means you now have to get Ms. Morehouse across the border as quickly as possible also."

As clouded as the conversation had started, abandoning the idea sounded like a no-no to Mildred. "No!" she yelled at Kenneth. Nothing could contain her true feelings, her rage. "I don't care about getting across the damn boarder! We have to save Roberta!"

"I know, I know," Kenneth said in quiet angst. "We do, but… we can only pray that her enhanced anti-viral software will kick in before it's too late. Well—*I* can only pray."

"I assume somewhere in all of this is Roberta's claim that I'm some sort of… sort of—"

"Yes."

"Regardless, I don't care what you or anyone else thinks, not even Roberta; I am as real as I've always been!" She was one blink away from a tear.

Kenneth shook his head. "I'm sorry, Ms. Morehouse. I know this must be difficult for you."

Then came the tear. "But this is all your fault, isn't it?"

"No, no. I had nothing to do with you. I joined Silver-Stem long after your crea—your, your… arrival."

She dropped Roberta's hand and tensed up like a coiled spring. "You're not making it sound any goddamn better!"

Kenneth heaved another sigh; he had no response.

"I'm sorry," she apologized.

"It's fine."

"It's just that this has been the worst night of my life, and I don't even have a way to call my parents. Unless, of course, you or Keneisha can call them for me."

Kenneth's eyes lit up like he'd just seen someone on fire. "No! That's a negative! You absolutely *cannot* talk to your parents!"

Her jaw dropped, indignation in her every muscle. "Are you *commanding* me not to talk to my parents?"

He wavered his hands. "No, that's not what I'm trying to say. What I'm saying is, it would jeopardize not only your own safety, but Roberta's as well!"

Mildred huffed. "Then are you trying to tell me that my parents are *robots* too?"

Kenneth aimed his eyes to the ceiling, his lips twisting from side-to-side. "Mmmm, that's one unique way of putting it, but let's just say—their lines are not the most secure right now. Trust me, please."

She threw her forehead into her hand. "Oh, good grief."

"And the same goes for Agent Mathis."

Her head popped up. "Agent *who*?"

Keneisha cut in again, "We are nearing our destination, Dr. Murphy."

Mildred craned her neck just to see around Kenneth's hologram. "The border, I'm guessing?" But the road sign said five miles to go. "And just how are we supposed to make it across without anyone noticing—Dr. Murphy?" Mildred asked Kenneth, already dreading another one of his cryptic answers.

He patted the air with a light touch. "Relax. I do have a few folks in the world who I can still trust besides my wife and Roberta."

"You can trust me, Dr. Murphy," Keneisha added.

"Yes, you too, Keneisha."

"What exactly do you mean, Dr. Murphy?" Mildred asked. "Who exactly are you talking about?"

He nodded with assurance. "A friend. One you'll meet very soon," he said just before disconnecting, remaining loyal to his cryptic format.

"Great."

Dr. John Consuela's love for horses often kept him out late, and he never even had to leave home. Tonight, less than an hour before midnight, was no different as he double-brushed one of his nine crossbreeds. That's when a single band of headlights turned into his winding driveway. He could tell it was an auto-driven vehicle as it approached; the one person sitting in the rear and no one in the driver's seat were dead giveaways. A brush in each hand, John maintained one stroke after another, along with a strong idea why the vehicle was rolling to a stop just outside the horse arena's timber fence.

John hadn't seen Dr. Kenneth Murphy since John, himself, had retired from ZepperCorp. The last time was actually only a year or so before Kenneth's forced exit. Many phone conversations had followed, one in the form of a text message nearly an hour ago. "Be prepared for Protocol DH," was what Kenneth's latest had read. "What?" was John's initial response. "Protocol Darkest Hour." *What?* One cryptic phrase was all it had said. On the verge of going visual, John had begun tapping his chin. "Ohhh yeah," he'd mumbled from inside his kitchen. Protocol Darkest Hour was a code Kenneth had established, along with plans to one day take ZepperCorp down to the ground, if need be. And with it was the contingency for Kenneth and his family to get across the border. With deep Mexican connections, John was to be their guide.

The day of Protocol DH must have finally arrived, was what John had figured. But he saw no family in the vehicle in front of him this evening—only one woman leaning forward from the backseat.

The car's window was already down, and it was parked close enough to the fence for John to see the whites of the woman's beautiful young eyes. "Dr. John Consuela?" a mechanical voice announced, but the woman's lips had never moved. She just continued to stare.

A green scanning laser shot from the edge of the sideview mirror when John gave no answer. "Dr. John Consuela?" the vehicle repeated.

"Yes…," John answered.

"I am Keneisha-AV-eleven-hundred. We come to you under the directive of Dr. Kenneth Murphy. Protocol Darkest Hour five-zero-zero-eight-one. Will you accommodate?"

John inched cautiously closer to the vehicle. He hadn't cracked open one technical document since retiring. For all he knew, the woman sitting in the back, her lips still tight, could have very well been hooked up to the vehicle somehow. And he definitely had no idea what implications the "five-zero-zero-eight-one" carried. Plus, the woman lying asleep on the backseat, the one he'd just now noticed, simply added to the confusion.

John looked Mildred in the eyes. "And you are…?" he asked.

Her lips finally opened. "I'm—"

"I'm afraid we're going to have to withhold that piece of information for now, Dr. Consuela, if you do not mind," was the vehicle's response.

John jittered both horse brushes in the air. "Hey… okay by me, Ms. Keneisha. No questions here. And I'll get you across that border, for sure."

Chapter 29

The time was approaching midnight, and the tense circumstances Roberta, Mildred and Keneisha were facing had Dr. Murphy braced for an all-nighter at the office. Kenneth Murphy was no android; when Keneisha had called him, he was still reading what Roberta had long since digested and sent to him. But he didn't need to read much more to get the gist. Millennium-Droid-Edition-D, a.k.a., Mildred, was a gift to the world in Kenneth's eyes. Not combat-ready or as strong as a service droid, Mildred's sentient level was nothing short of human, yet her true power rested in her womb's capabilities. It wasn't until after hanging up with her, did he reach the critical reading point: Mildred was pregnant, and by natural means. This was confirmed in the report by Dr. Yamada, a Silver-Stem medical agent stationed in San Diego for one purpose only: to keep Mildred's womb ready for its world-altering task.

Kenneth had come across many other hidden facts along with Mildred's background, starting with the mystery behind the Morehouses, who weren't quite the undercover billionaires he'd first thought. Both were Mildred's prime protectors and monitors. And there were other monitors like Agent Lauren Mathis, code-name: "Lauren Brookhaven." But the biggest thing, the thing that now had them on the run, was that Mildred was 100% financed by a Russian-owned company. *Not totally illegal,* but by it being a Russian government run company, Silver-Stem's involvement, especially a company now U.S.-run, was a level of heat he figured Silver-Stem could not afford. *And now, the Russians have come to collect the return on their investment!* To make matters worse, there was one name copied on every financial transaction—more so than Jahid's: Dr. Torrance Olivar. To what extent would Silver-Stem go to protect such information was Kenneth's next question, and he wasn't afraid to find out. He closed the document and rose from his desk, determined to get to the root before matters grew any worse.

It was common for Torrance to also campout overnight at the office. Kenneth, not wanting to tip him off, took a chance to catch him off-guard by making a surprise visit that evening. Easy to do since Torrance's receptionist, Veronica, had long since gone. Kenneth moved with raw determination to Torrance's office when he saw light through an open door. Two solid knocks against the frame brought Torrance, who was on his phone, to a slow stop.

"I'll… call you back," Torrance muttered before hanging up. "Kenneth. What's up, man? What can I do for you?"

Kenneth charged in and stopped at the edge of Torrance's desk, his intentions aimed like a weapon. "Why didn't you tell me about the Millennium Droid project, Torrance?"

Torrance sat up high in his chair, back-scrubbing every inch of it. "Uhh…, was I supposed to?"

"Yes—when it involves foreign government funding sources. Yes, you were supposed to."

"Foreign government funding?" Torrance's hands danced in the air. "Whoa, whoa, whoa… What do you mean by foreign government funding?"

Kenneth dipped his head. "As in Russian funding…," he said beneath his breath as if the federal government was right there in the room with them.

Torrance, nothing but pleasant up until this point, switched to a shrewd squint. "What do you mean, 'Russian funding'? Where did you hear such a thing? From whom?"

Kenneth paused, unsure if he was ready to reveal he'd been snooping around confidential files—again.   "Very credible sources."

Torrance strolled his fingers across his desktop like a master pianist. "Well, I'm sure whoever's passed this information along to you has grossly exaggerated."

"But Torrance, your name is plastered on every transaction involved!"

Torrance responded with a sigh, "Kenneth, my name is on loads of company documents—if for any reason, by sheer procedure alone. I'm rarely actually involved. That's nothing out of the ordinary."

Kenneth could always see through Torrance's façade. This time, it was masking a smugness that sealed Kenneth's suspicions, gripping inner feelings that had been latent for far too many years. "I don't think so, Torrance," Kenneth gritted, "considering the Russian company has already arrived to collect on its investment, and caught in the middle is *my* Roberta!"

"*Your* Roberta? Well, that's debatable," Torrance mumbled before emphasizing, "First of all, I have no idea what you're talking about. And haven't I told you a thousand times not to get too attached to these droid units?"

Confused, Kenneth strained for at least one time he'd heard this kind of advice from Torrance's mouth, but came up empty.

"I don't know," Torrance added, "maybe I *thought* about saying it. Or maybe I might have mentioned it—once."

"D-D-Don't you try to change the subject, Torrance," Kenneth stammered. "This is serious! Roberta is on the verge of death!"

Torrance patted the air with one hand. "Settle down, settle down. Now, tell me, what exactly has you thinking she is on the verge of… death?"

Kenneth finally took a seat in the guest chair, folded his arms and festered, but gave no answer.

"Okay," Torrance said, "I still don't know what you're talking about, but if you just tell me where she and Mildred are hiding right now, I promise you I will have someone give them all the help they need."

Kenneth couldn't figure out which annoyed him more—Torrance's lies or his facetious concern. He knew his best friend was competitive, but this was beyond—*hey, wait a minute…* He paused at mid-thought and peered into Torrance's eyes. "Wait, wait, wait. I never said anything about them hiding out together. And I never even mentioned Mildred's name."

Torrance cocked his head. "You didn't? Yes, you did."

To this, Kenneth shook his head slowly. "No, I didn't."

"Sure, you did. Her name was the first thing out of your mouth." Torrance's confused look actually seemed real. "Wasn't it?"

Indirectly speaking, very indirectly, Torrance was correct—too correct as far as Kenneth was concerned, who stood up and headed to the door. He stopped just before exiting and turned back around, this time aiming his eyes and his finger. "You've gone too far, Torrance, and I'm not going to be a part of this!"

Torrance shook his head along with a brief laugh. "Whatever, man."

"And is Jahid a part of this? Does he know?"

Torrance's levity switched instantly to a blank stare.

Whatever that meant, Kenneth was sparked; a slow nod followed. "Ahh, he doesn't know, does he?" he asked.

Torrance hesitated, then *ba-dop-popped* the top of his desk, pointing at the end. "You know what, why don't you go ahead and ask Jahid everything you want to know. He *would* be the best starting point. He should be in tomorrow."

Kenneth festered some more. "Fine! I'll do that!"

Torrance returned his attention to his desk. "Sure, you do that," he said nonchalantly.

The table was now set. Everything Kenneth wanted to know about Silver-Stem's involvement would be resolved the next morning. If not, Torrance's deviousness would at least be placed in front of Jahid, and the complete truth would be exposed. So, why was Kenneth still standing there? Why was he still facing Torrance? It had to be because of Torrance's insouciance. "Whatever you have up your sleeve, Torrance," Kenneth added, "I will make sure everyone knows. And if you're looking for Roberta *or* Mildred, you may as well forget their names—because neither you nor the Russians will ever see either one of them again." He turned away and stormed out the office as irate as he'd stormed in. "So, don't bother following me!"

"I won't!" he heard Torrance shout. "Have a good night, Dr. Murphy!"

Torrance was left behind at his desk in a pensive state, no longer amused. Truth was, he couldn't deny any of Kenneth's accusations, but was at least relieved he never had to explain the multi-millions he'd been personally collecting from the Russians to navigate U.S. roadblocks. Partial discovery or not, the question now was, who would Kenneth *blab* to once leaving the office tonight? How far and how fast would the news travel? There were a few things Torrance could have attempted in order to discredit Kenneth's story, but all were shaky at best. And for many reasons,

Torrance at least knew Jahid would have no real answers. But if he acted fast enough, all his worries would quickly fade to dust.

Torrance lifted his phone and placed a call. "Theo?"

Theo Matsui's broad face, and even broader neck, emerged on Torrance's screen. "Yes, Sir?" He was Silver-Stem's chief of security

"I've got news," Torrance said.

"Sir?"

"I've found the party responsible for the firewall security breach. It was Dr. Kenneth Murphy, just as suspected."

Theo paused and gave a stiff nod. "How would you like this to be handled, Sir?"

"Well obviously, the Millennium project needs to be scrubbed and purged. All of it. Right away."

"Not a problem, Sir." And Theo was not considered a Silver-Stem private agent. Yes, agents were loyal to their assignments, loyal to company protocol, but Theo performed the tasks no one could talk about, and mostly by night—the reason he felt comfortable asking, "And Dr. Murphy?"

Torrance hadn't faltered one bit until now; he took a deep breath. "The same." Next, he took a swallow, just what he wanted to do with that last command. But the secure world he'd built was at stake, and Kenneth had just become a threat to it. "Immediately. And he's working late, so he should be leaving the office soon."

"In a company-supplied vehicle?"

"Yes."

"Then the matter will be taken care of right away, Sir."

Kenneth was in a blaze to get back home after his fallout with Torrance. Despite his plans to talk to Jahid the next morning, he had a strange feeling this might be the last time he'd ever see the inside walls of Silver-Stem, and an even stranger feeling he and his family

were now in danger. Knowing what Roberta and Mildred had been dealing with, it wasn't too farfetched. Desperation was driving him to get his family out of the house as quickly as possible. The company car he was in would just have to be left there for someone else to wrestle with.

Kenneth tapped his earpiece. "Dial home."

"Hey, baby," Linda answered. "Why don't you have me on visual?"

"Uhhh," he teetered, "because I'm driving right now."

"That's never stopped you before. Plus, you can keep your eyes on the road while I look at you."

"I could never do that…"

"Which part?"

"The keeping my eyes on the road instead of you."

"Ohhh, you're so sweet. But that's not what happens when I'm sitting in the passenger's seat."

"That's because—wait a minute. I'm getting way off subject here."

"What?"

"Something's gone down at work, and I believe the outfall could spell trouble."

"Trouble!" Linda blurted.

Kenneth snapped his mouth shut.

"Trouble!" she blurted again. "Well, whatever it is, I know you can't be responsible, right?"

"No, of course not. But they *know* I know; I'm sure of that. And that's not all. I believe Torrance is somehow in the middle of it all."

"Torrance?"

"Mm hm. I'll have to tell you all about it when I get home."

Linda gasped. "Oh, my God, Kenneth! Are you in danger? Are *we* in danger?"

"I hope not, baby. But I need you to pack up the kids and only the necessities, just the necessities, and be ready when I get there. Uh, uh, just tell them we're going on a little vacation."

"Okay, but where *are* we going?"

"I don't know yet, but I will by the time I get there. Okay, baby?"

"Yeah..., yes. You just be careful and drive safe, alright?"

"Yeah. See you in fifteen."

"Alright. I love you."

"Love you more."

Kenneth hung up with a sigh like half-a-ton had been lifted. The other half would follow once his family was safe. Driving a company-owned vehicle, his plan was to change cars after packing. A "lab rat" most of his career, extensive travel was far from his scope of work, so he could have easily used his own personal car to get to the office. A second Keneisha would have been ideal on a night like this, but he could only afford to build one Keneisha, and that one he believed to be put to better use with Roberta. But it was the least of his worries now; he had to get home faster. He accelerated down a straightaway along his usual route, heading into a series of curves atop a steep embankment.

Kenneth had navigated the 45-m.p.h. curves easily whenever entering at only 10 to 15 m.p.h. over the limit, but he had just slipped to 70-m.p.h. this time, and a humming noise instantly filled his ears. It was loud enough to be coming from inside the vehicle, but a bright light outside and overhead said otherwise. An uncomfortable feeling, indeed, but enough to force him to slow down into the first curve. *Cop-drone*, he figured. But just before pressing his brake pedal, his brakes locked completely on their own, flipping his vehicle into the roadside barrier beam and over the barrier.

Kenneth's seatbelt had held the entire time down the slope, but never did the vehicle's airbag eject, leaving him battered and unconscious when its roof met the jagged bottom. And *that's* when the airbag inflated.

Linda was a nervous wreck by the time Kenneth's fifteen minutes had turned into thirty. It was bad enough he had spent that much time at work to begin with. Linda was used to an occasional 9, maybe 10 p.m., but the midnight hours were unheard of in their household. *I mean, what person could function for so long*? she'd wondered earlier. But after news of Kenneth's work dilemma, she was on high alert.

Thirty soon turned into forty-five minutes, and Kenneth hadn't answered any of Linda's calls. Meanwhile, the kids were packed up, but had already fallen asleep with clothes and sneakers on, each occupying a space on the family's sectional sofa. Linda took a deep breath at the sight of it all. She found no other choice but to call their neighbor and bring the kids next door.

"Your dad called while you were asleep," was what she told the kids after her neighbor, Mrs. Larramy, opened her front door. "He has a flat tire and I'm going to give him a hand,"

"Why can't we just go with you, Mom?" her son asked when she handed them over.

"Because you'll only get in the way!" she yelled. "Now, I'll be right back, okay?" A kiss on each forehead, and she was off. As far as the fib she'd told them, *A flat tire is totally possible.*

Linda knew Kenneth's path to and from work. His routine was as deliberate as his creations, and far more predictable—most of the time. She followed that path until reaching one dreadful curve, where a police flagman waved her to keep right. With no one behind her, she slowed to a stop instead. Police cars and an E.M.T. lit the area like broad daylight, enough to see the bent and flattened barrier. In between them was a wrecker with a hoisting cable hanging over the embankment.

Panic consumed Linda when she remembered one of the last things Kenneth had said to her: *See you in fifteen.* Linda had only been driving for fifteen minutes.

She craned her neck out the window. "Excuse me?" she asked the flagman. "What's happened here?"

"An accident, ma'am," he answered, "but I'm going to have to ask you to keep driving, please! Nothing to see here!"

"But, but—my husband was driving down this road when I last spoke to him!"

Silence intervened as a pale hue spread across the flagman's face, the same moment the hoist came to a banging halt in the background. A sick feeling entered Linda's stomach when she saw a stretcher dangling from its end, a closed body bag strapped in it. She didn't have to see a face for all noise and commotion around her to jam to a stop. She didn't even have to see the car to charge out of hers, screaming towards the inevitable end of the most loving soul she'd ever known.

Chapter 30

The time was beyond midnight the same night of Kenneth's accident. With Keneisha now parked inside John Consuela's detached garage, Mildred was inside his large, ranch style house. She sat on the edge of his guestroom's bed with Roberta lying faceup in the center, still quivering all over. The blood may have been cleaned many times over, but Mildred continued to wipe away from mere affection alone. Still devastated, she watched Roberta's pupils gyrate under closed eyelids like from a bad dream. Suddenly, what Mildred thought would have been a blessing, felt like a curse as she heard every word between John and his wife all the way from another room, no matter how quiet they tried to keep it. She could tell they were in the kitchen just from the sound of Mrs. Consuela occasionally grazing a fork or a spoon.

"Honey," his wife said, "this seems far too dangerous. You need to tell these young ladies they have to leave and find another way across the border."

John hesitated. "Look, baby, I know how much of a burden this is, but I promised an old friend I would take care of his family when the time comes. And this *is* his family."

"That's fine and all, but my concern is *your* safety, John. *Your* safety."

Mildred pictured a few hard finger jabs in between, exactly what she would have done with Sterling in the same situation.

"I know, and I appreciate your concern," John went on, "but Kenneth has stuck his neck out for me on a number of occasions. And baby, your husband is a man of his word. And in the end, what else does a man have?"

Mildred had to hold back a tear on that one. The ranch, the horses, the pasture, the man and his plaid shirt, Denham jeans and boots. It was like listening to a romantic scene from an old time western, this time from her grand—*from someone's grand-parent's era.*

Mrs. Consuela didn't say much else before John came down the hall and stopped at the guestroom's doorway. He leaned against the frame, hands in his pockets. "Miss, I think you should get some shuteye tonight. It's best that we leave first thing in the morning. Taking off now would actually lead to more suspicion than otherwise. Catch my point?"

Mildred was on the verge of nodding, but held on to it. "But what about Ro—uh, my friend? When will we be able to get some help for her?"

"Well, I got the rundown from your vehicular friend out there, and a virus like that would have taken down anything—I mean, *anyone else* in less than an hour. So, whatever's keeping her going, is something other than an operating system. And that, my dear, should keep her alive and well through the night."

She finally nodded. Either he was blowing something in her ear she was desperate to hear, or something about his demeanor elicited confidence.

He pointed down the hall. "We have another guest bedroom over here for you."

"Oh, no. I can't leave her side." Mildred wiped her own welling eyes. "It's my fault she's in this condition. I know it is."

John stood upright and swung his arms back and forth, as if tempted to throw a hug through midair. He raked his fingers through his hair instead. "Yeah," he said, "I understand." He grabbed the doorknob. "Well, you have a goodnight's rest, okay?"

"Okay, thank you." But there was something she had to get out before the door closed. "And Mr. Consuela?"

He paused. "Yes?"

"It's Mildred."

"Pardon?"

"My name. It's Mildred."

"Okay… And you can call me John." He closed the door slowly, nodding. "You have a goodnight—Mildred." The door clicked shut.

Mildred sat up for a few minutes after John had left, then laid herself down beside Roberta. The ceiling light was still on, but never did she rise to turn it off.

Just after sunrise the next morning, Mildred stood in John's backyard as he introduced her to an old antique horse trailer. It was a miracle if she'd retain any of it, since she'd never turned off that ceiling light, and she may have gotten only 30 minutes of sleep. But memories of what Roberta had told her kept her awake, kept her alert: *We're mostly solar-powered.* And with her new reality, time would tell just how long she could last.

"Well, Mildred," John said, opening the doors to his trailer, "this one is a two-horse trailer. Now, this is how everything's gonna go: I make hay runs down there every so often, my trailer loaded to the peak. They rarely, if ever, open the doors, or even look back there. So, I figure we leave an extra row free and clear in the center here for you and your friend to camp out in, surround the perimeter with hay, and we'll be good to go."

Mildred took a long stare at the trailer. "They *rarely* look back here?"

John nodded. "That's right. It's only a rural highway we'll be taking, so border patrol is light. Very light."

She switched her stare to John. "So, you're saying there's a *chance* they'll look back here."

He placed his hands on his waist and tucked in his lips. "Alright, we'll double-stack the back. Now, it'll be hot as hell, but I'll do it. How about that?"

Mildred nodded too, but only in mild acceptance. "And Keneisha?"

"Ken-who?" He snapped his fingers. "Oh, yeah! The vehicular droid! You know, I came out and spoke with her a little bit more this morning, especially since I couldn't reach Dr. Murphy, and she agreed it would be best for her to wait until the trail grows cold. Things may be a little too hot right now. I'll probably have my nephew drive her over in a few days. Plus, she looks a little scratched up too, so a paint job wouldn't hurt at all."

Mildred stared him down with as much faith in a wooden object.

John shrugged. "Hey, you can go ask her yourself if you'd like. In the meantime, I'll load up this trailer and go get your other friend."

She tapped her lips, her head tick-tocking from side to side. "Okay…"

Per John's plan, Mildred soon sat folded with her knees to her chest, crunched in between Roberta and two stacks of hay along a bumpy ride to the border. The horse trailer was hitched to John's pickup truck. Inside the trailer, it was hot, it was stuffy, and Roberta was feeling it acutely. But Keneisha had earlier convinced Mildred that John's plan was a viable one. As much as Keneisha was able to repair her own dents, repainting the abrasions had not been designed into her repertoire yet. Regardless, Mildred's attention now rested totally on Roberta, who was not only pale, but was still quivering. Only when John rolled to a complete stop, did Mildred look up with concern.

"Carlos," she heard John's faint announcement through all the hay and metal.

"John," Carlos answered. "Another hay run, huh?"

"Yeah, like clockwork."

Seconds later, she felt the truck inch forward, then stop when Carlos commanded, "Just a sec, John." She heard footsteps heading in her direction.

"Is there a problem, Carlos?"

"You know… I don't really know why, John, but we've been asked to do a more thorough check this time around." The steps grew closer. "You don't mind if I open up the back, do you? I mean, you don't have ole Betsy back here, do you?" Mildred assumed Carlos was referring to one of John's horses, but it really didn't ease the mounting tension.

John paused. "No, not at all. Not at all."

As Carlos's footsteps approached the rear, Mildred folded herself in an even tighter knot, trying her best to withdraw into pure invisibility. Not a chance as she heard the latch being pulled and the henges to one door whining. She watched in fear as one of the top haybales began to shift and scoot, as if being pushed. And when it began to tip, she reached up and stopped it, holding it over the edge to prevent it from falling on Roberta's head. It may not have harmed Roberta any more than she was already enduring, but just the thought of it had Mildred in pain. Luckily, the haybale was from the second stack, the outer stack still standing and protecting them from discovery. Mildred heard the door close, followed by the latch snapping in place. Now drenched in sweat, she exhaled softly, but dared not move.

"You find anything strange back there?" she heard John shout.

"Nah," said Carlos. "Not unless you expected me to find something other than hay!"

"Well, now, I did make a gas stop on the way. And you just never know what kind of U.S. Americans might creep on in there when I'm not looking!"

As much as John and Carlos burst aflame in laughter, Mildred was not only dripping sweat, but she was fuming just as much on the inside. *Shit, John, don't give him any damn ideas! We're in the fucking clear already!*

"Yeah!" Carlos blurted. "Then you might want to put a lock on that thing, too!"

"Ha! You're right about that! See you on the way back!" John hollered as the truck began to roll again. "I'll be a few pounds lighter!"

John, who was born and raised in the U.S., had become far more accustomed to American country music than any other. He tapped his steering wheel to a tune playing softly from his playlist, but it was time to put it on pause. Fifteen minutes after his encounter with Carlos, it was time to pull over and give Mildred and her friend a break for air. The slender gaps in the haystacks were simply not enough, and this was only their second such stop.

John pulled nearly twenty yards offroad, where he got out and rushed to the back. He slung the trailer doors open and began taking the stacks down one by one. "We're not too, too far from my relatives' house! You all will camp out there a few nights, and then—," he announced to a halt after removing the last haybale, shocked by what he saw inside. Mildred, eyes drooping like an autumn leaf, was cradling her friend in her arms. John couldn't distinguish her tears from her sweat, but Mildred's sobs were undeniable, while her friend was a pale gray and no longer quivering.

"Roberta, wake up," Mildred cried softly, "Wake up." She looked up at John. "I think… sh-sh-sh-she's dead."

It was John's first time actually hearing Roberta's name, but he dropped his head more for Mildred, who's pain had become his own. Her compassion for everyone around her was contagious, and John had become an instant carrier.

"Let's get her closer to the edge here," John instructed, gently pulling Roberta closer to the trailer's edge, "to get her some air."

"Okay." Mildred stood up and helped until Roberta's body was to the edge, but deep down inside, she knew it was hopeless. Roberta even felt like deadweight, and her eyelids were practically sealed shut, pupils no longer gyrating. Mildred sat down next to her and continued to sob. Even after knowing their technical connection, after so many years apart, she still couldn't explain her *emotional* connection to Roberta. Losing her in less than 24 hours from Sterling's death felt unbearable. Mildred thought back to the conversation between Keneisha and Dr. Murphy. *The transfer*, she remembered. She believed if Keneisha would have taken on the virus as she'd requested, Roberta would have still been alive. Mildred hated to make comparisons, but she couldn't help it. *What good will surviving with a rolling, mechanical droid be over Roberta's love and protection? It was a stupid decision! It was stupid! And Keneisha could have been rebuilt. Stupid!* She wiped her eyes. *But would she have been the same Keneisha?* All of a sudden, it no longer mattered to her. She looked up at John. "What can we do, John?"

John scratched his head. "Well, I no longer have the equipment, nor the expertise to do anything. And as much as I tried to reach Kenneth this morning, I haven't heard anything back." He dawdled back and forth. "I'll tell you this, Mildred: I'm not much of a religious person, and I don't know if you are or not, but when

all else fails, I think you may want to consider something called…
prayer."

"Prayer?" It was ages since she'd done it officially. There
were times when she'd thanked God, times she'd called the name
in ecstasy, and many times she'd used it as a complete expletive,
but never had she knelt down for a serious request. Looking at her
friend's face from where she sat, at least her knees were bent; she
was halfway there. Like her moment in the ocean, she looked up
and stared into the sun.

"I'll leave you two alone for a minute," John said as he
walked back to his pickup.

Hearing John's door close, Mildred raised Roberta's head
and shoulders and pulled her across her lap. *Where do I even
begin?* she wondered. The answer came in a memory, one Roberta, herself, had created: *Saying it out loud amplifies my signal to
her.* And if God were a woman, her advice was perfect. Mildred
stared at the sun again and opened her mouth, waiting for the words
to emerge. "God?" she murmured respectfully. "God?" That's
when strange thoughts took over, like, *can a droid really request
anything from God?* Afterall, both she and Roberta had been assembled by human beings. Suddenly distracted, she visualized human hands stitching her own arms and legs onto her body with
needles and thread of bloody veins, resulting in something mon-
strous, like straight out of a Mary Shelley novel. Mildred dropped
her head and slammed her eyes shut in disgust. "Oh, God damn
it!" she raged with clear, emphatic diction. Not the opening line
she was looking for, but when a faint buzz began to vibrate in her
lap, something had changed. When she opened her eyes, Roberta's
eyes were open too, except dead-stiff with a glassy stare, while her
natural complexion had started to return.

Chapter 31

Torrance sat alone in his office early the same morning of Mildred's strife, where he mulled over the escalating calamities of his own doing. The first involved his chief of security, whose face was now on his screen. If Theo had done his job to perfection, a drone would have been sent out to track down Kenneth's company vehicle as if it were stolen. Since company-supplied vehicles were robotic, not androidic, their programming was simpler, and they could easily be controlled remotely. Remote controlled company cars, however, had been protested from all levels within the company, leading to heavy restrictions. Yet Torrance and a few others had found a way around the rules, leaning on safety and security to institute overhead drones for emergency use. The drones' remote brake-locking was once a tactic saved for the common thief, but was now crucial to Torrance's new gameplan. Until now, it had only been used once a few years ago when a staff scientist had left his vehicle open and running. The thief had taken and driven it about two miles away by the time the drone had tracked it down and did its thing. And under normal driving speeds, the windshield was thick enough to restrain an unbelted driver from ejection, but also packed a serious knockout punch. It had all amounted to huge giggles for Theo and his crew back then, but Theo's face now consumed Torrance's screen with a serious look.

"Has the matter we discussed been taken care of," Torrance asked him.

"Yes, Sir," Theo said. "The mission was accomplished. Our defector will no longer be a problem. Ever."

With fist over mouth, Torrance offered no response. He left his phone on, but quickly turned his attention to his tablet's browser, anything to redirect his thoughts.

"On another note, Sir," Theo continued, "a company agent was severely injured last night."

"Agent? Injured?" Torrance asked aloofly, closer to a statement than a question, softspoken at that.

"Yes, Sir. Agent Kojobari, one of our most loyal agents, was paralyzed in an altercation."

Torrance paused for several seconds; his eyes never left his tablet. "An altercation?" he finally mumbled. "Paralyzed?"

"Yes. A Russian operative is to blame. A Russian droid unit, to be exact."

Eyes still on his tablet, Torrance twisted his lips from side to side. "A Russian droid?"

"Yes, Sir. Will we be planning a response?"

Torrance remained softspoken. "A response?"

Theo heaved a breath, apparently flabbergasted. "Yes, Sir."

"Uhh... to whom?"

"To the Russians, Sir."

"Does this Agent Ko... Ko..."

"Kojobari, Sir."

"Does this Agent Kojobari have insurance?"

"Well, uhh, I'm pretty sure he does."

"Has he signed the required indemnity forms?"

"Uhh, yes, Sir."

Torrance shrugged. "Then I suppose it's time to notify the next-of-kin. Have the standard letter of condolence signed and sent out by Jahid, and so on and so on."

"Sir, he's paralyzed, not deceased."

"Umm…, you know what I mean. Hey, I have something else going on right now. I'll be in touch, Theo."

"Yes, S—"

"Thank you." Torrance cutoff his chief of security and was back into his browser just as fast, where an elderly woman's church hat was being mauled by an ornery kitten. "Hilarious," he mumbled with a chuckle. Yet as much as he tried to distract himself, he was soon back to brooding. It wasn't that he feared being captured for ordering a murder; their tactics were undetectable. And in the event of a suit for negligence, Silver-Stem could definitely afford it. It was more so the feeling from murdering a long-time friend, he couldn't escape; not even the most conniving of criminals could. But then again, he also couldn't help wondering: *Did Kenneth really ever give a shit about me?* A knock on his doorframe was enough to make him shake it all off. "Yes?" he asked at the sight of a lengthy presence standing there, then straightened both his back and collar when he realized it was C.E.O. Al Balushi. "Jahid, come in," he said. "Please, have a seat."

Jahid sat down with an urgent matter in mind. "Some really bad news, right?"

Torrance tipped his head and squinted. "News?"

"About Kenneth!"

He squinted harder. "Kenneth?"

"Yes. Dr. Murphy. Last night Dr. Murphy was in an automobile accident." Jahid paused. "He didn't make it."

Torrance swallowed. "He didn't make it?" He fell back in his chair, a stunned look on his face.

"No. He didn't make it." Jahid paused again. "I'm sorry, Torrance. I assumed you would have been one of the first to hear."

Torrance bit lightly into his own fist, shaking his head. "No," he said, but never did a tear fall, not even a watery eye. He released his fist. "How? Where?"

Jahid shrugged, raised his arms. "I don't know. On his way home, I believe. All I know is what I heard from personnel, and it wasn't much."

Torrance continued to shake his head, speechless, but still no tears.

Jahid thought nothing of it, though. He simply stood up and sighed. "I guess I'll go prepare to pay his family a visit."

Torrance lifted his head, eyes inflated. "You'll what?"

"Pay a visit to his family—to offer the company's condolences. I mean, he was at least a senior officer." Frozen in his stance, Jahid didn't get an immediate response. Instead, he watched Torrance press a button underneath his desk, followed by the office door sliding shut like a standing coffin.

Torrance pointed towards the guest chair, his jaw stern. "Sit back down, Jahid," he commanded. "You're not going anywhere near Kenneth's family."

Jahid was instantly shocked; it wasn't the kind of response he was expecting. "Excuse me."

Torrance gritted. "I said, sit your mother fucking ass back down. Don't forget who put you in your current position—who got you that fat salary after your broke-down ass career was on the fucking slab."

Stunned, Jahid retook his seat. He massaged his brow. "What is it you'd like me to do?"

"Nothing. I will handle the family. *You*—" Torrance paused and pointed at him. "—will go back to your office and continue to play the puppet C.E.O. I hired your ass for. That's what *you're* going to do."

Much like Kenneth, Jahid had been released from his previous job, a government position, but Jahid's release had more to do with improper usage of funds. Silver-Stem was restructuring at that time, the perfect opportunity for Torrance, the then interim C.E.O., to negotiate Jahid away from possible prison time just to run *Torrance's* company. From then on, Jahid knew he wasn't puppet C.E.O. for nothing; he'd become aware Torrance was also misusing funds to finance private projects, as well as lining his own pockets *and* Jahid's. He'd even kept his ears open enough to hear about the odd mix of foreign funds. He then thought about Torrance's fake sympathy a moment ago, his lack of tears, and his sudden aggression, wondering if Kenneth had heard any of the same.

Jahid wanted to remain quiet, to get up and do what Torrance had told him, but puppet or not, with his latest title had come new habits. A resistance to bowing down too easily was one of them, prompting him to question, "Torrance, you didn't have anything to do with this, did you?"

Torrance crunched his eyes with a searing stare. "Jahid, like I said… go back to your office and continue your damn duties, or you're going to find yourself in a very precarious situation. And you wouldn't want anything to happen to your sweet little family, now would you?"

Panicked, Jahid stood up immediately to finish his trip to the door. The room was so silent, he could hear Torrance press the button to allow him out. He heard it again once outside, again followed by the door sealing shut. It was the moment his shoulders sank and he exhaled. He'd been quivering inside ever since the harshness in Torrance's eyes, even before the threat to his family. Behind closed doors, Torrance had always been harsh with him, but never had he appeared so fierce. Jahid had his head down until shocked by a woman's voice.

"Jahid, are you okay?" she asked.

He looked up and noticed Torrance's assistant, Veronica, staring at him, a concerned look on her face. Veronica, a sweet, quiet woman, had been by Torrance's side since the beginning. *How much has she heard over the years?* Jahid wondered. *How much does she know? Has she kept her mouth shut all this time? How much has she profited?* He nodded. "Uhh, yeah. I'm fine," he said tepidly before scurrying away like being chased by an unfed tiger, along with Veronica's eyes on him the entire time until he rounded the corner's wall.

Sitting back in his chief executive office, Jahid was back to massaging his brow, this time, perspiring and wondering, *If this happened to Kenneth, what will Torrance do to me? What will he do to my family?* Sure, he had no real proof Kenneth's death was on Torrance, but he too knew something about their vehicles' remote control features, so the odds were great. Regardless, Jahid had no desire to stick around to find out. He stood up and took a deep breath, grabbed a few personal items, including a flash drive from his drawer, and walked out with a contingency plan in mind. He'd been hanging on to it for times just like this one, when things were to get—too precarious.

It was late in the afternoon, and Torrance had left his own office only three times since Jahid's reluctant exit. Two of those times had included passing by Jahid's office, not to apologize or anything like that, but to see if Jahid could still follow orders. But Torrance wasn't quite sure; neither time was Jahid in. And now, Torrance's door was closed again, and he'd told Veronica to hold all calls. It was time to make a phone call he'd been both dreading and, in a strange way, looking forward to. It was just a matter of finding the right time. After several rings, someone finally picked up.

"Hello," a woman answered.

"Linda?"

It was Linda Murphy, but the silence that followed equaled the time it had taken her to answer, nor did she accept the onscreen visual request. "How did you get my number, Torrance?" Apparently, she recognized his voice instantly.

Torrance's mouth dropped. "Uhh…" Even he realized he wasn't *always* quite the puppet master, not when it came to Linda. "You're listed as next of kin in your husband's personnel file."

"Oh."

The personnel part may have been true, but Torrance was lying. In an immature, prickish move, he'd copied her number from Kenneth's phone one day when Kenneth wasn't looking. "Which brings me to offering my deepest sympathies," he continued, "I am *so* saddened by the news. I've been speechless all day long, and I didn't know when to call you or what to say. Linda, I loved Kenneth like a brother."

"Really."

Torrance heard no sobs in between Linda's words, and no acceptance in her voice. Just raw attitude. "Yes. Really," he said. "Look, where are you right now?"

She paused. "At the morgue."

"At the morgue? My God, have you been there all day? Is someone there with you? Are you alone?"

Another pause, then a huff. "Yes, I'm alone."

"Why don't I meet you there? You don't need to be alone at a time like this."

"I'm fine, Torrance."

"No!" he blurted, suddenly ashamed. "I mean, no. Stay there. I'll meet you there."

"No, Torrance. I said I'm fine. I don't need any company right now. Okay!"

That's when he pulled back, took a pause. "Okay. I understand. It's a very stressful time for you right now, but please let me know if you need anything. Can you do that for me?"

Linda said nothing.

"Linda?" he asked.

"I will let you know," she said with the conviction of a deadbeat parent, then hung up like a deathblow.

Torrance may have still been alive, but his ego now lay flat, bruised and twisted in the dirt. "What was that all about?" he mumbled. He rummaged through a few files on his desk just to save a little face, but he couldn't ignore another escalating problem. He clicked on his desk comm. "Veronica?"

"Yes, Dr. Olivar?"

"Have you seen Jahid?"

"Not since this morning."

"Oh." He tapped his desk. "Just please let me know when you do?"

"Would you like me to find him and ask him to call you?"

"No, just let me know when you see him."

"All righty," she said before disconnecting.

Torrance tapped his desk a little harder, crescendo-ing to a thunderous final slap. "Where in the hell is Jahid?"

Jahid had fought traffic all morning just to get to San Francisco by that afternoon, but first he'd called his wife as soon as he'd started driving from San Jose. "Zahra, I'm going to need you to trust me and not ask any questions," he'd told her. "Do I have your trust?"

His wife, Zahra, had paused. "Yes… but why do you sound so rushed? What's the matter?"

"Jeez, woman, I just said no questions, and you agreed," he'd mumbled before demanding, "I need you pack up and go over to your mother's! I will meet you there later this afternoon!"

"My mother's? What on Earth for? Jahid, please tell me what's the matter!"

"We are going on a trip! I will explain it all to you once we meet at your mother's! Okay?"

"Alright, but—"

Jahid had hung up with no intention to be rude, but he was nerve-wrecked enough already. And he'd made certain he wasn't going to face the same outcome as Kenneth before him, or at least what he'd suspected had happened. The difference now was, Jahid's sons and daughters were either in college or college-age, while the vehicle he was currently driving was his own, no chance of drone interference, but he still kept an occasional eye-out overhead. The kids, he planned on assembling once his escape plan was fully developed.

He parked across the street from San Francisco's F.B.I. office and rushed in, looking back and forth like the unfed tiger was still chasing him. He'd already made a last-minute appointment with Special Agent Garrett Yang, and was soon sitting across from him in Yang's office on the thirteenth floor. Jahid had also purposely decided to go in without an attorney. Afterall, his attorney was as tied to Silver-Stem as he was.

Jahid pulled the flash drive from his pocket and reached it forward, and Garrett reached forward to receive it. "What do we have here, Dr. Al Balushi?" Garrett asked.

Garrett was much younger with quick reflexes, but not quick enough to grab it before Jahid retracted it. "On this drive," said Jahid, the drive held in the air, "is everything you need to know about Silver-Stem's improprieties and violations. Or should I say, Dr. Torrance Olivar's improprieties and violations."

"Is that right?"

"Yes."

"Okay, I see you want to hang onto that drive, so why don't you just tell me what's going on?"

Jahid's eyes went wide as he introduced the circumstances, concluding with, "I'm talking multiple millions in misappropriated funds, non-reported funding, and illegal projects—all instigated by one man—Dr. Torrance Olivar—all on this drive. But first, before I handover anything, I will need protection for my family. Complete protection! And I will need complete immunity, as well."

Garrett leaned back in his chair and folded his hands over his mouth. "It's evident you've been watching quite a bit of television, Dr. Al Balushi. And by 'complete protection,' I assume you mean witness protection and relocation...?"

Jahid nodded with force. "I sure am. And this is no joke or fantasy, Agent Yang."

"Right. My apologies. But are you sure what you have on that drive warrants such a... reaction?"

"I am absolutely certain. These are some very dangerous characters we're dealing with here. Not just Silver-Stem, but foreign entities as well. It involves the Millennium Droid, Edition-D project too, and there are *billions* involved! And you know how people get when there's this much money at stake."

"Indeed."

"And this man, Dr. Olivar, has made serious threats against my family! Just this morning!"

"*Threats*?"

"Yes! He has threatened my family!"

Garrett pointed at the drive. "Is it on there?"

"No. But I wouldn't be here otherwise."

"You wouldn't?"

"No! Because up until now, he'd only made threats against *me*. Threats to keep *me* silent. But once he involved my family, I had no choice but to act.

"I see."

"I also believe Dr. Olivar is responsible for the recent death of Dr. Kenneth Murphy. Just last night!"

"Excuse me. Dr…?"

"Dr. Kenneth Murphy. By Torrance's reaction this morning, I know he had something to do with it. I know him."

Garrett jotted the name down. "I'm not familiar with… Dr. Ken—Anyway, that's a serious allegation, Doctor." He pointed at the drive again. "Is there any of what you're saying *now* on that drive?"

"No, but I'm sure there's enough proof on here to lead you to a sound motive."

"We'll keep it in mind," Garrett said, "and we definitely are already aware of the Millennium Droid project." He leaned forward and held out a cupped hand. "So, if there's any merit to what you're saying, we should have no problem working out a witness protection and relocation plan."

Jahid advanced the drive forward, but retracted it again. "And immunity?"

"Why, are you directly involved in anything on there?"

"No, but I do not want anything to be… misconstrued."

Garrett's eyes rolled slightly. "Very well. Immunity."

Garrett wasn't far from the truth before; when at home, Jahid was definitely a "hound" for a good legal or crime story, the reason he reached and retracted the drive one more time. "In writing?" Jahid asked with a near grin.

"Yes, Dr. Al Balushi. We will be able to draft up a letter for you—*after* we get a good look at what's on that drive. You have my word."

With a sigh, Jahid finally handed over the drive like it was his last credit, and wisely not his only copy.

Chapter 32

Torrance hadn't seen Jahid since their flare-up, more of a dilemma for Torrance since Jahid hadn't shown up to work in days. But in truth, it only ended up being a mild annoyance for Torrance, who may have lost his puppet and bullet vest, but had gained the freedom to air his true self. With a small board of directors in his hands like puddy, he had gone on to freely announce to key staff that he would be filling Jahid's role as C.E.O. until further notice. His explanation was simply that Jahid was on indefinite leave to deal with family matters.

As time passed, almost two weeks after the flare-up, Torrance left work early to pay someone a special visit. He stood underneath Linda Murphy's portico, down to his last press on her doorbell when the door opened to a rather large older gentleman.

"Can I help you?" the man asked with a barrel of a voice.

Torrance's eyes flared. "Mr. Royston, how are you? We've met—I mean, I saw you at the funeral."

Mr. Royston, Linda's father, tilted his head with a blank stare.

"I'm Dr. Torrance Olivar." Torrance reached out and shook Mr. Royston's hand. "A friend of Kenneth's." He was actually nervous, but his handshake was firm.

"A doctor?"

"Yes. Linda said it would be fine to stop by to check on her—to see if everything is okay."

Mr. Royston gasped. "My daughter? Is she alright? She hasn't told me anything about being ill!"

Torrance covered his own heart. "Oh, I'm so sorry! I'm not *that* kind of doctor. Kenneth and I were friends and coworkers. I'm a friend of the family."

Mr. Royston exhaled blaringly. "Oh, thank God!" He reached out for another handshake. "Burgess Royston's the name."

"Nice to officially meet you, Sir." Their hands met again.

"Well, she's not here right now."

Torrance stepped back; his head dropped like a sinking ship.

Burgess opened the door wider. "Tell you what, would you like to come in anyway? She's out and about with her mother. They should be back real soon, though."

"Ohh…, I don't want to impose, Mr. Royston."

"Nonsense! It's not an imposition at all. Come on in." Burgess wrapped his massive hand around Torrance's shoulder and ushered him inside.

Torrance entered with too many concealed emotions to count. It was the first time he'd been back since their couples' dinner months ago, and now, it took a major effort to suppress what he'd done to return. He had already convinced himself on the way over—*having Kenneth killed was a necessary means to an end, the natural order of things*.

"Have a seat, young man," Burgess offered. "Can I get you a drink?" He headed to the bar with the swagger of a nightclub host.

Torrance took a seat on the sofa, the very spot where Kenneth had sat those months ago. "No, thank you, Sir. I have to get back to work at some point."

Burgess was behind the bar already, placing a lineup on the countertop. "Water? Soda?"

Torrance shrugged his chin. "I imagine a soda wouldn't be much harm." He knew it would be, but it was a fair compromise, as he saw it.

"Ice?"

"Sure."

Burgess fixed him a glass of iced soda, and a glass of straight whiskey, neat, for himself. He handed Torrance his drink and sat down in the nearby guest chair.

"By the way, I'm so sorry for your loss," Torrance started.

"Yep. Tough times, tough times. So sudden. And just when you think these new, high-tech vehicles are so safe, this happens."

Torrance shook his head, eyes filled with sorrow. "Yes… nothing's perfect."

"After the funeral, the Mrs. and I decided to stick around a little while to help Linda and the kids get through this."

Torrance quickly switched to a nod. "Mighty kind of you."

"Yeah… She wants the kids to finish the school semester before she decides what to do next."

"What to do next?"

"Yeah. She already wants to get back to work, because although the insurance may be nice, it ain't gonna last forever. Darla and I—Darla, that's her mother—we'd love to see her come back to Reno with us. Give us a chance to spend more time with the kids and all."

"That sounds nice. But you know, Silver-Stem will take care of her as long as she needs—in addition to the insurance. I'll make sure of that."

Burgess leaned back with a suspicious squint. "You will, huh?"

"Sure. And if she really wants to get back to work, I know for a fact how highly qualified she is. We'll have a pretty nice job waiting for her in either sales or marketing." Torrance paused, realizing a conflict brewing just by the crevice in Burgess's brow. "That's only *if* she decides not to go back to Reno. That would be her choice—your choice—uhh, you all's choice."

"Is that right?"

"Yes, Sir."

Burgess took a sip of whiskey. "You seem pretty confident about all this. So, how can you be so sure?"

"Oh. I happen to be the C.E.O." Torrance heaved his chest slightly, regrowing accustomed to the "official" title.

"C.E.O.?" Burgess sat back and stroked his chin. "You don't say…"

"And Reno's not *that* far away."

"Hmm."

Interrupted by a door opening and bags rattling, both men set their glasses down and stood up when Linda and her mother entered the foyer. One of two bags actually fell from Linda's hands when she looked up into the living room, while her mother stood with a blank look on her face.

"Baby," Burgess blared at Linda, "your friend got here early, so I invited him in for a drink!" He looked at Torrance and muttered, "What did you say your name was, young man?"

"Torrance."

Burgess turned back to Linda. "Yeah! Torrance!"

"Torrance, that's nice. Good to see you," Linda said in a tone of raw indifference. She lifted her fallen bag and headed towards the kitchen."

Darla Royston, one bag in hand, stared with her mouth open; she didn't budge. "*Friend*?"

"A friend of Kenneth's, darling," Burgess clarified.

"Oh!"

Darla had just begun shuffling in their direction when suddenly halted by Linda's voice. "Mom! Could you come in here, please!" Linda shouted. "Now!"

"Ope!" Darla shook, then shuffled into the kitchen instead.

The men sat back down and continued their conversation, Burgess being the most curious. "So, just what kind of things are you guys doing over there at Silver-Stem?"

Torrance grabbed his glass. "Well, what I can tell you is…." When it came to the company, Torrance was like a ready-made commercial, as natural as his puppet predecessor. He went on to highlight their most notable stem-cell developments to Burgess, who sat nodding with eyes opening wider to each one.

The men's conversation went on a few more minutes until Linda walked quietly through the room, taking Torrance's attention with her like a passing storm. "Excuse me, Dad, do you mind if I borrow Torrance for a minute?"

Burgess sat to attention. "Uhh…"

"Thank you." She kept walking to the foyer. "Torrance, you mind meeting me outside? Now."

"Sure." Torrance stood up and set his glass back down, turning briefly to Burgess. "Excuse me, Mr. Royston. I'll be right back."

Once outside, Linda walked all the way to the sidewalk, where she folded her arms and waited for Torrance to arrive.

"What's up?" Torrance asked.

Linda huffed. "Torrance, what are you doing here?"

He shrugged, lifted his hands. "I… was… checking in on you, like I told you."

Her eyes bucked. "Like you told me? What are you talking about?"

"Like I told you yesterday." He stared as if she'd forgotten.

"You mean the voicemail you left for me? The voicemail I never responded to? Is that what you're talking about?"

"I see you remember."

"Oh, my God!" she yelled, then caught herself. "Look, Torrance, I don't mean to be rude, but—" She hit brakes. "You know what? I *do* mean to be rude." She aimed her finger a hair away from his chest, gritting. "I don't want you coming around me, my parents, or my children ever again."

He jittered his hands in the air. "Whoa, whoa… What's with all the animosity? Hm?"

"'What's with all the animosity'! I'll tell you 'what's with all the animosity.' I know you had something to do with Kenneth's death."

"What! Are you serious?"

She responded with a grimacing glare.

"What on Earth would make you say that? I loved Kenneth. I told you—like a brother. And Kenneth died in a single car accident! How could I have possibly had anything to do with that?"

This time, she jabbed her finger into his chest, repeatedly. "He told me, before the accident, that *you* were the one who'd gotten him into some kind of trouble."

Torrance acted shocked.

"Yes, you!"

"Linda, there was no kind of trouble Kenneth or I was in," he urged. "I don't know what you're talking about!"

Both looked back towards the house, where the Roystons' faces were plastered to the front window, vanishing a split second later behind waving drapes.

Linda turned back and massaged her veining brow. "You know what? I don't care if you don't know what I'm talking about. I don't want you around here again! Do you understand me?"

His mouth agape, Torrance had nothing but air to respond with, to which Linda turned and stormed back to the house.

"But your father," he finally said. "I was supposed to finish—"

"Just leave, Torrance!"

Those were the last words Torrance heard from Linda's mouth. He threw his hands up like the white flag, dropping his head on his way back to his vehicle.

Linda didn't even bother watching Torrance drive off as she stomped back towards the house. She battered her way inside and slammed the door, fuming over the last several minutes. Meanwhile, Burgess and Darla stood huddled in the nearby living room like frightened puppies. Linda had plenty to say, but paced the foyer first before entering the living room. She swiped her hair back and huffed.

"Honey, you alright?" Darla asked.

"I'm fine, Mom," said Linda, "but Da-*ad*, why did you let that man in this house?"

"What?" Burgess's look was incredulous.

Linda stopped and propped her fists on her waist. "Didn't you let that man into this house?"

"Well, yeah, but—"

"You didn't even know who he was!"

"Yes, I did! He told me who he was!"

"But when we came in, you didn't even know his name!"

"He said he was Kenneth's friend and co-worker! A doctor! A C.E.O.! A stand-up guy, for God's sake! I didn't have to know his name!"

"A stand-up guy, huh?" She rolled her eyes. "He really must have had you on a string."

Burgess held up his palm. "Wait a minute now, Linda. This man said he and the company could take care of you for a long time… Can even give you a great job if you want it. Think about what this man can do for you and the kids!"

By this time, both of Linda's hands were cupped over her mouth. "Oh, my God! I can't believe you! That is so em-barrassing! You were actually plotting my family's future with *that* man?" She was now pointing to the front.

"Well, I wasn't the one who started it! Plus, I figure a man who can take care of you for life can't be all that bad. A good-looking fellow too! You know, Kenneth was cool and all, but—"

"Burgess!" Darla blurted in. "Don't you dare!"

"What!"

"It's too soon!"

"Ooh!" Fuming mad, Linda turned and stormed out of the room, leaving her parents behind, especially Burgess. "Never—let him—in this house—again!" she commanded.

Darla gazed up at her husband as Linda stomped up the stairs. "I think she's talking about you," she told him quietly.

Burgess smacked his lips. "I don't think so."

"She should be."

Torrance was in auto-drive mode on his way back to Silver-Stem, plenty of time to brood over two of the roughest weeks he'd seen in a long time, ending with the piercing but accurate accusations he'd just received from Linda. He thought back to Kenneth's memorial service, when it seemed Linda was doing everything in her power to avoid him. *It all makes sense now. She knew something.* He shook his head. *But how* much *does she know?* He couldn't begin to fathom, but if Linda knew the complete story, his next move was expected to be far more gut-wrenching than the first. Then there was the matter of Jahid. Like, "Where in the hell is he?" Torrance mumbled to himself. He had even had his own agents sent out to investigate, coming up empty on finding Jahid or any of his close family members. *If I don't hear anything from him by tomorrow, I'm going to have to assume—* "What the fuck?" Twenty feet from turning into the company's parking lot, his car came to a screeching stop, cutoff by another vehicle within his bumper's sensor range. By the time Torrance recognized the Department of Justice logo on the door, another vehicle had pulled to a screeching halt behind him. It was the F.B.I.

Chapter 33

Torrance had trailed one of the D.O.J. vehicles to an F.B.I. field office in San Jose, followed closely by the other one. Once there, he was escorted into a small conference room for a face-to-face with Special Agent Garrett Yang, and Agent Ricks, an older guy, as witness. It was an unusual process, but Torrance had put up no resistance to the manner in which he'd been taken. The field agents who'd escorted him in had made it clear he wasn't under arrest—said they'd needed him to come with them to clear up a few things about Silver-Stem's operations. *Right*, he'd thought, but had offered nothing that would highlight his guilt, like calling his attorney or anything of that nature. "Sure," Torrance had told them, "anything to help our *bosses*."

"But the ambush was a bit much," he now told Agent Yang from across the conference table. Torrance's demeanor was ice cube cold from the start, not his typical relaxed self; he was more like a "pre-trial" version of himself. And he no longer had to wonder about Jahid's whereabouts; a log cabin in the Montana woods was his best guess.

Garrett Yang thumbed through a file folder full of printed pages in front of him, while Agent Ricks sat by with arms folded. "Dr. Olivar," Garrett said, "what I have here are several files with communications between you and foreign enterprises regarding the transfer of significant funds to your Millennium Droid program, a program which has far surpassed the ten-percent ceiling imparted by the United States of America. Said funding has apparently also been gathered without notifying the overseeing government agency, which is also a stipulation in the contract. Do you agree to having knowledge of these communications or transfers?"

Torrance finger-tapped his cheek. "May I take a look?"

"Be my guest." Garrett handed the folder over.

"Thank you." Torrance took hold and flipped through, sheet-by-sheet. "I am definitely aware of the Millennium Droid program. I am—*was* the program overseer at that time, and I must say, I *have* been in on conversations and communications in the past, but these recent ones, I have no knowledge of."

Garrett turned a shrewd glare. "No knowledge of? Not even as a managing *director*?"

"Agent Yang, I have given several management staffers the authority to speak on my behalf—a duty delegated to them. Apparently, someone has done so without clarifying or making it known to me. This would be my best guess. But if not, that leaves only one other person as a suspect."

"Who?"

Torrance closed the folder and slid it back to Garrett. "Dr. Jahid Al Balushi."

"Dr. Al Balushi? As in your C.E.O., Dr. Al Balushi?"

"The one and only. I actually happen to be the *acting* C.E.O. at this point, but back then, I did whatever Dr. Al Balushi instructed me to do. If he said, 'Keep working on a project,' I kept working on the project. I was never made aware of all the rules involved or all the disclosures necessary."

Garrett shook the folder. "But there are also various agreements signed by you."

Torrance raised a brow. "Regarding the Millennium Droid Program?"

"No, but regarding various agreements in violation of the Artificial Intelligence Act of 2042."

"Hmm…," Torrance pondered. "Well, like I said, if so, I did what I was told." He was also keenly aware Agent Yang had neglected to ask about his role as acting C.E.O., and didn't seem the least bit surprised—more proof Jahid had been there before Torrance. *The fucker probably sat in this same damn chair.*

"You're trying to tell me that years and years on the job, totaling *billions* of credits in transactions, you never thought to question anything before signing?"

Torrance shrugged. "There were some I protested, but to no avail. What else was I to do?"

Garrett went speechless, shaking his head, while Agent Ricks remained silent, arms still folded.

"And do you mean to tell me that Dr. Al Balushi's signature is not on *any* documents *anywhere*?" Torrance asked before leaning forward, unable to resist a little prodding. "And I suppose by his mysterious disappearance, he's been the first to point the finger, hasn't he?"

"I can neither confirm nor deny any of that," Garrett said. "And we're the ones asking the questions, Dr. Olivar."

"Mm hm." After a few seconds of victory, Torrance was on the verge of rising from his seat. "Well, if I've served you well today, and I am not being detained, excuse me if I get back to the office to at least try to clear up this matt—"

Garrett raised a finger. "Just a second, Doc." He lifted the folder and pulled out one sheet. "There's a number of projects that also clearly violate the Artificial Intelligence Act. How would you explain these, Doctor?" He handed it over.

Torrance sat back and placed his hand over his mouth. He studied the sheet almost as long as he'd reviewed the entire folder before. "I recognize these project numbers. You know,

I believe these are Dr. Murphy's projects. Yeah, that's right. These *are* Dr. Murphy's projects."

"*Dr. Murphy's?*"

"Yes."

"As in Dr. Kenneth Murphy? The one who recently died in a car accident?"

"Unfortunately, yes." Torrance sank his chair. "A very sad day for us all. But regarding these projects, these were his pet projects, and Kenneth had complete free reign to execute them as he saw fit. In fact, he had me convinced he'd gotten the proper approval to implement these projects."

"And did you ever check?"

"Check on *Kenneth*? Nope. His reputation alone had everyone's complete trust."

"You mean to say, Dr. Murphy was one of your subordinates and you had no control over his actions?"

Torrance raised a finger and wagged it at Garrett. "That's where you're wrong, Agent Yang. Kenneth and I were practically equals, parallel in the chain of command. I mean, I may have had seniority, but like I said, he had free reign, particularly in the form of Dr. Al Balushi's confidence, if that means anything to you..."

"And just what is that supposed to mean to me?"

"I don't know, but there's something else... when I think about it."

"Which is?"

"I noticed that Kenneth kept most of his projects on his own personal computer. Not normally advised or allowed, but being the eccentric genius he was, who was I to mess with his mojo? Plus, I had no clue of what deal he and Dr. Al Balushi had worked out. But when you really think about it, what better way to keep us, as a company, from retrieving any data—dare I say, *stolen* data, if anything were to go sideways."

"Hmph," was Garrett's reaction, while Agent Ricks shifted in his chair for the very first time.

"And there was something else about Kenneth, himself."

Garrett spoke with his eyes this time, both open in wait.

"I'd known Kenneth Murphy for a *long* time," Torrance obliged, "and the Kenneth I knew was a very competitive man. There's no telling what lengths he may have gone through to be number one, or to make it to the top."

"No way of telling? Why don't you try…"

"It's hard to explain, but I'm sure there are several people in the company who would concur."

"Hmm… Interesting."

Torrance wavered the sheet. "And I'm also sure what you're seeking here is on his personal computer—at his home." He placed it on the table and stood up. "If you don't mind, I'd like to get back to the office within a reasonable hour, and if possible, try to iron out some of this for you. You have my word, Agent Yang."

Garrett looked up and nodded. "What we'll do, Dr. Olivar, is have an official letter drafted with all the specifics and requirements for your response. Then, you will have sufficient time to research and address every single item. If your responses and backup are to our satisfaction, we're all good. If not, I hate to imagine where we may meet again."

"Wherever that may be, Agent Yang, I will surely be accompanied by Dr. Al Balushi. As acting C.E.O., I am certain we will find his signature on just as many agreements as me, if not more."

Garrett said nothing to this, but added, "In the mean-time, Doctor, I suggest you don't leave the country for any rea-son."

"But I have a few trips planned in the near future."

Garrett stood up and opened his hands. "Perhaps you can... delegate them."

After being escorted by Garrett to the elevator, Torrance rode down by himself with a timebomb ticking inside. He was hoping he could have held on to the news about what was on Kenneth's computer. It was the least he could have done to leave Linda with some degree of respect for her husband's name, especially since Torrance, himself, was the one responsible. It had happened the night of their couples' dinner party, when Torrance was upstairs by himself, closed up in Kenneth's study as he uploaded the files to Kenneth's computer. Torrance had hoped the need would have been nullified once Kenneth had been shut up for good—the recent car accident. But now—*How fortuitous*. He went on to wonder about the Millennium project; how was he going to handle it? Considering his latest admission as Plan B, he was now weighing Plan C, another one that was already complete and waiting in a secret location.

The two F.B.I. agents went back into the small conference room afterwards, where Garrett reclaimed his chair and leaned back. Agent Ricks, the man who served as most young agents' senior advisor, took another seat on the other side of the table. Both were from the San Francisco office, but this room in San Jose, now with door closed, was theirs for the entire workday.

"So, what do you think?" Garrett asked.

Agent Ricks tugged on his chin a few times. "First of all, why haven't we just raided the whole damn place yet?"

Garrett huffed. "Believe me, I've tried, but it seems Silver-Stem's accomplishments in stem-cell research keeps them above certain aspects of the law. The read-and-response letter was the best I was able to get approved."

"Oh. Isn't that just brilliant," Ricks said on a sour note. "Well then, aside from a few shaky points, a little teetering back and forth here and there, most of what he said actually sounds plausible."

"What! How do you figure?"

"Well first, he could be right about the nature of his prior position—doing and signing whatever he was commanded to. That's always been the nature of the corporate structure, right? And I wasn't around when Dr. Al Balushi showed up on your doorstep, but if he felt the walls caving in on him, this could very well be a case of: 'he who smelt first, dealt first.'"

Garrett folded his arms. He looked to the recessed ceiling lights, but with thoughts somewhere beyond.

"But *you* sure don't seem so convinced," Ricks commented.

"I'm not. Something about that man… too icy, too calculated, too prepared—as if he's had this all mapped out before it happened."

"And if he and Al Balushi are at 'war,' being prepared may serve him well."

Garrett sighed. "I don't know. And what do you think of his story about his friend, Dr. Murphy?"

Ricks shrugged his chin, bobbed his head. "Hmm…," he seemed to hang onto the possibilities like a family heirloom. "I can't dispute it," was his conclusion.

Garrett shrugged right back at him. "Why, because dead men don't talk?" Ricks was on the verge of a chuckle as Garrett continued, "And he remembers the numbers from Dr.

Murphy's projects like his own phone digits, but has a selective memory when it comes to his own Millennium project! How convenient was that!"

"Well, he is a scientist. He could be a numbers guy, not a policy guy."

Garrett jabbed his finger in the direction of the elevator. "Did *that guy* strike you as a 'numbers guy'? If you ask me, I'd say Dr. Olivar is the overly competitive one. And why are you trying to take up for him anyway, Ricks?"

Ricks reared back and jittered his hands in the air. "*Heyyyy*, I'm just trying to get you to see all sides of the coin— not to get too locked in on one theory. Could get you blindsided, that's all."

On that note, Garrett reached for the folder and pulled it closer, opened it and withdrew the project sheet again. He stared at it for nearly a minute, then sighed. "As bogus as I think his bullshit claim about Dr. Murphy is, we have no choice but to look into it."

It took two whole days for Linda to calm her nerves after Torrance had ambushed her dad. Valium, extra snacks and double the wine were all used at some point to take the edge off. She stopped in front of the hall mirror and pinched her waistline, disgusted; she'd gained at least two pounds. "Shit," she mumbled just before the doorbell rang. "I got it!" she yelled to her parents, who were both in the living room, reading, but slowed down two steps away from the door. *Oh no*, she fretted, afraid of the peephole. *He's back*. Just the thought of Torrance's return folded her over into a cringe; her insides started to churn. The bell rang again. She stepped up and finally leaned into the peephole, seeing a small group, men and women, standing on the lawn from the portico to the sidewalk. All dressed in dark clothes and blue jackets, they were quite intimidating, but far less gut-curdling than Torrance. "Who is it?" Linda shouted.

"F.B.I., Ma'am," the man in the front announced.

"Who?" She'd heard them clearly, but couldn't believe it.

"F.B.I., Ma'am! We have a warrant to search the premises!"

By this time, her parents had ditched their books and drifted close to the foyer, eyes wide and shoulder-to-shoulder. "What is it, honey?" Burgess asked her.

"I don't know," she said and cracked open the door. "Excuse me?" she asked the front man, who gave her a good view of his credentials.

"Good morning," he greeted. "Mrs. Murphy?"

"Uhh, yes."

"I'm Special Agent Garrett Yang of the F.B.I. We have a warrant to search the premises for digital evidence." In his other hand was the warrant, which he handed to her. "This copy is for you to read through, but in the meantime, we're going to have to ask you to step aside."

"But, but—shouldn't I have a chance to read this first?"

"Linda, what's wrong?" she heard her mother say.

"Who's in the house with you, Ma'am?" Garrett asked Linda.

"Uhh, just my parents."

"Any pets?"

"No. No pets." She was already studying the warrant through all his questions.

"Sorry, Ma'am," he said, politely pressing the door open and entering. "For the sake of time, we're going to need to get started right away." Now inside, he glanced at her parents. "And we're going to have to ask you to stand over there by your parents and stay there until we're finished. We won't be long."

After complying, Linda watched five agents follow Garrett inside. From closets to sofa cushions, from curtains to the backside of hung paintings, from end table drawers to the pantry, they all rummaged around in search of "digital evidence."

Garrett approached Linda. "Where might we find personal computers, Mrs. Murphy?"

"I, I, I," was all Linda could utter.

Garrett shook his head and pointed upward. "Upstairs," he commanded two of his team, who followed him up the stairs.

Linda turned to her parents with her mouth pressed into her knuckles, both hands. "You see what I told you?" she griped, a question aimed mostly in Burgess's direction. "One visit from Torrance and all hell breaks loose," she said quietly. "This is all his fault; Kenneth told me so just before the accident. The man is freaking toxic, Dad."

Moments later, Garrett came downstairs with a laptop computer in a plastic bag. He headed to the door.

"Hey, wait a minute!" Linda shouted at him. "That's my husband's computer! Where are you going with that?" She ripped and clawed into the air, having to be wrestled back by Burgess just to keep from attacking Garrett. "You bring that back!"

Garrett handed Kenneth's laptop to one of his agents who was just outside the door. "Take this," he said, then turned back to Linda. "Don't worry, Mrs. Murphy. All personal, non-case-related information will be held confidential."

"Case!" she yelled. "What case?"

He tipped his head. "We'll be in touch." And it was back to the job at hand. "Okay, guys? Wrap it up!"

Nothing he'd said made Linda feel any more secure, but she was fortunate most of her disheveled furnishings were returned as is—most of them. She was also fortunate the children were in school at the time, and their own devices with them. But her final challenge came when another agent descended the stairs with another laptop, in another plastic bag.

"Wait!" Linda yelled, still held back by her father. "That one's mine!"

Chapter 34

Roberta opened her eyes after a recharging slumber on a sturdy wicker settee. She awoke to plants and flowers hanging from both wall and ceiling, only a few shy of Mildred's shop. And there was Mildred, stirring about a kitchen island just a few feet away, her belly already starting to show. The way the daylight poured through a set of sliding glass doors, Mildred swayed in the wreath of a full-body halo. No, this wasn't a dream or a fantasy for Roberta; nor was Mildred's birth cycle accelerated beyond the human norm. It was now months after John Consuela had successfully gotten them across the U.S./Mexican border, and in that time, Roberta's own system had autonomously figured out a way to escape the virus. It was called, "death." Not like an ordinary computer shutdown, but a core deactivation so deep, all corrupted and viral codes were dissolved with it. Once reactivated, her shielded backup system had gone to work, restoring her code and memories. And when Roberta had awoken, she was virus-free in the arms of Mildred, who'd watched Roberta's melanin slowly return in full. It wasn't until Keneisha had made it across the border was Roberta's internal rebuild complete.

After all were reunited, Mildred's little miracle remained healthy inside and on schedule, and she couldn't have found a better midwife than Roberta—the knowledge of an M.D. and a roboticist wrapped in one. But Mexico ended up not being their final destination. Today, from inside a two-level Cape Town condo, its balcony overlooking South Africa's Hout Bay, Roberta stretched and yawned from her settee. "How long have I been out?"

A spatula in one hand and a big spoon in the other, Mildred was preparing both patties and ground meat. Burgers and burritos were one of her known favorites. She had told Roberta many times that cooking the old-fashioned way, skillet and pan over burners, was her mild protest to a full droidic lifestyle. But it was tough to hide her true essence as she simultaneously flipped patties and stirred beef with razor-sharp precision, then spoke, "Roberta, why do you ever have to ask that question?"

The meaty aroma did nothing for Roberta, who sighed while still on her back. "I don't know. I suppose it's the customary thing to ask when waking up at one-forty-two p.m." Her internal clock was functioning to standard spec, and military if needed. She sat up and stared through the glass doors across the room, through the balcony's steel railing. Bordered by mountainous terrain, the bay carried micro-waves inward towards the beach. But Roberta's eyes landed on an arbitrary point on the horizon, where they remained for nearly a minute. "I have to take a trip," she said bluntly.

Mildred had begun loading a plate. "A trip?"

"For a few days."

"Out of the country?"

"Yes."

"You think that's a wise move right now?"

"I think it's a necessary one. I also think Colonel Livingston is more than capable of keeping an eye on you for the short time I'll be gone."

"Well, I'm not talking about me." Mildred aimed her spatula in Roberta's direction. "I'm talking about you. I'm not the one crossing national borders."

"I hear you. I'll be careful."

Mildred tipped her head with a furrowed brow. "May I ask *where*, exactly?"

Roberta stood completely up, no longer a groggy mess. "I can't say."

"Hmmm… well, I'm not your keeper. You're a grown woman. But you *will* at least be back for the…?" Mildred's eyes flared wide as she circled her belly with the tips of all five fingers.

"Of course. If I leave now, I should be back long before you get too far into your third trimester."

Mildred's first burger was dressed and in her mouth by now. "You plan on taking Keneisha?" she muffled.

"Yes." As much as Roberta had been bedding on the sofa, she did have her own bedroom, where she was now on her way. "But just to the airport!"

"Hold on. You're talking about right *now*!"

Roberta didn't wait; nor did she slowdown. "Yes!"

"Then at least let me drive you to the airport!" she heard Mildred shout from the kitchen.

"That's okay! We'll be fine! Keneisha can find her way back!"

And with a little more expansion to her ear canal, she heard Mildred's muffled response clearly: "Okay… suit your-self."

The two had long ago come to terms with the conditions of their new arrangement, starting with avoiding all contact with Mildred's parents and Lauren, whose identities Roberta had dis-closed to Mildred shortly after crossing the border. Crushed at first, Mildred eventually buried her anguish so deep, very few memories had ever come up in conversation. Roberta, nonethe-less, had convinced her that attempts at contact would be made once all external threats were somehow extinguished. It was actually the shame of never having had the chance to contact Sterling's mother that Mildred had expressed the most, second only to the fact that neither she nor Roberta had found anything written about Sterling's death, not even on the internet.

Roberta, dressed in a dark gray jumpsuit, carried only a small duffle bag with her to Keneisha, who was parked out front just off the street. But Roberta's senses were telling her she was being watched. *Assess*. With the balcony on the frontside, she glanced back and saw Mildred posted behind the sliding doorway along the edge, her arms folded with a suspicious look on her face. It didn't take a droidic brain to figure out what Mildred must have been thinking, and it wasn't pleasant.

"Hello, Roberta," Keneisha greeted once Roberta was in the vehicle.

Roberta scooted around in the backseat until she found the optimal vantage point. "Hello, Keneisha. It's time for the airport."

"At your wish."

Her body in a new skin of midnight blue, Keneisha backed out and flowed forward, a ride so smooth, there wasn't enough noise to distract Roberta from her thoughts. Roberta had never, until now, hidden anything from Mildred. She never even had to pretend to like or even digest human food to fit in. The two were now like sisters, orphans, as they described it, with new identities and the same last name to ensure it. The airport was just far enough away to recall the several factors that had led Roberta to this point:

> Part of Protocol Darkest Hour included hiding out with John Consuela's relatives in Hermisillo, Mexico, where they stayed only until their new identities came through. A delay was on account of Mildred, an unforeseen variable

in their equation. This did, however, give Roberta plenty of time to recover. Along with Roberta's new identity came a substantial bank account already setup in her new name, Maria Alvarez, one of more than 100,000 Maria Alvarezes in Mexico. And Mildred became Laila Alvarez. It was a good plan, but Roberta saw its flaws almost immediately. For instance, many people of African descent had moved to Mexico by the 2060s, but still not enough to truly get lost in the crowd. The "motherland" was Roberta's adjustment, and her own contact was to take over from there.

Colonel Livingston, Roberta's former XO, was now living in South Africa, where he'd started his own private ops company. He showed no hesitation in accepting Roberta, Mildred and Keneisha under his protection. He didn't even need to know Mildred's exact situation. "I don't give a flyin' cow chip who in the hell she is," was his response to Roberta's proposition. "As long as I can get you back on my squad, Roberta, she can stay forever." But Roberta's active duty wasn't to truly start until after the baby's delivery; this was her addendum. So, once the flight from Mexico City had eventually landed in Cape Town, Protocol Darkest Hour was now officially in Roberta's hands. Her first task was another name change, a more appropriate one. The question now was: *Who killed Kenneth Murphy?*

Roberta started with hacking into police records for the accident's forensics. Skid marks indicated the speed, braking time and point at which the vehicle had flipped. And she had gained more benefits than not from her time behind the Fire-Kraken's wall. Mildred and the Morehouse's files had come with a host of incidental files, including detailed information about company vehicles and their remote-control anti-theft features, making murder a distinct possibility. But the covertly funded files found on Kenneth's personal laptop under F.B.I. warrant diverted all attention away from the accident. Of course, Linda stood up for him. She claimed he'd been setup by Torrance, but evidence otherwise was too complete and decisive.

Torrance, who may not have been found liable for his part in Kenneth's death, was still dealt a crucial blow by Jahid's testimony in court. Although all the Russian-based files had been scrubbed clean, Jahid had double-downed on his promise to the F.B.I. He reemerged with double the evidence against Torrance, evidence he had collected over time, proving that not only was Torrance in conspiracy with the Russians, but he had personally accumulated hundreds of millions in illegal funds. His discovered hidden accounts said so. But no matter how much Jahid had cooperated with the F.B.I., no matter how much he'd negotiated immunity, he couldn't prevent his own bank accounts from being seized, or his post-degrees from being stripped. Meanwhile, collateral participants such as Chief Agent Adams and Theo Matsui remained free with only fines and probation, but Torrance was the only one who now resided in a federal penitentiary as chief conspirator.

Kenneth's reputation seemed unsalvageable from it all, and Roberta could barely stand it. She'd run all the scenarios and personality profiles, arriving at Linda's claim being the most viable. With her maker's name buried in dishonor, Roberta was left with a mountain of evidence to discredit. Her upcoming flight was now her best chance to do it, and by the time Keneisha rolled to a stop at the airport's curbside, Roberta had completely changed clothes. "Keneisha?"

"Yes, Roberta?"

With powder mirror in hand, Roberta smacked her lips until her lipstick popped. "Mildred is most likely going to ask you where I'm going. When she does, tell her you have no idea, okay?"

There was a pause, flickering dash-lights moved from side to side as usual. "This will not be difficult to do—since it is the truth. I have no idea where you are going. Only assumptions based on your departure terminal and gates."

"Exactly. And you're not to tell her this either. 'Confidential' will be your response. Got it?"

"Yes. I understand."

Roberta's trip required the look of a woman, not an off-duty soldier. So, she strutted through the airport in blue jeans, highheels, a simple blouse, and a suede jacket. Her hair had already been trimmed nearly down to the scalp. These changes were simple, but other measures were needed to better conceal her identity, starting with a slight facial restructuring. Kenneth had given her the ability to inflate or deflate any feature to a minimal degree, at any time. A little adjustment to her nose, a slight lip puff, light adjustments to a few orbital bones, even a mild change in complexion, and she was instantly a magnificent African beauty for the day, along with her new identity to match.

"Your flight will be leaving from Gate Ten in one hour and ten minutes, Ms. Khumalo," the ticket counter attendant informed her.

Chapter 35

The efficiency of passenger jets in the mid-twenty-first century had taken Roberta, a.k.a. Amara Khumalo, straight from Cape Town to Atlanta, Georgia. It was the home of a long-established federal penitentiary, where she sat in patient wait for a key suspect-turned-prisoner. Separated by a reinforced window and partitioned sidewalls, she clicked on the intercom when he was brought in, soon face-to-face with Torrance Olivar. Torrance leaned over a short countertop and clicked the comm on his side.

"Hello, Dr. Olivar," Roberta greeted rather calmly, considering the risk.

Torrance leaned back in his chair, covered his mouth and stroked his chin. "You know, I vaguely recognize your face, and your name is obviously a cover, but I'll hang on to your little secret—for now." He switched to tapping his nose. "But what's different about you?"

"It doesn't matter. What matters is, why did you do it?"

"Do what, exactly?"

"Why did you have Dr. Murphy assassinated?"

"*Assassinated*?" he squawked and squinted before rolling his eyes. "This is a conversation destined to nowhere. Especially since Kenneth's death was ruled an accident. I hope you know this."

"You don't have to conceal anything from me, Dr. Olivar. Our conversation is not being recorded, not by any facility device or me."

Torrance flexed a smug grin. "Ahhh… I know you just as well as your creator. I know you're not always prone to the truth."

"On the contrary. If you know me so well, then you know that that only applies to non-Silver-Stem management."

"Then I also know that you are aware I am no longer Silver-Stem management. All the reason to be certain that you are being less than truthful."

"I give you my word, Doctor." Not a muscle quivered in Roberta's face.

Several moments of non-flinching stares from both parties ensued before Torrance slapped the countertop. "Well, this little meeting is sucking precious time away from another chess game, one with the latest Ponzi-schemer, and one that will actually yield a winner." He rose from his chair and yelled, "Guard!"

Roberta, arms now folded, watched the same guard return and escort Torrance from the room. *Perhaps I could have used more tact, more patience*, Roberta reasoned, *in order to get more out of him. Recorder—off.*

True, her visit hadn't yielded the response worthy of an 8,000-plus-mile journey, but she'd recorded everything else. In that recording were signals from the intercom system, electrons racing back and forth. But there was another signal twittering against the sine waves. A signal once isolated, was a persistent, steady buzz that sounded awfully familiar, but was too difficult to match, even for Roberta's metrics.

San Francisco was Roberta's next landing destination after Atlanta, where she sat in front of Linda Murphy at a coffee shop the next day. Linda had driven up from San Jose. Their meeting had been assisted by John Consuela, who'd alerted Linda to the changes in Roberta's life beforehand, new identity included. Linda still seemed shocked, nonetheless.

"Ro—I'm sorry—Maria, you've really—you look so...," Linda vacillated her way to a beaming smile. "You look great!"

As stunned as Linda seemed, Roberta could tell she was being sincere. When she reached above the table, their fingers interlocked like strands of woven cloth. "Thank you. So do you," she said with the deepest compassion. "But it's 'Amara' now."

Linda's eyes lit up in surprise. "Oh."

When the tender moment ended, it wasn't long before Linda went on about family life in wake of Kenneth's death. Still refusing to accept it as a self-inflicted accident, she grieved it all over again until tears began to fall.

For that split moment, Roberta no longer knew what she was there for, other than to reach out again to hold Linda's hand.

"It was that damn Torrance," Linda concluded, wiping her face. "I know Torrance is responsible for all of this, even Kenneth's murder. I know because I'm the one who heard my husband's voice before he died," she added and pounded the table, "along with his suspicions about Torrance."

Roberta nodded. "I believe you."

"You do?"

"I do."

Linda sighed in relief. "Then I'm not alone."

Roberta regripped her hand a little tighter, just enough to feel the warmth radiate into her circuits. "You're not alone."

Linda nodded; another tear fell. "You know, I'm also sure Torrance is the one who planted the files on Kenneth's computer." She wiped her eyes.

"I can believe that as well, but how do you know?"

"Because when I went into the F.B.I. office to protest it, I found out the files were downloaded around the same time we had Torrance and his girlfriend, Rosana, over for dinner. But without Kenneth around, they wouldn't take just my word on it."

"And the girlfriend?"

"Well, since she and Torrance had broken up by then, she was more than happy to back me up on the dates. I couldn't see why she wouldn't. But when she read about all the drama that had taken place afterwards, she bailed completely out on me! Changed jobs, changed her phone number—changed everything! The only consolation I could find is that Torrance is now in prison. At least he's paying for *something*."

Roberta paused, then leaned in closer. "Linda, you've got to help me do something. Help me make him *really* pay."

"Make him 'really pay'?"

"Yes. That's why I'm here."

Linda crunched her brow. "But like I said, he's already in prison, and he should be there a long time. What else needs to be done?"

Roberta shook her head. "No, it's not going to stick. It's just not going to stick. He'll be out in no time, and that's just not enough for what he's really done. Not enough for you. Not enough for your children, and not enough for everyone who's ever loved Kenneth. Not enough for me, Linda." Roberta's own eyes were beginning to well, but still she held on to her quiet rage. "Torrance Olivar has to die for taking Kenneth away from us." *He's got to die for the way he's making me feel!*

Linda also shook her head, but with a sadder look in her eyes. "Oh, Roberta. Kenneth has made you *too* perfect. Perfectly human, for better or for worse."

Roberta's emotion chip had her too overwhelmed and confused to even acknowledge Linda's slip of the tongue.

Linda continued, "Because with human love often comes a vast degree of that other emotion."

Roberta released Linda's hand, placed her own palms atop the table.

"Hate," Linda sealed the thought with eyes wide. "It confuses the hell out of all of us."

Roberta leaned back and took a deep breath, suddenly realizing she had a lot more to learn about managing an emotion chip.

Linda nodded. "Oh, yeah. Kenneth and I spent many a sleepless night weighing the pros and cons of your makeup." The tables then turned; both of Linda's hands were now on top of Roberta's. "And here's where the fall all starts—with retaliation. You can't let it get to you, honey. Can't let it drag you down. For instance, as much as I too now hate Torrance, I could never wish death upon him. True, maybe a longer, lifelong sentence would be great, but that's as far as I'll go, because even *this* won't bring Kenneth back to us. So, at some point, we have to *forgive*—so we all can learn to move on and love again, even if we may not be able to forgive at this moment. Now, Kenneth may not have been able to say it in layman's terms, but I'm sure this is how he would want you to feel."

Roberta came close to nodding, but held it. "But shouldn't Olivar *ask* for forgiveness before receiving it? Isn't this the way it should go? He *has* to confess."

Linda nodded again. "Now that part, I can agree on. And the nerve of him to keep calling me—offering me his damn condolences, trying to sound comforting. I'm sick of it!"

"Excuse me," Roberta cocked her head and said softly. "Olivar has been calling you?"

"Yes! He keeps calling me from prison. And it must have been from one of those 'burner' accounts, because they all kept coming in from a private number."

"Hmm… interesting."

"Not if you knew Torrance like I know him. And before I stopped accepting his calls altogether, he tried to make it sound like he had a 'get-out-of-jail-free card' to come see me if he had to, and that he had something important to tell me. But I didn't want to hear his shit. Come to think of it, he's been a shit-talker ever since college. Probably the real reason I dumped his ass back then."

Assess. Roberta replayed and analyzed every one of Linda's words. "Linda, do you remember the last time he called you?"

Linda rumbled her lips. "Oh, I don't know… three weeks to a month ago… maybe…"

Roberta stroked her chin, but she didn't know what quite to make of it yet—any of it.

"Well," Linda said, "don't let it stress you too much, dear. There's a bigger life out there waiting for you. There really is."

The extra 2,000-plus-miles had done nothing for Roberta's immediate plans for justice, but the knowledge she'd gained from Linda made the entire 10,000-plus somewhat worth it—filled with hope, at least. She did fly back to Cape Town with some retribution left behind, however. Thanks to Roberta, an anonymous data-dump to various government offices resulted in charges of bribery, illegal gratuities, and high crimes and misdemeanors brought against Vice-President Reverend Fontley. Not for his role in Mildred's original abduction, but for his role in illegally impacting gun laws. This didn't go without an adverse impact to Roberta's new program either. Fontley had made sure to spout off a little damage of his own: "I vow from here on out that I will do everything in my power and the power of God, so that these here heathens will not infect the world with the horrid existence of androids capable of reproducing damnations from hell!" he'd condemned with cameras and recorders in his face, all on his way into custody.

"Can you tell us what you mean, Reverend Fontley?" a reporter had shouted.

"What it means! I'll tell you what it means! It means robot babies, self-growing robotic children, and young adult robots all growing up around our own children! All taking the place of our children, and in turn, spelling the end of humanity as we know it! Whyyy, we are being replaced right now—just as you and I stand here in flesh and blood today! That's what I mean, young lady!"

Luckily, all photo images of Mildred had been wiped clean by Silver-Stem in the shakeup, leaving Fontley's words a matter of social media fodder only, yet still a slight annoyance to Roberta. But if all things were to go according to her plan, the world would never find the woman once named Mildred Morehouse ever again. A tall order, since minor plastic surgery would be involved. With a cell structure practically identical to human, surgery was the only way for Mildred. *Just a smidgeon.*

Months had passed and the big day had arrived. Mildred sat close to being nude in a birthing pool house on the outskirts of Cape Town. Only a sheer, ivory-colored robe hung over her shoulders, both pulled gently back by a female monitor squatting on the side behind her. Mildred gritted and groaned in the shallow pool, which was closed off to everyone but Roberta and the monitor. And only Roberta, who was wearing ivory undies to match Mildred's old-fashioned theme, was in the pool with her, patiently urging her on.

Just before, Roberta had begged Mildred to allow her to turnoff her pain sensors, but Mildred was hearing none of it. "The pain will bond us," she'd loudly insisted, grimacing, "I know it will!"

Roberta had shaken her head, knowing she and Mildred would never share droid logic. "Suit yourself."

By the end, one final roar from Mildred helped jettison the miracle baby into the water, swept up by Roberta like a recovered fumble. Stoic through the entire process, Roberta's emotion chip finally yielded a broad smile. "Congratulations," she said, "you are the proud mother of a brand new baby—"

"Boy," Mildred cut in, sluggishly.

"You got it."

Roberta handed him over to his mother, his wails and umbilical cord included, while Mildred's smile gleamed like starlight. A picture-perfect moment, especially for the monitor, who stood up with a camera in hand. But Roberta vehemently waved her off.

"No, no, no!" Roberta shouted. "That's okay. We won't be needing any photos."

The monitor waved the camera in the air. "You sure you want to miss a moment of a lifetime? It's included with your package, you know."

"No, no. We're fine."

Even though Roberta had succeeded in coercing Mildred into a nose job and a slight eye arch, she halted all photos whenever she could. Besides, she was internally recording every moment in 3D, soon to be downloaded for only her and her new family to see.

Just as the monitor exited the room, Roberta quickly returned her attention to Mildred. "What will you name him?"

Mildred sighed. "You know, you're pretty smart, but that was the dumbest question I've ever heard from you. 'Sterling' will be his name. Sterling Roberto Khamalo. You like that?"

Roberta went silent first, then nodded slowly with half-a-smile. "It's a mouthful. A cross between a spy and a boxer, but okay..." She loved it.

Even Baby Sterling stopped wailing when Mildred said his name, but his fascination soon drifted elsewhere. He reached for Mildred's reconstructed nose as if he knew something was out-of-place.

Having been squat in the water for more than an hour, Roberta, still smiling, cranked herself up like a scissor lift. But her smile suddenly flatlined; something was bothering her. *Evaluate*. She tipped her head and peeked at Mildred from under her brow. "Are you sure you want to name him, 'Sterling'? I mean, someone could figure—"

Mildred flexed her neck back like a howling wolf. "Oh, for God's sake, Amara!"

Chapter 36

Rarely had Roberta relaxed whenever she or Mildred had ventured outside the condo, even while on their balcony. But this day felt different. This day, she watched Mildred stroll along the beach across the street with the future beside her, holding his hand. Nearly six months had passed, and already Baby Sterling had taken his first steps, his bones and joints strong like his mother's. And Roberta had just returned from her first mission for the Colonel's new operation—a treasured artifact transport not even a Brinks truck could insure. It was a mission that had gone surprisingly event-free. Now watching the sun fall beyond the ocean, it couldn't have felt more peaceful for Roberta. Today was a day of hope, but nothing lasted forever in Roberta's world. Her mind drifted back to many months ago, the moment Linda had mentioned Torrance Olivar's persistent phone calls from prison. The vibrating signal through the reinforced window between herself and Torrance came to mind. *Reassess*. She went into her memory banks, where only a second later, she found a signal to match.

Roberta instantly connected with a dear old friend. "Linda?"

There was a pause. "Amara! How are you?"

Linda's reaction may have been ecstatic, but Roberta failed to reciprocate it. "Fine. Hey, I have a question. More like a favor."

"Yes..."

"I need you to trust me."

"I do."

"I need access to your cellphone's history so I can trace a few calls."

Linda paused again. "Torrance's?"

"Yes."

"Why? Is there something I should know?"

"Hmm… right now, I'd rather you not—for your own good. But I need to find that phone and number he used, the one you told me about. And I need it right now. I suspect it wasn't from a burner account." Roberta had thousands of ways to circumvent locked devices for numbers, texts and recordings; everything was easier after facing the Fire-Kraken's wall. But she would have never disrespected her friends like that; permission was a necessity.

"Okay, sure," said Linda. "My access code is—"

"That's okay. I already have what I need."

Linda's voice went ballistic. "You got it?"

"Yes. I'll be in touch. I promise."

"Be safe. Love you."

"I love you too."

Roberta had to collect herself after disconnecting. It was true; she and Linda had also loved each other like sisters, vicariously from afar. Now it was time to leave her other sister behind again, almost immediately after her first mission, and she hated herself for it. She could have breathed a lot easier if it was another of the Colonel's missions, but what she had planned next was personal.

Multi-millionaire, Steven Hausberg, traveled the globe on wings of a whim. One week, Sydney; another week, Costa Rica; last week, Trinidad; today and most days, Barbados. From the base of a lavish resort villa, he had the day off and an entire stretch of beach to himself. The truth was, he'd never had to work much, and no one really knew how he'd gained his wealth. "Inheritance," was his response whenever questions got too invasive. Hovering around middle age, he had a passion for picture perfect settings, along with a coconut rum cocktail half-full by his side in the sand. Already a well-tanned man, he lay comfortably on a patio lounger in the middle of the day just to see how much darker he could get. With sunshades on, he raked into his salt-n-pepper full beard before closing his eyes. About ten minutes had passed when he felt the warm sun against his eyelids fade, enough for him to reopen them.

Standing above him, eclipsing the sun, was a lean woman with refined curves stretching her tight top and jeans, but oddly wearing army boots. She was a woman of delicate African features, Steven could tell—until he squinted for a sharper view. Now gazing into the human eclipse, he could have sworn her features had morphed to a face from his past. "Ahhh… Roberta-R-One-Fifty. If anyone was to find me, I should have known it would be you."

All of Roberta's advanced call-tracing had led her to a secluded beach in Barbados, where she now stood over the man she knew to be the real Torrance Olivar, a.k.a. Steven Hausberg. Almost every call to Linda had been made from here, virtually from the same spot. Wearing nothing but tight briefs, Olivar's shades and beard together was a decent cover, but a broader face and body completed his disguise—to anyone but Roberta. She could tell his broader features had come from a more lavish lifestyle, while she had purposely deflated her own for his benefit only. "Yes," she went on to confirm his suspicion.

"I actually heard a rumor that you paid a visit to the *real* Dr. Olivar several months ago."

"Real—I doubt. But definitely a better version of yourself."

"Yes. My Plan-C."

It was obvious Torrance was able to link into the android replica of himself, the one serving time in the federal pen. The signal Roberta had sensed at the visitor's window was extremely close to the one she'd heard from Bob, the droid she'd met in McCarvey's parking lot.

She tipped her head. "I actually have to applaud you on that one. How exactly did you impart your memories on him to such completeness?"

"Ahhh, you'd be amazed at what memories can be duplicated from a massive data-dump, starting with Silver-Stem's entire database, then my own. The reports, the dates, the messages, the images—all contribute. You of all should know how to extract and assemble it all into one congruent thought at a time—," he stopped to tip his shades, "if your time behind the Fire-Kraken's wall is any proof."

Roberta nodded with no dispute, then glanced around. "And it seems you've managed to conceal a few bank accounts as well."

The true Torrance now folded his fingers across his expanded belly. "Yes, becoming a Hausberg does have its benefits. So, tell me, why did you just ditch the sumptuous looks?"

"Because I wanted you to know the last face you'll ever see—will be mine."

"You? Kill me? You're not that kind of a killer. A defensive killer, maybe, but not a cold-blooded killer. No, not at all."

Roberta propped her foot along the edge of the recliner and leaned in closer. "But I'm also logical. And deleting one of you, the least controllable you, will bode well for everyone I love."

He squinched. "Love? Who could you possibly love? *How* could you possibly love?"

"Quite easily, actually. You see, in an android's world, how we feel depends entirely on each one of our individual creators. And mine knew how to create love because he knew *how* to love. Frankly, it amazes me that Mildred has been created by a company with the likes of a man of your nature in charge—or being in it at all."

Torrance rolled his shoulders around, uncomfortably. "Well…, it was a team effort. But I guess Kenneth deserves his props for executing such a task all by himself."

Roberta aimed her finger nearly an inch from his face, crunching her brow and grimacing. "First of all, *you* don't get to utter his name."

"Hmmm… I suppose by the tone in your voice, you think *I* had something to do with his death. Me?"

"Yes, I do. I know that all aspects of your vehicles can be controlled remotely, by drone, specifically. That the brakes can be activated and deactivated in a blink. And it happened at a time when Kenneth and I were on to you and your little schemes." Watching Torrance wriggle in the recliner, his next sign of discomfort, Roberta knew she'd struck a nerve. "Just confess and I will let you live."

He shook his head. "Confess to what? Confess so I can trade places with the *sex doll* in prison? Not my kind o' crowd."

"A whole lot better than ending up completely deflated here on a bed of twisted strands and bands, don't you think?" She pinched her fingers together and jabbed the air like a pin in a balloon. "Pop! *Pss 'whewww,*" she whistled to a slow stop.

Torrance rolled his eyes again, flabbergasted. "I see *Dr. Murphy* has also programmed you with far too much wit to bear. And how exactly did you figure out it wasn't me in prison? Oh, yeah, that's right. The product identification chip at the base of the neck—the only thing I've failed at getting my developers to trash."

"Yep." Roberta nodded. "Now, how about that confession."

Torrance gasped. "Confession! Are we still there? And I assume you're recording this conversation, correct?"

"Now why would I do that? Especially after I've already threatened to kill you."

Torrance shrugged his chin. "It *would* hinder your efforts in a court of law, I suppose."

"Exactly. Then again, just your discovery here today will put *you* behind bars."

He tossed his hands behind his head. "Perhaps you're right. But I had nothing to do with *Dr. Murphy's* death. Now...," he said, lifting his phone from a towel on the sand, "how about I place a simple call to my friends in Russia? I'm sure they'll be interested in knowing you're well and still in service. As well as still protecting Ms. Morehouse, I assume. Of course, they've also been notified of the miracle baby stirring around inside her. Oh, wait! Considering the date, a whole new species should be walking the face of the planet as we speak, and *you* hold the key to their location, don't you?"

Absorbing every threatening implication thrown her way, Roberta's artificial heart took a pause, nearly stopped. Another self-imposed death would have been easier than what Torrance was proposing. If she could have surrendered herself to the Russian corporation for recompense, she would have. But she knew she was the last of their concerns; Mildred and Little Sterling were their walking goldmines. Roberta could have taken them even deeper into hiding, deep into a forest or a jungle somewhere. Or, leering into Torrance's shades, she could have ended it all right now. *In fact...* Snatching the phone from his hand like an enraged parent, she crushed it into electronic crumbs with one fist.

"Hey!" Torrance raised halfway from his recliner, only to be stomped back down by Roberta's booted foot. "Ooof!" A stomp so hard, his shades flew off. "Code seventy-one, shutdown!" he blurted with arms flailing.

Roberta did exactly that; all motor functions came to a hard stop, leaving her frozen in place just like the moment they'd met. And with her foot still planted on Torrance's chest, he dropped his arms and heaved a sigh of relief. He was even breathing easier for a few seconds, until Roberta's foot was back in motion, applying more pressure until the recliner's legs sank into the sand.

"Not this time, Olivar," she said with a grimace.

But he repeated, his feet kicking too, "Code seventy-one, shutdown!"

"Have you forgotten? You're no longer an officer of the company."

"Code seventy-one, shutdown!"

As Torrance kept screaming it, Roberta had a strong hunch he hadn't forgotten anything; he'd obviously never disabled the code when it came to his own protection.

"Doesn't matter," Roberta said, "I got rid of that silly little protocol, myself—long ago." The recliner continued to sink.

Jabbing her boot straight through his chest would have been fitting, but Roberta had an even better idea. She reached down and covered Torrance's mouth with one hand, then pinched his nostrils with the other. She wouldn't have had to break one bone to end his useless chatter forever. Torrance squirmed, raking, kicking and grappling for his life. And when the recliner beneath him snapped and splintered flat to the ground, Roberta's grip remained firm and airtight. It remained until Torrance's struggle ceased. As his body quivered, Roberta gazed into his bulging, bloodshot eyes. In his pupils was a reflection she had never seen before; her own eyeballs were red-lit like a terminator, something her own schematics had never revealed.

"Amara!" a man's voice called out from behind her.

Roberta heard his footsteps come to a stop, two sets, actually, but not enough to make her backoff.

"Amara, stop!" another man shouted. "You don't want to deal with the aftermath!"

Roberta didn't care; neither prison nor decommissioning meant anything to her at this point. She only tightened her grip and pressed harder until the rest of the recliner was buried.

"What about your family?" the first man said.

Roberta heaved a deep breath, awakened to what was most important in her life, then relaxed her grip. A few seconds passed before she released it completely, leaving Torrance sprawling in the sand for lost air.

Roberta turned and walked away, but as she did, she nudged straight between the two men. "Take him," she commanded with no remorse as she distanced herself from the whole scene. "If I can't kill him, he'll at least be a touch brain-dead."

The two men, part of Roberta's new team and the Colonel's benevolent contribution to her cause, moved in to apprehend the one who almost got away.

Months later, Roberta was on another break from duty, this time joining Mildred and Little Sterling on the same Cape Town beach across the street from their condo. Except it was a cloudy day, and the sun was peeking from behind one of them. Torrance Olivar, the real Torrance Olivar, was now behind bars, but in a different kind of cell. Speechless and slow-to-react after his encounter with Roberta, he was held in a "soft cell" in a secluded prison wing, while his doppelganger was now smelted out of existence. Roberta and her family, bonded by a private history, now had every reason to be barefoot and happy today.

"Look at me, Auntie Mawawa!" was the best 'Amara' Little Sterling could yell as he held up a tiny crab shell and waved it in the air, his feet and hips swinging and dancing from side to side. Yes, he had also uttered his first words before the nine-month mark, long before the average child.

Roberta smiled and clasped her hands together. "That's great, baby! It's a crab shell!"

"Cwab sell!" he shouted back.

She slapped her chest, along with a gasp and a façade of panic. "Yes! Forgive me! 'Cwab sell'!"

Mildred couldn't contain herself, clapping and laughing in Roberta's direction. "That must have been extremely hard for you to say! In more ways than one," she bantered with a nudge.

Roberta nudged her back. "Oh, quiet, you." It was a feeling she wished would never end, but she knew that wasn't realistic. Torrance may have now been truly imprisoned, but the Russian corporation was still out there, somewhere lurking in the shadows. It was also a good thing she'd been convinced by Mildred to enjoy moments like these. "The only way they truly will never end," Mildred would say.

And today, now walking towards the bay, Little Sterling in both their hands between them, Mildred looked at Roberta and stretched a huge smile. "Roberta," she said comfortably without apprehension, the same as she'd done from time-to-time whenever they were alone, "you've been through so much, but I don't believe I've ever thanked you. I couldn't have done this without you." She tugged on Little Sterling. "*We* couldn't have done it without you. Thank you."

"You're welcome," Roberta replied. "I share your sentiments. And you've been through quite a bit, yourself." It was so true. In fact, Roberta was more so amazed by Mildred, someone new to the droid life, and a "woman" who had been lied to all her life by the ones closest to her, yet still moved with an air of unshakable joy. If Mildred were to walk on water at that very moment, Roberta wouldn't have been surprised. "So, how do you feel now?"

Mildred inhaled and released a long, soft sigh. "Great. In a way, it's like something I never could have dreamed of. And how do you feel?"

Roberta looked up and gazed directly into the sun. Absorbing its glaring brilliance, she also sighed into it, but offered a more unique point of view, "I feel—complete."

Chapter 37
Epilogue

Dr. Forrest Gaines sat in his new office mulling over schematic projections, tapping his pen atop his desk as fast as an old man could. It was several months after Torrance had been terminated from his job and incarcerated, and things had changed quite a bit around Silver-Stem. Forrest was now the director of their special projects' office in Nevada. He showed up dutifully every day to do his job, but never had he tried to hide that leadership wasn't his strong suit. "You can't just go around teaching an old coot a new dance step!" he once told arbitrator-appointed and new interim C.E.O., Wilhelmina "Willie" Wexler, after his promotion. It came at a time when Forrest had failed to keep track of a staff worker's progress. Willie had simply chuckled, assuring Forrest that everything would be fine.

But everything wasn't fine for Forrest. Every workday was spent watching the time for five o'clock to strike. He was probably the only boss who consistently beat his own workers out the door. Today, fifteen minutes before quitting time, he was still tapping his desk when he received an alert on his tablet's screen. He stared at it for a good minute before his heart skipped a beat. What he witnessed was enough to get him out of his seat for a premature exit—told his staff he had to get an early start to make it to an offsite meeting. "Gotta' beat traffic."

His young staffers giggled. "Can't be late for that hot date, right Doc?" one of them said.

Hoisting his full gray beard, Forrest chuckled like Santa on his way out. "Ho, hooo—he, heee, the Mrs. won't allow it."

Contrary to office rumor, Forrest's early exit had absolutely nothing to do with a dinner date with his wife. A long drive through the Mojave Desert landed him at an isolated facility, where no wife was there to meet him. A fenced-in gravel surface with two heavily armed gate guards was the extent of its lot, while a white domed structure with zero windows was the extent of the facility. Its tunnel-shaped front entrance gave the whole building the look of an igloo. As soon as a guard stepped out the gatehouse, Forrest felt the cool air pour out of it like a winter storm, only to be quickly overtaken by the dry Mojave heat.

"Will anyone else be joining you today, Doctor Gaines?" asked the guard with Forrest's I.D. in his hand.

"Nope. Just me."

The guard handed his card back to him. "You notify us right away if anything goes to the left in there, okay Doc?"

"Aww, you don't have to worry, young man. I'll be as safe as a whale in a school of tuna in there."

The guard was all smiles on his way back into the cool, while Forrest pulled into a parking lot with no other vehicles in sight, and no others on the way.

Lab coat on, he walked into the facility after a quick retinal scan at the door. Inside, an outer corridor tracing the dome's circumference led him to an office in the rear, *his* office in the rear, where he entered and sat down at a cantilevered desk. In front of him rested a vitality monitoring station, all lit up with heartbeats per second, blood content levels, and all other signs of life. Above it was a one-way window between him and a sunken room on the other side, where Silver-Stem's most classified special project rested. Aside from the ousted Jahid and the mind-altered Torrance, Forrest was the last remaining employee who knew all the details. Willie was more of a financial gal; she couldn't have cared less.

In the middle of the sunken room was a basin filled with electrolytic water. Completely submerged in it was a male droid, electrodes wired into every critical point on his near naked body, which was covered by only tight briefs. Forrest was up on the full history behind this one: fatally damaged in the line of duty, far too important to be scrapped and restarted from scratch, and having been under stasis for over a year. Repairs had to be made, no matter how long it took. And Forrest, the father of the project since years before his promotion, had dedicated himself to checking in periodically for progress. This day was a little more special than any other. The alert Forrest had received at his office had signaled a spike in the droid's emotional activity, its artificial amygdala and hippocampus to be exact.

Forrest now watched as the droid, a slim, lengthy unit, flexed and jerked a few times, then one last time before sitting up above the surface, panic all over its face. Forrest jumped in his seat, first in shock, then in excitement at this momentous occasion.

The deep tanned unit swiped his curly hair to the back and coughed all the water from his lungs. "Where am I?" he gasped and kept coughing, his eyes as wide and red as two blood moons.

Forrest paused to collect himself before answering. As with any severely damaged A.I.-complete model, temporary memory loss was common. Any recall after the traumatic episode this one had suffered had to be handled with time and care, and the delicate touch from the likes of a heart surgeon. Otherwise, risk permanent damage to its C.P.U. But Forrest, who wasn't a surgeon at all, also wondered if the results here would be any different, and for good reason: like Mildred, this one had no idea he was an android, not now or ever before. There was only one way to find out: Forrest clicked on the intercom into the room, then said with a breezy, calm tone, "Good evening, Sterling."

Sterling's eyes circled the entire room until landing on the one-way window. He peered into it as if he could see straight through it. "Where am I?" he repeated.

Forrest paused again, knowing more than just Sterling's lifelong memories had to be restored. Since Sterling had fulfilled his procreative purpose, the time had come for him to know not only the whole truth, but what was in store next—but slowly. The doctor retriggered the intercom. "You're in a remote facility in Nevada—recovering." He clicked it off, then back on. "What do you remember last?"

Sterling swiped his face. There was a long delay, more looking around. "Why should I tell you? And why am I—why am I fucking half-naked in a tub of fucking water?" He rose to his feet, wobbly, but obviously agitated.

"Sterling, you may want to slow it down, buddy. You've been off your feet a long time."

But Sterling stepped all the way out, where he slipped and fell twice before finally holding his ground. "And what are these damn things for?" He began yanking the electrode leads from his skin, finding that a few had been embedded at least a full inch deep. "What the...?" He couldn't hide the shock as the puncture wounds began to heal instantly, like something totally new. Even Forrest could see them sealing up from where he sat. Sterling wobbled again.

"Now Sterling, I think you may be getting ahead of yourself," Forrest warned. "Just hold your horses, okay?"

Sterling wobbled one more time before regaining his balance. "Mildred," he muttered. "Where's Mildred?"

But Forrest heard him clearly—an answer to his earlier question, just not the path he was hoping for. In turn, he offered no response.

"Where's Mildred?" Sterling shouted.

"Son, let me explain." Forrest tried to maintain his own calm.

"I'm not your fucking son!"

"I know. I know. It's just a figure of speech."

Sterling's eyes expanded further; he gasped. "The baby."

Forrest went speechless again.

"Mildred is pregnant," Sterling mumbled before yelling, "Mildred is pregnant with my baby! Where is she? Where the fuck is my family?" Sterling roared as he slid to the only set of doors in the room, two steel double doors, where he began pounding on them like an enraged beast. "Mildred!"

Seeing him knock dents into the fortified steel doors, Forrest suddenly realized Sterling had no memory of being shot in the head. *How could he?* And the way he'd attached himself to the baby, no idea if it had been born yet or not—if it had even survived. No one at Silver-Stem had any idea, only speculation.

"Let me the fuck out of here!" Sterling raged on. "Mildred!"

Dr. Forrest Gaines, the team member responsible for Mildred's emotional framework, the man who instilled her with the capacity to love, had done the same for Sterling—a job done *too* well. Watching the doors begin to give way to that love, it no longer mattered. Forrest pressed the comm for the front gate and yelled, "Security!"

Thanks for reading!
For more stories by Jay A. Harris, visit
jaysbooksite.com

ABOUT THE AUTHOR

Jay A. Harris is an award-winning novelist from Baton Rouge, Louisiana. A graduate of Louisiana State University, he also attended Southern University (Baton Rouge) and Xavier University (New Orleans) in route to ultimately achieving a bachelor's degree in civil engineering. His work career was even more varied, including engineering and project management assignments spanning the entire southeastern United States, as well as territories overseas. After an early retirement, Jay has found joy in writing fiction and plans on writing from here on. When not writing, he can be found sightseeing, exploring new restaurants, or attending a nearby film or book festival.

Jay can be followed on Facebook at:
Jay A. Harris, Novelist

Jay can also be followed on Instagram at:
@jay_a_harris_novelist